FLESH
OF THE
BLOOD

To

BY

E.A. CHANNON

WATCH OUT FOR
DRAGON FIRE!

CHEERS

Flesh of the Blood

E.A. Channon
ISBN-13: 978-0692275603 (Custom Universal)
ISBN-10: 0692275606

To Troy, Paris and my wee Priam

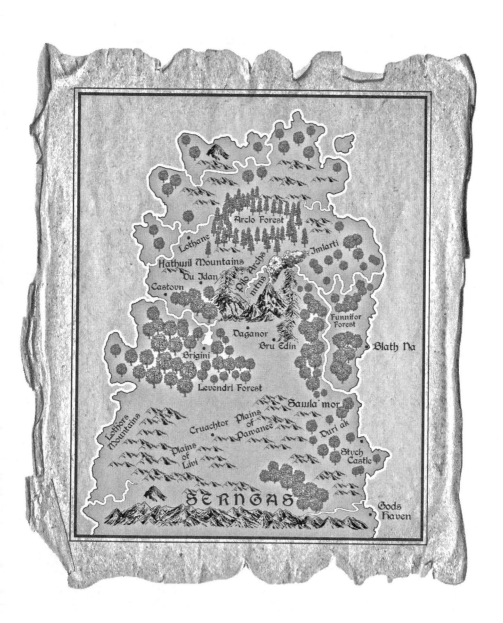

Chapter One

The hawk was perched atop a large branch tearing apart the mouse she had caught but a few moments earlier. To the hawk it had been a normal day, spent soaring hundreds of feet above the ground, looking for the smallest movement. Here and there she would either catch a mouse or a rabbit or scavenge the remains of something a much larger predator had left behind. She had eaten well today and was no longer driven by hunger.

Startled by a loud bang of metal, the hawk abandoned what little remained of the mouse and quickly flew away. The hawk looked to see what had made the sound and saw a group of small beings encased in shiny metal shells emerging from the tree line. Instinctively recognizing potential predators, the hawk gave up her prey and flew out of sight.

If the hawk had been able to distinguish between the predators of her world, she would have recognized the beings as the dwarves who ruled the underworld. There were five of them, each standing between four and five feet in height and clad in polished armor. Each of them sported either a grey or white beard and was armed with an axe. Four of the five dwarves were laughing about what the day had in store for them. The one not laughing, Malor Spinebreaker, was the one with the longest and whitest beard. He was the oldest and, in his mind, the smartest of the dwarves, his deep-set wrinkles and intelligent gaze serving as visible signs of his years of experience.

As he walked through the forest with the laughing pack, Malor let his thoughts wander to days past. His father had once traveled this route, during the last war between his clan and man over 350 cycles ago. Malor had only been a child at the time, but he still remembered the fireside stories told by veterans of the long-ago battles. Malor also recalled what his father had told him about Brigin'i — how it was naught but a small village with a lone tower — but the home of King Dia's ancestors had also been the main military stronghold in the area to the north of their home.

A bark of laughter drew his attention back to his companions. Despite being the youngest of the group, as evidenced by his nearly fully black beard, Holan Orcslayer was the best storyteller in the entire clan. So good, in fact, that he had been banned from telling humorous stories in the presence of the king after the latter once literally fell from his chair in mirth over one of Holan's tales. Looking at the faces of the others, Malor suspected that he understood why. Olan Orcslayer, Holan's older brother, an exact replica of Holan with just a bit more grey in his beard and a few battle wounds on his face, was nearly doubled over in laughter. Koran, Olan and Holan's equally strong but far more heavyset cousin, was not laughing aloud, but only because he seemed to be, as usual, chewing on something. Bringing up the rear of the group was Elawic Glenmaker, the tallest and thinnest of the party. While his slender physique made him stand out among the other warriors, his striking blue eyes and whitish blond hair and beard made him stand out among the rest of the clan, especially in the eyes of the ladies.

Malor smiled as he thought about how all of them were like family to him. So caught up was he in his own thoughts, it took him a moment to realize that the group had gone silent. Smiling fully now, Malor turned to the group and said, "I guess the joke is on me!" before slapping his own knee in amusement over their momentarily shocked faces.

"Blimey, he speaks!" Holan retorted laughingly, but also, Malor noticed, with a sense of relief. While their chief and king had been immensely proud to send these dwarves to the human king's challenge, the fortnight-long trek from their underground city of Cruachator to Brigin'i had not been entirely trouble free. Reports of strange, troubling forces in the human world had reached Cruachator just as they were preparing to leave. Though only rumors, the tales being spread were worrisome enough that their king felt compelled to keep the majority of his warriors close to home.

Consequently, Malor and his companions had set out north toward Brigin'i alone. As they had been traveling through the dense woods, the first thing they had noticed was uncommonly large bands of orcs — so large, in fact, that the group had been forced to spend days maneuvering around them. Although the other dwarves had wanted very much to fight them, Malor knew that they didn't have the strength in numbers to battle more than fifty at a time, and so there had been no laughter during those days of sneaking around and evading what had seemed like hundreds of orcs filling the forest.

The sound of an approaching horse, huffing and puffing, could be heard just beyond the rise in front of them. All smiles were gone in a second as the group quickly prepared for battle.

Coming over the rise toward them was a horse-drawn cart driven by an elderly man. Malor laughed a bit to himself because this man could almost be mistaken for a dwarf based on his long beard, cracked face and stooped body. The driver tipped his hat as he passed, causing the dwarves to laugh a bit. Malor and his band watched for a moment as he drove his cart in the direction of the nearest farm, about five miles away.

"Dwarves ... what's the world coming to?" the old man grumbled as he passed the bunch of dwarves.

* * *

As Bennak approached the huge main gate of the city, he could hear the racket that a large city produces from inside its walls. The massive stone gate — one of five surrounding the city — was an impressive structure in itself and boasted the biggest metal portcullis Bennak had ever seen.

Coming through the main gate as Bennak entered was a group of human warriors who were laughing and hitting one another, each holding onto a tankard of ale. Noticing Bennak, one of the men, drunk and unsteady on his feet, pointed to the half-orc coming his way.

"Hey, look at the ugly orc-man, my kin. He thinks he can come into our city … I don'na like that," he said as he bumped into a cart that had stopped so the driver could be questioned by the guards standing at the gate. All the warriors stopped laughing and looked toward the spot their friend was pointing to and then started laughing once again.

"Orcs. I hate orcs. They smell of mold, dirt and death," one of the drunken warriors grumbled to his other friends. They all laughed as Bennak approached them with his hands motioning peace.

"Friends … we are all friends here. I am not here for a fight with you. I have come at your king's request." In truth, Bennak wanted to beat the foolish men into a heap, but he kept his temper. He had not traveled this far into the kingdom of men only to end up fighting humans and getting locked in a dungeon somewhere.

"Friends? You are not a friend to me, orc-man," one of the men shouted. His friends soon joined him in hurling insults at the half-orc, who merely stood with his arms crossed over his massive, scarred bare chest as the drunk fools stood far enough away to avoid any blows he might send their way.

Soon enough, the commotion caused by Bennak and the drunks caught the attention of one of the gate guards, who motioned to the other three near him to come with him. Each was carrying a halberd and short sword belted to his hip.

"What is going on here, Volgr?" asked the nearest guard. "We don't stand for things like drunkenness and fighting within the walls. You know that. So either get out of the city or prepare to spend some time in the tower," the guard continued as the other guards came up and surrounded the group of drunken men.

"Nothing is wrong here, my friend. We were just welcoming this orc-man to the city," Volgr stated, waving his tankard toward Bennak.

"And now you have. Move along now. I'm sure your women

are wondering where you are," the guard answered as the others smiled and giggled quietly.

Mumbling under his breath, Volgr led his own group away from the gate, weaving their way down the road amidst raucous laughter.

Looking toward Bennak, the guard grunted with a slight smile. "I am sorry, my friend. Sometimes the warriors of this kingdom have little enough to do except drink or fight. Are you here for the challenge?"

Bennak looked at the guard and raised his eyebrow before answering. "Yes, I am here for the challenge. Will any of them be participating as well?" Bennak nodded toward the departing group of drunks.

The guard looked to the group and then back to Bennak before smiling. "No, I don't think there's a one of them capable of giving a small child much of a challenge in the arena, let alone a warrior of your stature."

"Pity. I think I would have liked to run into that Volgr creature in the ring," Bennak groused with so much feeling that the young guard smiled even wider and laughed.

"I can certainly understand that. Still, let me be the first to properly welcome you to our beautiful city."

Bennak nodded, happy to have at long last arrived. Now all he had to do was win his challenge. And not do anything to dishonor his people.

Chapter Two

*M*aking her way past local merchants and shoppers, Amlora found herself literally awed by the city of Brigin'i. Everything was so much … "more" than she was accustomed to seeing — the shops, the houses, the high towers of the temples and the huge castle that overlooked the city below — which, in turn, made her feel smaller and more insignificant than ever. "How could I have ever thought to win a competition?" Amlora chided herself after watching a man on the street control fire with his fingertips.

Experiencing the sights, sounds and wonders of the human city was something new to Amlora, who had spent most of her life in seclusion at the convent. Since arriving in Brigin'i, she had seen elves, gnomes and more domestic animals than she had ever known existed.

After a bit, the man wowing the crowd with the fire trick mentioned that he was a bit tired and wanted to taste a pint of the local brew. Amlora decided to follow the crowd that accompanied the man into the tavern behind him. She smiled to herself as she noticed the dwarves in the group nodding approvingly at the sign at the door which depicted an orc losing its head.

As the crowd sat down on both sides of a long table, Amlora was anxious to enjoy her first trip to a town tavern. Suddenly, however, the mood was broken by the arrival of two very muscular men wearing the uniform of the royal guards. One of them opened a pouch hanging from his side and yelled out what sounded like "Chansor." Amlora watched as a small, wiry man cautiously approached the guard, who handed him a rolled parchment before turning and exiting the tavern with his companion.

The crowd had gone quiet when the guards arrived and now

looked to the small man who had been handed the message to learn its contents. One of the dwarves who had come in with the crowd was the first to notice the man's hesitation to share. Not being the most tactful of the group, Holan yelled out, "Need help with that? I can read royal script."

The small man grinned and held the parchment out for Holan's view. Holan read the parchment to himself first, sorely testing the patience of the waiting crowd as they saw his eyebrows move around while he read. Amlora feared that the dwarf was close to being attacked himself when he finally looked to the crowd.

"Well now, it says here that Chansor — that be you, right, lad?" Holan looked toward the man as he nodded. Satisfied, Holan continued reading the message. "It says here that Chansor can participate in the games. Congratulations, son."

"Congrats, lad!" yelled the man who had been performing the fire trick. "Drinks all around. Put it on my tab."

The young barmaid near the counter gave the man a look. "Just make sure you pay your tab, Harbin. You may be my brother, but nobody drinks for free in my place."

* * *

The inn had once been a large manor house. One of the finest buildings in the city, it now served as a very comfortable bed and breakfast with stables and a large public house, which had been converted into a venue for welcoming the contestants to the city. To Birkita, it was a splendid example of human architecture, with ornate decorative features that still managed to be far less flashy than buildings of the elven folk. Looking up at the sign hanging from the front, which read "The Dancing Clown," Birkita thought it seemed very pleasant and inviting. As she ambled through the front entrance, a large, somewhat handsome man caught sight of her and walked over to confront her.

"I can always spot a ranger. And now you have to be one, else no one will ever believe me again. Tell me that I'm right, dear lady."

Birkita laughed. "Yes, you are. My name is Birkita. And you?"

"Jebba, at your service, milady," Jebba replied with a friendly smile and bow.

Birkita smiled back and chatted comfortably with him as others arrived. Soon the room was filled with elves, gnomes and humans. Outside, a few giants milled around carefully. Stepping on a fellow contestant was no way to start the games. Everyone was getting along quite well by the time the herald stepped out into the open by the fireplace to formally welcome the contestants.

The herald boomed, "Welcome all. His Majesty, King Dia, welcomes you to his city and to this, his favorite inn, 'The Dancing Clown.' Rooms have been provided for those of you who can fit into the establishment." Laugher and giggles filled the room as the competitors shared the joke. The herald held up his hand to quiet the contestants. "We have provided accommodations for our larger friends at their campsites. Tomorrow, at sunset, please be ready to go to the castle to meet His Majesty. Until then, His Majesty would be most pleased if you made yourselves comfortable here. The servants have been directed to get you anything you need. That is, for the competition."

The herald chuckled at his own joke, then bowed slightly and turned to depart. As he watched the variety of contestants, he thought of Baron Parnland's wager with him that this year's competition would be the most interesting yet. From what the herald had seen thus far, he thought the baron might just be right.

Chapter Three

King Dia presided over a meeting with his councilors inside his immense castle. He sat at the edge of a huge table, surrounded by a few chiefs of tribes that lived within the kingdom. Besides the inner circle that sat at his table was an elven prince from the northern forests who had come to watch the challenge as well as a few other royals and diplomats of various races dispatched by their respective kings or leaders. All had come to enjoy the unique wonders of the city that King Dia was so proud of.

Himself a formidable man, sturdier and taller than most of his race, King Dia stood and opened his arms to welcome everyone in the room. Cycles of training and fighting had given him an impressive and intimidating physique. One had to be tough to survive in a world with a nearly constant threat of warfare and vile creatures bent on ravaging outlying villages at the edges of the kingdom. It had taken several cycles of leading his army in battles and skirmishes throughout the northern lands, but in the end, King Dia had succeeded in uniting the independent settlements of men. Some grumbled that this feat had been accomplished less from his efforts to conquer local chieftains and more from his ability to vanquish marauding orcs, but Dia knew that his critics could do no more than whisper their displeasure, as he alone had managed to provide a lasting peace to the people under his rule.

Now all was relatively quiet. No major wars or battles had occurred for many cycles, giving Dia time to expand on his dream of a peaceful land by ensuring the goodwill of his people and others across the region, who were no longer having to spend their lives in battle.

"Friends, diplomats, princes and chiefs, welcome to my city of Brigin'i. I'm sure you all have had the chance to explore the city, and if you have not, please do so." Slowly walking around the table and behind most of his guests, Dia continued. "As we all know, war and the death and destruction it brings had been part of our lives for many cycles. Some of you suffered loss more than others. These games or challenges I have created help seal our brotherhood, strengthen our resolve and enable us to forge the lasting peace that will carry us far into the future," he said while watching the nods from many of his guests as they all agreed that war and battle death had to come to an end.

Dia kept circling around the table as he spoke. "Again, I bid you welcome to my beautiful city. Tomorrow the games will begin. And I can say that this year my ending challenge has brought forth some very interesting people from across the region. The gods, and you my friends, will surely be entertained." Raising his hands to the ceiling, Dia said a soft prayer to his god.

The other guests joined in this solemn moment, quietly praying to their own gods, and when they were finished, they all got up and commenced bowing, slapping backs or shaking hands, according to their customs, wishing each other well as they took their leave to follow Dia's request to enjoy his city.

After shaking the hand of the elven prince and bidding him well, Dia walked over to one of the large windows and stood alone, looking out at his city and smiling with pride.

Oh how hard I worked building this city, and how much I love it. My sons and daughter, their children and children's children, will continue to enjoy this city long after I am dust, Dia thought as he remembered his sons.

Dia and his wife, the lovely Queen Shermeena, had raised six children, including five wonderful sons who had all grown up strong and determined to fight for him when he needed captains for his armies. The memories of his two sons who had died cycles ago fighting orcs in the western province still saddened him and remained as fresh wounds, never completely healing. But even in his sorrow, his heart swelled with pride, knowing they died protecting him and their people. Queen Shermeena was still grieving their loss, but she too understood that the price of leadership, of royal privilege, was a life of total service to your people, despite what many might assume. Of his remaining three sons, two were off patrolling the borders. The eldest, Prince Frei, was now coming into the city, according to the captain of the city guard. Dia was pleased with the news. It would be good to have his son here with him as the challenge began.

Looking to one of the towers of the castle, Dia thought of his only daughter, Princess Shermee. She was widely considered one of the most beautiful women of the kingdom, but Dia knew her to be a major thorn in his side as well. Shermee was a spoiled young woman who enjoyed her money and privilege. Dia had been trying to tame his rebellious daughter so that he could marry her off to some prince in one of the other kingdoms. Some of the royals were of an age to be perfect potential suitors, but so far no suitor showed the slightest interest. Her rebellious nature was a quality many royal houses neither liked nor wanted to tolerate.

Shrugging his shoulders, Dia walked over to the table and picked up some paperwork as he left the room. Commanding a passing servant to inform his queen of her son's return, Dia walked to his own chambers to change into something warmer and perhaps a bit more appropriate for welcoming his returning son.

After a few minutes, he heard a soft knock on his door and, after calling out permission to enter, watched impatiently as a servant humbly excused himself for interrupting the king in his chambers.

"Sire, your son, the prince, is waiting for you in the private reception room."

The king thanked the servant, who quickly exited the room and scurried down the hall. It took only a few moments for the king to reach the private reception room. Upon entering, Dia found his wife and his eldest son already embracing each other with obvious delight.

Spreading his arms to welcome Prince Frei back home, Dia stepped forward to grasp his son by the shoulders. "Welcome home, dear Frei. It is very good to see you and see firsthand that you are well and unharmed." The presence of his son brought such joy to Dia's heart, but then he saw that Prince Frei looked tired and was still wearing his armor. His armor was splattered with blood, dark orc blood. Dia gave his son a concerned look.

Gesturing with his hand for his son to sit down, Dia crossed over to the queen, and they both sat in front of their son to listen to what he had to say. Frei poured water from a pitcher placed on the table next to him and drank deeply. Then he looked at his parents with an intensity born from the thought of never seeing them again, something he had really expected to be the case just a few days earlier.

"Father, I've returned to you to give you news ... news that I do not believe you will like," Frei said in an exhausted voice.

Dia leaned closer to Frei and told him it was fine and he understood, begging Frei to continue.

"As you know, I've been patrolling our farthest borders, just north of the Hathwil Mountains. Last week, my battalion of nearly 500 soldiers was attacked by an overwhelming, yet still unknown force. The loss of life was truly devastating." The solemn looks from both Dia and Shermeena confirmed to Frei that they were totally focused on listening to their son. Neither said a word.

"We fought well, quickly organizing a defensive action as we were ambushed by them. After three days of fighting for our lives, we were finally able to make it to Selkie, where the village guard helped our injured and wounded. From there, only my private guard and I rode south to a border tower. And though we made it home at last, of the thirty men who had come with me, only seventeen survived to reach the city proper." Leaning closer to his father, Frei continued. "Father, we were attacked not only by orcs but by giants as well, and I am sure I observed other, darker beings among the enemy, giving commands."

Standing up, Dia walked over to the fireplace to warm his hands. Dia knew what Frei said to be true. Over the past month, his own spies had confirmed the sight of orcs, giants and other, darker beings marching along their far northern borders. But so far, none of the creatures had attempted to enter his kingdom. At first, Dia had suspected that the recent attacks on settlements along his borders were merely a ploy to provoke a response. Now he realized that he was not dealing with a renegade group of malevolent creatures, but rather a well-organized army trying to provoke war.

Looking to Frei, King Dia asked, "Did you get a look at these other beings that were with this army? Did they seem in control of the orcs?"

Frei shook his head and then glanced at his mother's worried face before leaning over and placing his hand on hers. Shermeena smiled back at him.

"I'm just glad that you made it back, Son, and I'm sorry for your loss."

"Thank you, Mother," Frei responded, turning back to his father. "Are you going to continue with the games?"

Dia nodded and looked to Frei and then his wife. "Yes. We must. This event, although tragic, cannot be shared with our people. We must continue to act as if nothing has happened." At Frei's frown, Dia added, "But I will send out messengers to the other kingdoms and cities to see if they can shed any light on what is going on outside of our borders."

Dia sat down next to Frei. "Son, again I'm relieved that you are alive and well, very much so, and now you will surely want to rest. I am sure that there are many in the kingdom who will be most eager to see you at the opening ceremonies," Dia said with a wink.

Getting up slowly and groaning because his muscles had tightened since sitting down, Frei smiled at both of his parents and walked out of the room to his own room a few floors away.

"Are you sure that keeping silent is the right tactic, my husband?" Shermeena asked, still watching the door.

Glancing at his wife, Dia grunted then smiled when she looked over to him. "I'm sure that the city could use the coin. Like I said, whatever these creatures are about, thus far they have not breached our borders. I think we can get through the games before the situation changes." Smiling again to reassure his wife, Dia kissed

Shermeena on the forehead before leaving the chamber, motioning a servant to follow him as he made his way down the hall.

Truth was, Dia was worried. Having those creatures attack the city during the games could lead to disastrous effects. He needed to make a plan. Turning to his trusted servant Opto, he quickly ordered the man to find the captain of the guard, the captain of the cavalry and all of the top generals.

"Tell them to come to my private chambers at sunset. And to tell no one of the meeting. Their utmost discretion is required."

Dia watched as Opto bowed deeply before running off to carry out his orders.

"Let the games begin," he uttered as he turned to make his way out to the courtyard.

Chapter Four

The small bird sat atop the wall, viewing the competition. A nearby noise startled the bird, causing her to take wing and fly to where a small girl was resting with her eyes closed near a lower wall. When the bird landed, the girl reached out and gently grabbed her, bringing the bird up to her face. Nothing was said as the bird and girl connected, talking to each other silently.

A few moments later, the bird flew away chirping, freed of the rare spell cast on her by the girl, who slowly stood and stretched her arms back while adjusting the light grey cloak that identified her station. It was sometimes annoying having to wear light clothing, especially when it came to keeping dirt and dust at bay, but that was just part of the life of a druid, a life she would not trade for anything. Niallee smiled to herself. *Yes, this is going to be an interesting day,* she thought as she finished her primping. She was neither the most beautiful woman nor the best dressed in the land. Still, she knew that she possessed a mysterious allure that enchanted many males. For those she did not appeal to, she had more than enough tricks up her sleeve to compensate for whatever she lacked in beauty.

Hearing the trumpets and shouts from within the walls, Niallee finished plaiting her light brown hair into a long braid, picked up her bag and followed the other druids who had gathered since the most recent bells had rung. Walking up to Niallee was Hrliger, who, like her, was a follower of the druidic ways, but he was a gnome. The two had become friends instantly when they had met years ago.

Leaning close so only Niallee could hear, Hrliger whispered to his friend, "Niallee, I think this will be fun, but I have seen some of the other druids here, as I know you have too ..."

Looking around, he poked Niallee to get her attention.

"See the one wearing the long black cloak? He doesn't look friendly to me."

Niallee nodded. She had seen him and felt something was amiss with him. Something beyond the taboo black cloak, that is, but she had no time to respond to Hrliger as they entered the main arena to an eruption of shouts and roars from the crowd.

The contestants were motioned by guards to go to the middle of the arena, where they could see the king above standing in a booth with his queen beside him. Royal banners surrounded them, and they were dressed in robes interwoven with gold, silver and jewels. The crown that King Dia wore shone brightly, giving both him and Queen Shermeena an unmistakable air of wealth and power.

When all were assembled, the trumpets signaled for silence. The crowd grew quiet as King Dia began to speak.

"My lords and ladies, people of the great city of Brigin'i and all who join us from beyond our borders, I thank you for attending the first day of this grand challenge. For those who have not been here before, take note as I explain the proceedings. We will have three days of heavy combat among all those assembled before us now. This will include sword fighting among knights, battles of strength and strategy among mages, and beings and creatures that will amaze you. When it is over in three days, we will have selected a team of players from among the very best of the contenders, who will then take on the ultimate challenge for the glory of all our land."

Looking down to all who had gathered before him, the king continued. "There are no rules except this: You may not kill or mortally wound your opponent. If this rule is broken, then that contestant will be disqualified from competition and subject to severe penalties." Dia paused to allow the gravity of his words to sink in, making certain that the competitors below clearly understood that uncompromising rule. When he was satisfied, he continued.

"Over the cycles, these challenges have brought our kingdom great joy and exciting competition, and I'm sure that this challenge will be the best of all. Let us commence with a demonstration of the skills and magical power of the knights and druids."

King Dia lifted his arms, and the trumpets blasted their song as the druids below readied themselves.

* * *

"Are you sure that we should be doing this?" Fagor whispered to Cann as the latter was trying to open the wooden box they had just found. Outside, they could hear the trumpets from the arena. Stopping what he was doing for a moment, Cann looked over to Fagor and smiled.

"Yes, our employer wants whatever is in this box so he can use it to hurt King Dia. We've always wanted to hurt King Dia as much as possible too, and the money is good, so why not take advantage of the opportunity? Do you not agree, Brother?"

Cann, not waiting for an answer, looked back to the box and pushed his lock tool further into the lock, twisting and trying to manipulate the mechanism, and upon hearing the click from the lock, snorted in excitement as the lock fell away. Fagor caught it just before it fell to the floor, groaning at his brother's carelessness. The loud bang would have echoed throughout the castle, attracting unwanted attention.

At least he could be confident that the two guards they had left unconscious outside the door would remain so for a while longer. Fagor also knew that few guards came to this part of the castle, except in the evening when the guard changed.

Standing, Cann looked over to Fagor and motioned for him to move to the other side to help lift the lid of the huge box. Both grunted as the heavy lid rose slowly up and off the box. Strong as dwarves are known to be, they couldn't believe how heavy this thing was. Cann remembered how their secretive employer had told them that the box would be too heavy for them to lift, which was why they needed to break into it. Both took a moment to rest as they leaned the lid against another box to the left.

"Get the bag," Cann whispered as he peered into the box. Fagor rushed over and picked up the bag. He wanted to see what was inside now too, especially after hearing Cann say, "By the lords."

"What did you find, Brother?" Fagor looked inside the box and then at his brother. Both looked at each other in disbelief.

"Are you sure this is the right box?" Fagor asked with a puzzled look on his face after seeing what was inside. Looking at the outer panel, Cann was able to discern the symbols his employer had drawn.

"I was told to look for these symbols. This is the only object with such an inscription." Cann pointed to the words in front of him, seeing Fagor question him with a quizzical expression.

Fagor walked around, carefully examining the words, and then looked at Cann. "That may be, but I do not think that our employer was looking for this," Fagor said as he reached in and pulled out a corset made of black leather as well as a leather whip and other, smaller leather articles, "unless King Dia is using this as a present for his daughter." At that, both laughed a bit while continuing to rummage through the contents of the box.

Within fifteen minutes, they had a pile of things, including clothes and equipment such as whips, chains and a few other things the two thieves couldn't believe King Dia would have in his household. Leaning up against the box, Cann no longer cared why it contained such unusual items. He was too busy worrying about the other risk he had taken on with this job. If he didn't find what his employer had asked him to find, there would be no reprieve. They would be killed right away with no questions asked.

Cann was thinking about giving up and leaving the city to hide when he heard Fagor grunt and pull himself out of the large box to show Cann a smaller box. "I think I found something, Cann."

Cann looked over to see what Fagor was talking about and saw the small box in Fagor's hand. He jumped up and grabbed the box away from Fagor, slapping his brother on the back so hard that Fagor almost fell back inside.

"This is it, or at least, I think this is it. The boss said that the box would have these markings on it." Cann pointed to the small black marks on the side that seemed like claw scratches.

Fagor looked down at the markings and nodded his head. "We should leave this place now, before the guards or someone else finds us here. The last thing ..."

Cann nodded and interrupted Fagor. "I know, I know. Toss this stuff back into the big box while I pack this in our bag." Cann did his part in a just few seconds, then gazed in amusement while Fagor put everything they had scattered about back into the large box. Nearly finished, Fagor stopped and glared at Cann with a "what the hell" look on his face.

"What if that's not the box, Cann? What if it's something else for the King?"

Cann smiled. "This is the box. It has the right marks on it. What are you thinking? I should open it to make sure?"

Fagor nodded, raising his eyebrow. "Yes, I think you should, Cann. I don't want to show up and give the boss anything other than what he sent us to get."

Cann looked down into the bag and frowned at this brother. "If I open this, Fagor, you must not tell our employer that I even took a small peek inside because he told us not to open it."

Cann took the box and studied it to see where the opening might be. When he found the concealed latch, he looked over to Fagor. "Stand aside in case there is a dangerous surprise." Fagor watched Cann as he backed up to stand a few feet away. Cann thumbed the marks and then opened the box slowly. He peaked in the box and saw something interesting, something he had never seen before, something strange but incredibly beautiful.

Fagor saw Cann's eyebrows purse together in serious thought. "What is wrong? Is it not what we came for?"

Cann smiled at Fagor. "I believe it is exactly what the boss wants —."

Suddenly, a beautiful, intense blue light shone from the box, covering Cann's face. Fagor shook his brother, who appeared to be in a trance.

"Cann, Cann, what is it? CANN!"

Unable to speak or move, Cann was consumed by the light. A woman's face materialized and slowly floated toward him. She was smiling, seemingly at him alone, and the image became more distinct as it grew ever closer. Cann wasn't terribly frightened by the visage, although he was uncomfortably aware that he was not in control of anything at that moment.

The woman's face appeared to stop only inches in front of Cann as they both stared directly at each other for what seemed like a very long time. Cann attempted to ask a question, trying to formulate the words, any words, but he remained mute. After what felt like an eternity, the apparition finally spoke to him.

"I am sorry, but you are not the person that I am required to speak with. I am truly sorry for this."

At that, the female face dissolved, and a flaming skull quickly appeared in its place. Cann could feel the heat growing in intensity until it became unbearable even for a seasoned warrior. Cann screamed inside his mind as the flames enveloped his face and body.

To the now-terrified Fagor, Cann's expression went from alarm to interest to stark terror and pain. The screams followed, and his face and body erupted into flames. Fagor jumped back when he, too, felt the heat from the flames and almost wet his trousers watching his brother disappear before his eyes, screaming for help. When it was over, the only thing left of Cann was a wisp of smoke that rose up from the ground near the box that Cann had opened.

Fagor stayed for quite some time, collecting his wits and considering his options. His brother was dead, and the mysterious box had been the instrument of his death. At long last, Fagor got up, grabbed his bag and looked at the slightly open box lying on the ground. He was now in charge and responsible for getting this box to their employer. And he knew that not returning with this prize would result in an even harsher death than poor Cann had suffered.

He bent over slowly and closed the lid, hoping the flames wouldn't do the same thing to him. Curiously, the box wasn't even hot from the flames as he speedily dumped it into his bag and rushed out of the large room into the hallway, almost tripping over one of the unconscious guards. He ran with purpose until he eventually came into a crowded area of the castle. Fagor was nervous. With the loss of Cann, he no longer had anyone to watch his back.

Coming to a street corner, Fagor scanned the road to his left and right to be certain he wasn't being followed by guards and made his way to the main gate. Ducking in and out of crowded areas and cubbyholes, Fagor took some time to reach the main gate. Guards were positioned on either side of the gate, ten in all, each very well armed, but he knew they weren't searching for him. They were observing the people and goods coming in and out of the gate area, anticipating troublemakers on their way to the games.

Taking a deep breath, Fagor left his hiding place and ambled toward the gate. Not even glancing at the guards, Fagor just passed by, almost bumping into an old lady coming into the castle. Mumbling an excuse, Fagor continued making his way into the city proper. At last he was free of the castle. It would be difficult to find one thief in the midst of such a huge and diverse crowd. Sighing with relief, Fagor disappeared into the throng dispersing everywhere in the city. It would take another thief or a mage, maybe even a mind reader, to find him now. Fagor could at last breathe easily as he melded into the crowd and became one of many, and yet no one in particular.

Chapter Five

The blast from one of her opponent's spells hit her in the face, causing Niallee to fall hard to the ground. Luckily, she was able to scurry behind one of the protective walls that sprang up from below the arena at unpredictable intervals, offering a diversion or obstacle. Niallee had initially found them very distracting, but she learned to use them to her advantage. Gently touching her face with her fingers to see the extent of the damage, Niallee painfully discovered that, while her face was only slightly burned, she now suffered the total, yet unnatural, loss of her vision.

"A blinding spell? Great," Niallee muttered. Off to her left, Niallee heard shuffling in the dirt and knew that she was now exposed to the other druids, who would either attempt to help her or take her out of the competition. Fearing the latter, she pushed herself up and away from the wall just as the ground under her feet turned into mud, making the wall pitch forward toward her.

"Bastard!" Niallee muttered again as she blindly ran into the arena wall behind the fake wall. Suddenly, she heard another blast off to her right, followed by the muttering of an incantation. A moment later, she heard someone fall hard into the dirt nearby with a loud groan.

"There you go, Niallee. I'm always protecting your back."

Recognizing the familiar voice, Niallee couldn't believe her good fortune. "Hrliger? Is that you? I thought I saw you go down a while back." At least she hoped the sound of the rapidly approaching footfalls were those of her friend. Magic could disguise the voice of an enemy, making him, or her, sound very much like a trusted friend.

"Indeed I did, Niallee, right into a worm spell. Good thing too, since my opponent chose that moment to violate the rules and send a mortal spell in my direction. Luckily, he did so right in the view of the judges, so they took him out of the game. You should have seen what happened to him."

Hrliger put his hand on Niallee's arm to reassure her that the immediate threat had passed. "Here, take this potion. It should restore your sight."

Niallee took the small vial and pulled the cork, taking a careful sniff of the potion. It smelled of earth and herbs, neither pleasant nor vile, so she took a sip. Instantly, the feel of a growing warmth spread from her throat to her stomach before radiating throughout her entire body. Her pain eased, the weariness dissipated and, to her delight, her eyes gained light, then shape, then color and, finally, a clarity of vision that was sharper than normal. Standing before her was Hrliger with a big smile on his face.

"See, it's me, Niallee." Suddenly, Hrliger stiffened, turned and pushed Niallee down as a fiery bolt nearly hit them, slamming into the wall just above their heads. The bolt spread into flaming tendrils and grew along the wall for a few feet.

Both recognized the crawling heat spell and spun around quickly to see who had conjured the attack. A short human druid approached with an evil grin across his face. The spell wouldn't kill them, but it would hurt like the devil.

"May I suggest that we leave this spot and … ah, run!" Hrliger suggested to Niallee as he turned and took his own advice.

Seeing the druid's gleefully wicked intent, Niallee nodded and took off after Hrliger, narrowly avoiding another blast. Toward the end of the wall, Niallee could better observe the rest of the arena and blinked with surprise as she realized that there were few contestants remaining. Another flash of light, accompanied by a loud "BOOM," drove the pair back to the ground in an attempt to shield themselves from whatever it was that had exploded near them. Whoever the diminutive druid was, he was unexpectedly powerful.

Hrliger took stock of the druids left standing. The dust from the explosion made it hard to see, but excluding himself and Niallee, he was sure that only three remained. Nudging Niallee, he held up three fingers to signal the number of remaining competitors, then suddenly grinned naughtily.

"I was thinking maybe after this, we either go straight home or make our way to a local pub and really get pissed tonight. What do you think, Niallee?" Hrliger asked as he attacked another opponent, mangling the druid's shoulder in the process.

The lift of Niallee's eyebrow was the only answer Hrliger received, as she was intently focused on the most powerful of the druids. Pointing to this human, Niallee whispered loudly that they must work together to defeat this dangerous opponent.

"I agree. Why don't we do what we did to that giantess we met last year?" Hrliger removed a small seed from a pouch he carried, placed it in the dirt before him and began a new incantation.

Niallee nodded and had almost finished her own spell when the druid returned his attention to them and yelled, "Why do you keep fighting me? You know I can easily destroy you both."

His taunting ended abruptly as the ground beneath him turned into deep mud. Vines spread out from Hrliger's tiny seed and quickly arose all around the small man, encircling him and forming a dense web that trapped and immobilized their enemy within the mire.

"Aha!" cried Hrliger as he stood and looked over at the druid. "Take that, you evil turd."

Niallee was equally surprised by the power of the spell, but before she could comment, the ground was rocked by a large explosion. Apparently, the trapped druid had been interrupted while intoning a deadly spell. When he had lost his concentration, the spell had backfired, causing him to explode from the pent-up force. The body that had once been that of a man was now scattered everywhere. Niallee shuddered in horror when she noticed a piece of bloody meat on her shoulder, which she brushed off quickly, a loud squeak coming out of her mouth as she did so.

Hrliger looked back to Niallee and gave her a confused look. He wondered why his friend was brushing her shoulder frantically like there was a huge spider on it or something.

"Niallee, what are you doing?"

"That explosion blew apart one of the druids. Some of his gore was on my shoulder, Hrliger," Niallee said as she continued to brush her shoulder.

As Niallee finished brushing off the blood and guts on her shoulder, she spied the last two druids positioning themselves behind Hrliger. "Ah, Hrliger, turn around," she said, bringing the words of a spell to her mind and fingering in her own pouch to find some objects that would help.

Hrliger also gathered words for a new spell. Seeing the druids coming their way, he directed his spell towards the one whose shoulder had been damaged by Hrliger's earlier attack.

Hrliger's spell hit the injured druid with the force of a hammer blow and knocked him back as it took effect. A huge tiger materialized in front of the druid, instantly pinning him to the ground. The smaller druid stopped in his tracks, knelt down and removed his hood, revealing to Hrliger that he was not a he but a she, and she was preparing a retaliatory spell.

During this entire combat, none of the competitors paid much attention to the crowds of spectators above them cheering and shouting as things progressed and contestants were eliminated by failing to either protecting themselves or eliminate another contestant using their skills of combat. Now, with only three druids left, the cheering got louder and louder until those yet remaining could barely hear their own thoughts and voices.

This cacophony interrupted Niallee's focus, and she forgot some of the magical words of the spell, causing nothing to happen. This failure was, in fact, very fortuitous because behind the female druid, the large gate into the arena opened and the king's mages, flanked by armed guards, entered.

The contest was over according to the guard captain who had raised his hands for all combat to cease as he walked out onto the field. The three remaining combatants finally acknowledged the cheering crowd, stopped what they were doing, and looked around with smiles. Hrliger and Niallee couldn't believe they had survived the contest. They heard the booming voice of King Dia as he congratulated the contestants on their victories. Hrliger released the small druid from the tiger's guardianship as directed by the guards. He and Niallee were led away from the arena into a small chamber. Here they were offered water and any medical help they might have required and told to wait until the king arrived to speak with them.

Within moments, the two were laughing at Hrliger's bawdy jokes as Niallee had healing salve applied to her burns, reminding Hrliger of her condition as he turned to Niallee with a concerned look.

"Oh, I'm fine now — just a slight burn from whatever that human hit me with," Niallee said. "Nasty spell. I thought druids couldn't, or wouldn't, cause that kind of harm."

Hrliger leaned over and looked more closely at Niallee's face. "I thought much the same, but maybe he didn't tell the truth about who he is," Hrliger mentioned quietly, hoping the guard couldn't hear.

They paused at that thought, then looked up when they heard the sound of heavy boots coming down the hall. The door opened and three guards entered, telling them to stand. They rose just as King Dia arrived with a mage behind him who looked fearsome himself.

King Dia bore a huge smile across his face, approaching them with open arms as he again congratulated all three contestants on their victory.

Together they bowed to the king and, in turn, thanked him for the chance to demonstrate their skills.

"I am glad you are here and thank you for the excellent competition. You gave us all a great show. Now, I'm afraid I must ask that you stay here within my castle until I call for you two days hence when this contest is finally over." The confused looks on the druids' faces made Dia smile again.

"I understand your confusion, but the captain of the guard told me that some grudges between contestants can linger a long time after the games, and I do not want battle in my own city. I hope you understand."

Niallee frowned. "Not particularly —"

Hrliger interrupted Niallee. He had his suspicions about such a strange request too, but he knew better than to speak of them before the king himself. "We do, Your Majesty, but are we to remain in this very room while we wait?"

"You will be shown to more appropriate accommodations. Everything you would desire will be available to you — food, rest, women," looking over to Hrliger and Niallee, he added, "or men, if you care — and you can resupply yourselves as you wish."

Dia gestured to his mage standing behind him. "My counselor, Bogwa, has provided all you will need for your comfort." Niallee felt the king's eyes on her as she nodded to acknowledge Bogwa with the other druids, having picked up on Hrliger's signals.

"Now you must excuse me, but the next contest is about to start, and being a warrior, I will find this exhibit the most interesting. Setting steel against steel is what I call fun." With that pronouncement, King Dia bowed very slightly, turned and left the room.

The druids bowed deeply to the departing king, then to Bogwa, who nodded to each and followed his king after speaking to one of the guards, who nodded and gestured to the druids to follow him. They looked to each other and then accompanied the guard up to the castle.

* * *

Fagor made his way to the forest edge east of the city. He was sure that he was safe now. If an alarm had gone up, he would have heard something by now. Walking into the forest along the main road, he came around a sharp curve, only to be surprised by a person in a long black cloak coming out of the tree line. Fagor could see that he wore light armor underneath his cloak and could just make out the image of a silver horse emblazoned on his breastplate. The person's visage was hidden in shadows beneath a hood. Fagor's first thought was that behind the hood and armor was an elf, but like druids, elves in this forest did not wear black clothing.

"Are you waiting for me?" Fagor asked as he walked closer to him, but cautiously.

Not raising his head to look at Fagor, the cloaked figure replied so quietly that Fagor had to lean in closer to hear him.

"Did you bring the box?" he asked in a raspy voice.

"Yes I d-d-did, but my br-br-brother ..." A chill went down his back when he heard the voice come from underneath the hood.

"I do not see your brother. Did he open the box?" At that, the creature raised his head so Fagor could just see the mouth and chin of the being standing in front of him.

Fagor nervously answered the figure. "Ah ... no, no, no. I mean he didn't open the box. He merely touched it," he said, hoping that his employer would not catch his lie. "You d-d-did not say it would kill one by touching it, or we would have brought something to protect us."

Faster than Fagor could react, the being reached out and grabbed him by the neck, almost breaking it as he lifted the now-choking Fagor into the air and tightened his grip.

"Only one of royal blood can open the box. Your brother could not die from touching it, meaning that he died because he opened the box, which you were told very clearly not to do." Fagor was gasping for air as he tried to explain that he didn't open the box, but he just couldn't get the words out.

"Where is the box, Fagor?" the being leaned forward and whispered again as he pulled the hood back and revealed himself to Fagor for the first time. Fagor felt himself soiling his pants. What had once been a human male now seemed dead with skin ripped, decayed and falling off in places and maggots crawling in the open flesh. But it was the eyes that frightened Fagor, sending an instant chill up his back. Set deep in his skull where the eyes were supposed to be were small points of glowing red fire.

Finally, the black cloaked figure seemed to understand that Fagor could not answer him. He relaxed his grip long enough for Fagor to catch his breath and whisper that the box was in his bag that lay along his side. The creature nodded and grunted to Fagor, "You are no longer needed," and before Fagor had a chance to beg for mercy, the creature broke his neck with a quick twist of his hand and threw Fagor's lifeless body to the ground. Satisfied, the ghostly creature grabbed the bag from the body and looked inside.

Packed alongside some useless things such as coins and bits of dried meat was the box he had asked these foolish dwarves to find. Lifting his head, he laughed a haunting laugh before disappearing into the wood.

Later that day, a horse and grey cloaked rider passed the area. Seeing the body on the ground, the rider stopped the horse and dismounted to examine the now dead dwarf.

After tilting his head and listening for any potential attack, he picked up Fagor's body and tossed it upon the back of his horse before remounting, turning and galloping back to the city he'd just left.

Saying a quiet prayer for the dead, the elf rode toward Brigin'i City.

Chapter Six

Those assembled in the arena for the upcoming combat were anticipating a great display of traditional battle skills. Many in the audience placed bets on who would stand victorious at the end of the day. Matching steel against steel and wits against guile was something they could all understand, unlike magic, and therefore, it was one of the biggest events of the games.

King Dia was considered a great warrior in his own right, once even killing a frost giant and a few orcs single-handedly during a skirmish in the mountains. Fighting for his people and kingdom was a great honor for him, just as it had been for his father, the mighty King Muutlor, who was known as one of the greatest warrior kings in history.

Seeing the fighters assembled below brought back memories of past conquests. Dia missed the feeling of power and purpose that came with the wielding of his sword in righteous combat. Those glorious days were only memories now. Among the certain changes afflicting the race of men was the inexorable physical frailty wrought by the passing of too few years.

Hearing a commotion behind him, Dia turned to see Prince Frei entering the royal booth. Dia rose and hugged his son, happy to see that he was fully rested.

"This year we have the strongest field of contestants ever, and more than ever have assembled to compete. Come, sit and enjoy them with your mother," Dia said as father and son walked back to a set of large, comfortable chairs.

Frei waved to the crowds as they enthusiastically cheered their favorite prince before taking his seat beside his father.

"Father, I'm very happy to watch your games, but we will

soon need to speak about the gathering of orcs to the north." Frei spoke with a smile on his face despite his concern. He didn't want the people around them to believe that anything was amiss, and he surely didn't want rumors spreading that their prince had come back hurt and with a loss of many of their soldiers.

Nodding that he agreed, Dia jumped up when one of the fighters fell hard to the ground and another ripped his shield away in a swift and precise move. Dia clapped his hands and cried out to congratulate the winner of that particular match before sitting back down to speak softly with his son.

"Dear Frei, you just returned from a terrible battle and need to rest. It will do our people no good to have their prince killed. So please, Son, enjoy these games and know that I am doing all that I can for our people while you recuperate. Our scouts and spies will find out what is happening outside our borders and act accordingly." Dia laid a hand on Frei's arm, patting it to reassure him.

Queen Shermeena, sitting on the other side of Dia, leaned over to the king and pointed to one of the warriors below.

"Husband, who is that fighter there?"

Dia followed her gaze to a brightly armored knight whom he recognized instantly as one of King Eathu's knights. He was the only king among the human kings to have his knights wear ornate and highly polished armor to show that he had money to spend lavishly.

Lifting his hand and motioning to one of servants to attend him, Dia asked for the name of the knight the queen had pointed to in the arena. The servant bowed and left to find out the information.

"Why do you want the knight's name, my love?" Dia asked, still watching the battles below, but with a curious amusement.

"Oh, he looks like he is going to be one of the winners today, and I merely desire to know who that gentleman is."

Dia knew that his wife did not really want to know that particular knight's name but believed if he was a winner that she could bed him that night.

The queen smiled and pretended to be completely innocent.

This was a familiar game between them, neither faithful nor jealous. And it was a game that neither would soon tire of playing.

"Why do you laugh, my husband?" She already knew the answer, and knew that her husband knew well that she fancied the knight. It was all part of the game.

"Oh, nothing, my dear," Dia said, still snickering when he noticed the servant was back.

Bowing to the king, the servant leaned down and gave him his answer. The king dismissed the servant and turned to his wife with a wide grin. "The knight that you fancy, my love, is called Winsto lu Kinflod. He is one of King Eathu's men."

"Winsto. Why thank you, my love." The queen settled back into her chair to continue watching the knight as he took on another armored fighter, quickly besting that warrior with a few strokes of his sword. The queen knew that a true knight of the realm would probably not join her in her bed this night, but it didn't hurt to admire and tease her husband a bit.

King Dia was more than a little surprised that his wife would want to entertain a knight. Maybe a knight would prove an interesting challenge. They were not known to be the most cultured and gracious people, but what could he do? She was a woman, after all, and each and every one remained a complete mystery to him.

After hours upon hours of steel upon steel and triumph and defeat, the second day of contests finally ended. King Dia, as was customary, had the winners brought to the castle to await his congratulations.

Walking into the large room smelling of sweat and used leather stirred even more memories of Dia's youth. Surveying the room, he saw the winning competitors positioned at different parts of the room to give themselves enough room to remove their armor. There were over two hundred knights who had taken up the challenge, making for a long, long day.

Those competitors who were seated rose when the king's contingent arrived. As Dia stepped into the room, the competitors bowed as one. Dia heard a distinct groan from one of them and resisted the urge to smile. He himself had felt that way after many a fight in his youth.

Walking up to the nearest competitor, Dia clapped him on the shoulder. "I'm honored, my friend, that you survived the challenge and that you are doing well. May I ask your name, and is there anything I can get for you as you rest?"

Grunting a bit because his muscles were hurting from the ten and more battles he had just fought, the warrior looked down at the king's feet, then looked at the king himself.

"My lord, my name is Whelor. I come from nowhere special. I only need rest, my lord, and maybe a bit of food."

Smiling at the answer, Dia nodded and reached out so the warrior could kiss his hand before turning to his personal servant and motioning for him to get Whelor what he had asked for.

"You shall get food, but please rest for now."

As Whelor bowed again, King Dia turned and walked over to the next fighter, who was leaning up against one of king's servants who had volunteered to help out.

"Ah, and who do we have here?" Dia cocked his head to one side as he took in the man who stood before him.

"Name's Malor, Your Highness. Malor Spinebreaker," the dwarf answered, taking a step back in order to look up at the king towering over him.

Dia nodded and extended his hand. "You demonstrated excellent showmanship and warrior skills, my good man. Know that you made your people proud today."

Malor grunted and bowed slightly with a weak grin. As it seemed Malor had nothing else to say, Dia turned to the next warrior.

"And you are?"

"My lord, my name is Jebba. I was once a soldier for you until all my family died from the black sickness three years ago, except for my son whom I now take care of."

"Your son, ah, I understand, and I am sorry for your losses.

That sickness was nasty. I also lost family from it." Dia had a nephew whose whole family had died from the scourge. Their deaths had been quite painful as he recalled. "But now that you have won the day, you will have to leave your son for the final challenge. You do realize this, yes?"

Lowering his head slightly, Jebba thought of his son. They had both understood from the day he decided to take part in the games that he might win and have to leave his son behind. Now came the hard part. Raising his head, he forced himself to stare Dia directly in the eye, praying that he wouldn't be struck down before he finished speaking for committing an obvious breach of protocol. Ignoring the shocked gasps around him, Jebba spoke with grim determination.

"Yes, my lord, King, I do understand, which is why I must ask a favor of you, if I may."

"King Dia does not do favors, citizen," barked the raised voice of Bogwa, standing behind King Dia. Dia held up his hand to quiet his guard. He was curious as to this soldier's request. And impressed by his boldness.

"What is your favor, soldier?"

Jebba took a deep breath. "As you said, my lord, being one of the winners of your games, I will soon leave my son behind as I engage in the quest. As he is still too young to fend for himself, I ask that you take in my son as one of your … wards while I am gone." Jebba released his breath slowly, trying not to give away how nervous he felt. He had told his son that he would ask the king to make him a lad-in-waiting, but the competition this year felt … different. Maybe there was something going on, maybe there wasn't, but Jebba was determined to protect his son at all costs.

Thinking for a moment, Dia turned and walked away from Jebba without giving him an answer. Jebba stood firm, even though his knees felt like jelly with the worry that he might have just ruined his son's life. As the king approached the next fighter, he suddenly stopped and turned back to Jebba.

"I will honor your request, Master Jebba, but know that if

and when you come back from the challenge, your son will have to stay here in my castle until I release him from my charge." Dia gave Jebba a hard look, making clear to all who listened that he would not be dictated to by anyone, including a favored soldier. Do you agree to this?"

Jebba smiled in relief and nodded before lowering his eyes and thanking King Dia for his generosity.

Satisfied with Jebba's response, Dia continued the round of congratulations until he finally approached the knight whom the queen seemed to fancy so much.

His first thought was that the man seemed a little too sure of himself. Maybe that was what the queen liked about this knight who had fought a frost giant, four elven knights, three human knights and even a dwarf. To Dia's annoyance, his still-gleaming armor looked like it hadn't taken a single hit.

"Knight, I believe a 'thank you' from me is needed here. You put on a most impressive display against some of the hardest opponents in the games," Dia said, looking the knight up and down. "And you did so without being struck very often yourself. Being a warrior myself, I would be most entertained if you could tell me how you acquired such skill."

"My lord, King, I was well trained by my king and our captain of the army, but most of my skills come from fighting on the edges of my own kingdom and in the wilds of our land."

Dia frowned and eyed him skeptically. Seeing that he had not convinced the king, Winsto leaned in a little closer to the king and said, "I also had the benefit of my armor. It has properties that protect me very well, except for from the pain of blows."

Smiling, Dia laid a hand on the knight's shoulder and whispered in his ear, "I understand, my knight, and will not tell your secret." Leaning back and pretending to laugh at a joke, Dia stepped away from Winsto and turned to address room of contestants.

"You have all done yourselves and your lands proud. You will now accompany my guards to the castle, where arrangements have been made for you to stay until the games are over." As the warriors were the most prone to attacking each other, Dia had Bogwa ensure that a large number of his guards escorted them to the castle.

As he walked out of the room, Bogwa reminded Dia that the last warrior — a frost giant — awaited them in the open air garden. This was the first time one of their kind had come to the games since Dia had made an alliance with their king some five cycles past.

Walking into the large open area, Dia saw that the large frame of the frost giant as he leaned against a tree. Standing over ten feet tall, he wore leather clothes and carried a shield strapped to his back, but it was his sword, larger than anything a human could wield, that most impressed Dia. When the giant saw Dia walk into the area, he stepped away from the tree and bowed to him, startling the guards as he spoke for the first time.

"King Dia, the king Zakalesa sends his greetings. I am glad to have the chance to meet you finally."

"I am glad to finally meet you as well, my friend, and congratulate you on your performance in the games. Normally, all winners are housed in my castle until the competition is over, however your great size presents me with a problem in extending the same invitation to you, as you can well understand. Thus, I have decided that you will be allowed to return to your campsite outside of the city to rest and relax until the games are over completely. Do you require anything between now and when we meet again?"

The giant raised a hand and scratched his beard that was longer than some men were tall before answering Dia.

"A wagon of food should suffice, my lord."

"Bogwa, see to it," Dia replied.

"Right away, milord," Bogwa answered as he gestured to one of the guards, who immediately left the garden to pass on the order. .

The giant smiled and turned to pick up a large bag that was leaning against a statue, ready to be escorted away.

Dia turned to leave, then stopped himself short. "What is your name, my good giant, so that we may enter it into our records?"

Dia inquired, thinking himself rude for not asking that question when he first met the large creature.

Adjusting the bag on his shoulder, the giant looked at King Dia and smiled before speaking loudly enough for all in the area to hear. "My name is Ame-tora, good king."

"Good name for your people and one to remember. Thank you, good giant." King Dia saluted Ame-tora and then continued on his way.

Chapter Seven

The next day, the games continued with the thieves and clerics competitions. Although far from the most popular segments of the games, King Dia had always enjoyed watching the thieves. While he never tolerated the use of their skills within his kingdom, he did find it interesting to watch them solve traps that had been set up to stop them or get through devices set up by the other thieves around them.

The audience laughed when one of the thieves, while trying to solve a trap, was thrown high into the air to land in a pool of water that was set up not far away to catch him.

In the end, only four thieves survived the trials, and thus, won immunity for themselves for anything they had done in the past. This was a way for a thief to redeem himself. As most thieves didn't have glorious pasts like knights and mages, the smiles of those who had won were more about their freedom than anything they were now winning.

At the end of the thieves' portion, Dia met with the winners and delivered the same speech as he had with the others, offering rooms in the castle and asking them to stay until the end, reminding them with a pointed look that their immunity was only for past crimes.

One small man who wore a ripped cloak and looked more like a small child than a grown man constantly smiled while the king was about and even jumped when Dia shook his hand.

"And who do we have here?"

"Chansor, sir. My name is Chansor Mmm I mmm am from mmmm … wow, I forgot, sir, but I mmm I won!"

Dia laughed at the excitement the thief was showing, and as he walked away, he placed his hand on Chansor's shoulder, reassuring him that he was going to have fun now.

At that, he turned and walked away with the captain of the guards, who reported that all was well within the kingdom but things were stirring outside of his borders.

Nodding at the comments, he followed his guards back up to his balcony, from where he could start and then observe the next competition, the clerics.

Though he never understood how they got their powers or abilities, it was interesting to watch how these warriors fought each other without really hurting their opponents.

The arena had been changed quickly and within the hour was set up to take on the 20 or so robed men, women and even a few elves who had come to try out their skills.

"Might be interesting this cycle, my lord," Bogwa whispered into Dia's ear, making him nod slightly.

"Many, I see, are older than the contestants of previous cycles, though, my friend, so who knows, eh?" Dia said, smiling.

The cheers erupted in the arena as the trumpet blasted away, informing everyone that the competition had begun.

Instantly, a bright flash exploded in the middle of the arena, and 4 out of the 18 clerics who were standing were quickly knocked out of the games.

Cheers for and against those fighting echoed loudly as everyone enjoyed what they saw, not really caring who won. It was just fun to watch.

The number of clerics shrank down faster than ever before, with only 5 still standing against each other after just 20 or so minutes.

Dia stood up and walked over to fill his glass with some elven wine that had just come in from the east as he turned and watched that final group. He leaned on the edge of the wall to watch closely as they swung their maces and staffs. A few even lifted rocks that had been put there to use for defense-to-offense attacks.

He couldn't watch them all, of course, so he leaned down to watch an elf maiden and a man who seemed to be the size of a stick fight each other. They threw a few spells that they could bring out of themselves, knocking each other down, but it was the elf who was able to get up more quickly and run over, slamming her staff hard on the chest of the man. Even from where Dia stood, he could hear her tell the man to stay down, making Dia laugh out loud.

At that, he raised his hands to show that the competition was over and that the clerics still standing were the winners of this portion of the games.

Like before, the winners were escorted out of the arena to gather in a room where they could relax and clean themselves up before the king came in and spoke them.

As he walked back into the royal booth, he saw that his son and daughter were both engaged in conversation with others. Frei was standing off to the side, speaking to a man in a dark green cloak that covered his face. Shermee, his daughter, was sitting in her chair, watching the crowds and talking to one of her ladies-in-waiting.

Dia felt his anger stir at the sight of his daughter, thinking as he always did at the sight of her: *How could I have raised such a child? All she thinks about are her own needs and desires. Her mother has always spoiled her and allowed her to do whatever she wishes. Every lord I have entered into negations with has left once meeting her. I will never marry her off. Ohhhh, but I do love her.* Looking then toward Frei, he smiled, thankful that things were not the same with his sons.

When Frei saw the king, he and the cloaked man stopped talking and, after bowing, the cloaked figure walked out of the booth. Watching the man walk by, Dia turned to his son with a puzzled look on his face and asked, "Who was that, Son?"

Frei walked over to his father and leaned in so that his voice could only be heard by his father. "Father, that was one of my own spies. He informs me that another gathering of orcs and other creatures is approaching from the east."

"Where are they at this moment?" Dia asked with definite concern in his voice. This was all he needed: two armies of orcs and other creatures gathering on his borders during the games.

"They seem to be waiting near the Forest of Dreams, near the eastern border of the Hathorwic Forest. The elves there informed my spy of the happenings, as they are also watching with concern, of course."

Frei needed to make his father understand the extent of the danger. "Father, whatever the orcs are up to is obviously much worse than either of us thought. My sources inform me that many lands are under attack not only by orcs, but also by goblins, giants and seemingly darker creatures bent on just killing just about everything they encounter. Both Nakalor to the east and the capital city of the elves, Fuunidor, have been attacked, which hadn't happened in ten cycles. In Blath 'Na City, there are reports of landings of army upon army of creatures coming from the eastern and southern seas that destroy village or township and then move either back out to sea or march further inland."

Slumping down in a nearby chair, King Dia was getting a little nervous at his son's words. Was this the beginning of the end of their kingdom and the peace he and many others had worked on for many years? Who were these armies, and who was their leader or leaders? When he heard the name of Blath 'Na City, Dia looked up with a pained look, knowing that the large port city was one of glory and strength in many ways

"You say that they are reporting this? How did you get this news since Blath 'Na is over a fortnight's ride to the east from here?"

Taking the seat beside his father, Frei waited for the noise of the crowd to subside before answering. The cheering was growing now with the arrival of the mages, who were slowly entering the arena shooting sky bolts of fire into the air as entertainment.

"Father, you know that I have forged my own connections with many kingdoms and people around our great lands. Throughout the years, I have amassed quite a network of information gathering." Seeing his father's confused look, Frei shook his head. He and his siblings had indulged their father's bad habit of treating his children as babes in nappies for far too long. "There is no need for worry, Father.

I did not give away parts of our land nor form alliances with people you do not know of. I just have ways of speaking to others over great distances, and with this, I hear things," Frei said with a slight grin.

Nodding to his son, Dia looked over to see that the game announcer was waiting for his signal to start. As he raised his hand to give the signal, he noticed the murmuring and realized that his posture and demeanor were giving the impression that something was wrong. Forcing a smile onto his face, he sat up a bit straighter and waved for the games to continue.

The crowd erupted loudly as bolts of fire, lightning and more exploded below them all as each mage fought against mage. Worried, Dia turned to his son again, asking that he be informed of any movement from these gatherings of orcs and more as soon as Frei found out.

"Have you told General Comitay of these new developments?" Dia asked, still somewhat annoyed that he was learning of this news from his son's network instead of his own. In fact, he was still waiting to hear what his generals had learned since yesterday's meeting.

Frei turned. "Would you like him informed?"

Dia hated seeing the look of contempt on his son's face, for he knew that Frei felt that the general wasted time contemplating when action was needed. "That would be best."

Frei stood up and bowed to his father before turning to leave, moving so quickly that he barely gave his mother a nod as he passed by her on his way out. Shermeena could see right away that Dia was not paying any attention to the explosions and screams in front of him. Shermeena was no fool. Whatever he and Frei had discussed had been of deep concern and importance. She had been queen long enough to know when to not ask her husband questions. This was one of those times.

Besides, in truth, she had no need to. It was she who had taught Frei to develop such extensive networks. Knowing that she would have the answers to what she sought by the end of the evening, Shermeena turned and watched the games in front of her.

Prince Frei walked out of the arena and up the hill toward the city and the castle where the generals were in conference. As far as he was concerned, many were only there because they were just happy with the security and comfort King Dia had given them. However, Frei conceded that a few were actually good at their jobs. Problem was, they weren't the ones in charge at that moment.

As he hiked up the main stairs to the large conference room, he heard the voices of the generals arguing. "Typical," Frei muttered. He stopped down the hallway and listened while they argued about trivial issues.

"They do not understand what is coming our way," Frei said quietly to himself, absently rubbing the battle wound he had kept hidden from his parents. To Frei's annoyance, the wound was starting to throb again. Frei almost welcomed the pain as he pushed forward to confront the generals.

He walked into the room, pushing the two large doors open at the same time, and paused on the threshold as he waited for the assembled crowd to acknowledge his presence. Within seconds, all talk ceased as those within the room all turned and bowed to their prince.

Frei entered the room where ten generals of his father's defense forces were gathered around a large table covered with maps, paperwork and many mugs of beer.

"I do hope that you have come up with something and that the spirits have not taken over your minds, generals," Frei declared as he walked over to sit in the large chair that his father normally sat in.

General Comitay, who was King Dia's favorite and the most powerful of all his generals, looked at Frei with a concerned smile. Despite being only forty years of age, Comitay commanded seven legions of soldiers and four regiments of armored cavalry. Although Comitay was well-liked by the people of the kingdom, Frei knew that the general had his share of jealous enemies in this council due to his power and closeness to the king. Not only was he young for a general, but he was also quite brilliant on the battlefield, which made him dangerous to his enemies, whoever and wherever they might be. Luckily, Frei was not one of the general's enemies.

"My prince, you being here ... does that signal that your father, the king, is not interested in what we have to say?" Comitay asked quietly.

"No, of course not, General," Frei smiled to reassure him. "As you know, the king is very busy with the games and thought it would be prudent for me to get news of your progress so that I might inform him." Frei looked at each face in the room to see what they might be thinking. Only concern was registered on their faces.

Comitay shook his head and looked back to the rest of the council. "So far, my prince, we have come up with a few different plans, but we just received newer information on another sighting of orcs and goblins east of here,"

"Yes, I know of that news. I asked the servant to bring it to you myself." interrupted Frei.

"Ah, then you know who they might be, my prince?" asked General Suop, who commanded the heavy and light engineering regiment.

"No. I do not know who or what they are, only that the contingent has a large number of unidentified creatures with the orcs and goblins. "

Both knew, as did all in the council, that if their kingdom was attacked from the north and east, the city-state would fall. The southwest, where the high mountains of the Loth'ors shielded the city from attack, provided their only source of natural protection. Plus, his two brothers held castles in that mountain region and guarded the passes with their own armies, making it very hard for any sizable force to venture toward the city from that direction without being attacked from behind.

Comitay looked at the other council members and, trying not to sound too concerned, asked if an advanced troop of soldiers could be sent east to Castle Dagonor, which lay on the eastern edge of their kingdom. The castle was controlled by Prince Frei's cousin, King Dago. According to rumors, Dago wasn't the most liked royal due to acts he had performed on some of his subjects a few cycles back. From torturing his people to get money from them to using a few as entertainment for some games to show anyone that he could do anything he wanted. Such rumors had never been confirmed, so that didn't concern Comitay now. Castle Dagonor provided the best chance of protection for Brigin'i from the east.

General App, who patrolled that area of the kingdom, checked some paperwork then nodded. "Yes, General, I do believe enough soldiers can be sent. It is high time we showed a presence there," he said, looking at Prince Frei.

Frei looked up at General App. "Then by all means, let's get all the soldiers that you feel we can spare out there immediately. Be sure to give my cousin a warm welcome from me when you pass his gates."

Bowing to the prince, General App turned and walked out of the room. His voice echoed down the hallway as he barked out orders to his men.

Comitay picked up a map of the lands to discuss possible strategies when King Dia's private servant, Opto, walked in, getting Frei's attention as he came up next to him and whispered in his ear. The council waited patiently until the servant left, then looked at Frei.

"The king is sending his private mage, Bogwa, north to Whisleneck to speak to the mage council that gathers there. Hopefully, he will be able to learn more about these new attacks from the east."

General Comitay nodded and directed the council's attention to the area on the map where Whisleneck lay. All understood. If the attacks coming from the eastern seas and the attack that the prince experienced up north were in anyway related, or worse, converged, the city could very soon be on the front line of battle, if it wasn't already.

After a few more hours of discussing possible battle plans, the council felt ready to present their conclusions to the king. Prince

Frei dispatched a message by a servant, then accompanied the council into the king's private council chambers, where Dia awaited them after retiring from the games to rest himself from the excitement of watching them.

King Dia listened without saying a word while the generals and his son shared their ideas. Once everyone was finished, Dia got up and walked over to the balcony to think. Prince Frei stepped out to accompany him after dismissing the generals.

"Father, what are you thinking?" he asked, standing by the table.

Dia shook his head over the disaster he had created with his arrogant silence. Only one day was left of the games; he needed to be at the games and the ending ceremony tomorrow night. He still believed that secrecy was the best tactic for now, but it was getting harder and harder to keep the secret. Once the rumors got out, he would have a riot on his hands, if not something worse. Not to mention the fact that his northbound and eastbound visitors would be traveling into certain danger at this point. He knew the time was coming to admit to his people that there was an upcoming battle and to encourage those who joined the games to join him in this battle. He knew that he could still salvage his reputation by denting some of his pride, but the timing had to be just right, or he would lose his people and any potential help those from the games would be able to provide. First he had to get the dignitaries on his side.

Forcing a smile onto his face, Dia turned back to his son.

"Father?" Frei repeated.

"My son, tomorrow is the last day of the games, and our people are having a great time. The money is flowing into the city coffers, and the captain of the guards says that the city is peaceful. Do you not agree that all of this is good for our people, my son?"

"Well, yes, but —"

"With General App sending soldiers east toward Castle Dagonor, which is good as I have always believed that King Dago needed reminding here and there that he does not rule the entire kingdom, the city will be safe for the time being."

Worried over his father's answers, Frei walked over and placed his hand on Dia's shoulder. "Father, I am with you no matter what happens. You know this. But may I ask, do you truly believe, as our generals do, that we should continue to do nothing at this point?"

"Oh, I believe that these things are attacking and destroying villages and killing innocents, and that cannot be allowed to continue. I also believe that they are the most evil beings we will encounter and only together with allies can we defeat them. This must be done very soon." Dia turned and placed both his hands on his son's shoulders and gave him a huge smile.

"But for now, we need to ensure that the people have no idea what is amiss. However, I will concede that the royals must know of the danger. Please tell Opto to invite all attending royals to my private council chambers to break the fast tomorrow at the sun's rise."

Frei sighed, but nodded and smiled back at his father before turning to leave, only to be stopped by his father's final order.

"Oh, and Frei, please ensure that none of those in the competitions leave for home just yet. We may need to call on their services if these threats get worse. Offer drink and food if need be to keep them happy."

Frei stared at his father for a long moment before replying. "I do not pretend to know your mind, Father, but of course, I will do as you ask. Meanwhile, please go and get some rest. Plus, I am sure that Mother already knows that something is wrong. You should fill her in."

Smiling absently at Frei, Dia turned and stared out over the balcony, dismissing his son, both from the room and his thoughts. Frei sighed, then turned and left the room to find Opto.

Chapter Eight

The sounds of the forest made Caed smile a bit as he spied his brother, Jarmc, fanning away the flies that buzzed around his head as he scanned the forest. Those flies meant that summer would soon be upon them. Most elves welcomed the springtime as a signal of life waking up in the forest, but even as youths, he and Jarmc had always preferred the summertime, as the sun felt warmer on their faces.

Suddenly, Caed felt a wave of unease flow through his body and instinctively felt for "The Object" he always carried. As its appointed guardian, he had been trained since childhood to protect it from potential thieves. For the past week, however, he had felt something more urgent about the sense of a real threat.

A whistle brought his attention back to the present, and he finally noticed Jarmc pointing due east, past the fields near the forest border, where more than twenty fires now appeared in the far distance, and large ones at that. Worse, those fires were being set by groups of orcs. Knowing that they would not have much time to prepare for the attack, Caed hurriedly gestured to his brother in the hand language of their people, making motions and finger wiggles to indicate words and more.

WE HAVE A PROBLEM, MY BROTHER. MANY FIRES. MANY ORCS. I NEED TO INFORM KELIC.

Jarmc shook his head and responded back using the same signals. NO, BROTHER, YOU SEE BETTER. KEEP WATCH. I GO. STAY SAFE.

With that, Jarmc quietly shimmied down the tree to the forest floor. Turning back up to Caed, he waved farewell and disappeared into the forest in the direction of their village, which was about half a day's run from their current position.

Knowing that he would have quite a while to wait, Caed turned his attention back to the advancing threat. Over the next four hours, Caed observed about fifty or more orcs arriving from the east, joining the first bunch. Even from this distance, Caed could hear the chanting and loud singing of the orcs.

Caed covered his ears, but it wasn't enough to block out all the crying and screaming. *By the gods, that noise is terrible*, he thought.

Suddenly, the singing stopped. Caed looked around to see the source of the blessed quiet and observed yet another large group moving toward the campground. Even with his superior eyesight, Caed could not make out who these beings were as they approached. What he could see is that they were moving faster than orcs or even humans on horses.

"I wish I had a mage or someone here who could see what is out there," Caed said out loud, then fell silent when he heard something move in the branches. Feeling that sense of unease return, he again touched The Object and gripped his knife before recognizing the form of a cat moving around, trying to find food along the forest floor. Shaking his head over his own nervousness, Caed sheathed his knife and wished for a moment that he could be as carefree as a cat with no worries about things around it.

A whoosh of air from Caed's right brought his attention back to situation around him as he suddenly felt a sharp pain in his side. Looking down, he saw a small arrow poking out from his side.

"How ..." That was the last word that escaped Caed as the blackness overcame him.

Caed slumped against the large trunk of the tree as a figure wearing a black cloak jumped from branch to branch, finally coming to rest next to Caed. Unconcerned with whether Caed was dead or not, the cloaked creature began rumbling through Caed's pouch.

"Where is it, you bastard elf!" the creature screamed at Caed, having found nothing in the pouch. "I know you have it," he said as he kicked Caed, making the elf groan.

As Caed had been rendered unconscious by the poison on

the arrow tip, he could do no more than moan softly as the creature searched his jacket and body until he found what he was looking for.

"Ahhhh, here you are," the creature cried out as he held what he was looking at up to see it in the moonlight before looking down at the unconscious body of the elf. "You foolish elf. Only you would be stupid enough to carry this while out on a patrol and this close to the edge of your kingdom." The creature kicked Caed yet again, evoking a louder moan this time.

Suddenly, a commotion of branches and leaves breaking below reached the creature's ears. It had no choice but to move quickly away from Caed as his brother and another ten of his comrades burst into the clearing below.

Seeing Caed slumped on his branch, Jarmc raced up the tree and instantly saw the small arrow sticking out of his brother's side. Turning to the other elves, Jarmc used hand signals to order them to spread out to find the culprit.

From his perch about a hundred feet away, the creature watched silently as five of the elves jumped into the nearest trees while three others ran along the ground. One even passed underneath his position before moving out of sight. The creature thought about using their movements to cover his own escape until he noticed another, finer-dressed elf approach the base of the tree, where Jarmc now worked to get his brother out of the tree. This elf looked like royalty and held some command over the others.

For a moment, the creature considered capturing the elf lord. Only the precise orders of his master stayed his hand. He was not the type to appreciate any deviations from his plans. The creature would just have to wait out the elves.

* * *

"Caed is not dead, my lord, but he has been hurt badly by this arrow. Do you recognize its markings?" Jarmc asked as Kelic sat beside him.

Leaning closer, Kelic carefully studied the base of the arrow, trying not to move it for fear of hurting Caed further.

After a few minutes, Kelic's mouth formed a line as he clenched his jaw and shook his head, knowing that the answer would not help Jarmc feel any better.

"Jarmc, we must move your brother to a safer area. He will not survive for long if one of our priests does not see to him," the elf lord said quietly.

The expression on Jarmc's face was one of frustration, pain and anger as he hugged his brother's still form. "Yes, my lord, Kelic, but what of the orcs?"

Standing up, Kelic nodded grimly at Jarmc. "Let me worry about that," Kelic said. Peering into the darkness of the forest, Kelic brought his fingers to his mouth and whistled a series of tones that sounded like a signal before turning back to Jarmc.

"Your brother will be well, Jarmc. Remember, he is very strong and will not fail you or your family." Kelic reassured him by placing his hand on Jarmc's shoulder before quickly shimmying down the tree.

The white horse that emerged from the darkness was one of the most magnificent creatures Jarmc had ever seen. All of his life, he had heard tales of such creatures, as they were revered among the elven people.

As it approached, Kelic jumped down to the ground and walked up to the horse, speaking to it quietly. Though Jarmc did not speak the language of the magical beast, he could tell by the looks that Kelic kept giving him that the two of them were either talking about him or his brother, Caed. Jarmc hoped it was the latter, as his brother was growing weaker with each moment.

Nodding, Kelic turned and motioned to Jarmc to bring his brother down from the tree. Jarmc did not hesitate, so desperate was he to get Caed to the priests. However, as Jarmc approached the beast beside Kelic, he realized that it was the first time he had had the privilege to stand next to one of these large beings. "Magnificent" was the first word that came to his mind as he saw the being up close.

"Thank you, my elven friend," replied a voice of peace and beauty directly into Jarmc's mind, shocking him so much that he stopped in his tracks. He looked helplessly to Kelic, who smiled gently at the stunned elf.

"Do not be afraid of my friend here," Kelic said, motioning back to the beautiful creature behind him. "Lord Lugtrix is one of our oldest allies. He has chosen to reveal his voice to you so that he can give you his personal promise to take care of Caed, is that not right, my friend?"

At that, Lord Lugtrix lifted one his front hooves and stood on his hind legs before opening up the huge wings situated on the side of his huge body. Jarmc had not noticed them before but now stepped back and ducked to avoid being hit by one of the wings as he heard Lord Lugtrix in his mind assuring him that Caed would be fine and well with him.

"Do not worry, my elven friend. I will get him back safely."

Jarmc nodded as he helped the others place the unconscious body of his brother on Lord Lugtrix's back, working quickly but carefully to secure Caed so that the arrow protruding out of his body wouldn't be moved as the creature carried him.

As soon as he had finished the final tie, Jarmc watched in amazement as Lugtrix turned away from them and began to gallop away and gasped when Lord Lugtrix jumped into the air and used his great wings to fly toward the center of the forest, where their large village was.

The creature waiting in the trees did not gasp at the sight of the unicorn, though he, too, had never before seen a being of the like. He wondered if his master knew of them, then decided that there was no need to mention the creature. Keeping this little tidbit of information for his personal use might prove fortuitous.

Looking up at the sky, the creature noticed heavy clouds moving across the horizon, covering the moon. Now was the perfect time to move without being seen by the elves. Using the shadows of the trees, the creature made it to the edge of the forest, confident that he had evaded all of the elves as he began to run across the open field.

Suddenly, a cry came up from behind informing him that he had been seen by the elves. "A creature has been seen running away from the forest," one of the elves screamed. Kelic and Jarmc ran toward the elf who had cried out as more elves above quickly dispatched arrows toward the target.

"I believe our brothers have found the culprit, my friend," Kelic said as he ran out into the open field, watching where the arrows of the other elves were landing. He called for Jarmc to ready his bow and follow him as he ran toward the center of the field. Kelic frowned as he watched the creature evade some of the pitfalls that would slow most humans with their poor night vision. Hoping that more light might blind the creature, Kelic raised his arms and, with a single word, caused all the arrows flying over their heads to burst into bright flames as they streaked across the night sky. As each arrow landed, the magical flames that had engulfed the arrow spread along the ground, lighting up the area quickly.

As Kelic had suspected, the light seemed to slow the creature. In fact, the creature stopped and turned back to stare directly at Kelic and Jarmc. As Kelic drew his sword, the creature saw that the other elves in Kelic's contingent were closing in on his position as well.

Suddenly, a cry that sent a chill down Kelic's back burst out from the creature as he took off running again with such lightning speed that he was almost able outpace the elves. Having seen the creature in the light, Kelic knew that this being was something unusual, maybe something of the underworld. Whatever he was, Kelic needed to catch him, preferably alive, so that he could find out why Caed had been attacked, which was still a mystery to him.

"Stop or you will be shot," Kelic cried out, wishing that he was as proficient with an arrow on the run as he was with his sword on the battlefield. Jarmc, however, was more than proficient with an arrow whether standing or on the move, and so hearing Kelic's threat, he quickly aimed and released three arrows that literally brushed the cloak of the creature as he continued to run.

Instantly, the creature stopped and again turned back to stare at Kelic and Jarmc, who had yet another arrow notched and ready to fly. Kelic could see the creature was annoyed, but he cared not.

The being had thought to simply retrieve the device and return to his master, but now, it looked like he would have the opportunity to kill more elves. Not that the idea bothered him; he quite enjoyed attacking elves.

Kelic was the first to speak. "Who are you? Why did you attack my people?" Jarmc stepped up to stand beside his lord, his bow up and ready.

"You heard him," Jarmc growled, never taking his eyes, or his aim, off the creature. Kelic knew the look on Jarmc's face all too well and realized that the only thing staying his hand was his own desire to find out why his brother had been attacked.

"Tell us or die here in this field and be left for the vultures," Kelic continued.

Hearing a commotion in the distance, the creature smiled a little.

"No, I think it is you who will die on this field and be left for the birds," the creature rasped as a loud roar of approaching orcs reached the elves' ears.

Glancing at Jarmc, Kelic knew he only had a moment to get this creature to talk before they themselves had to turn back to the safety of the forest.

"Last chance, beast. Who are you, and why did you hurt one of my brothers? Speak or die," Kelic pressed as the sound of the orcs came closer.

Waving his hand at Kelic, the creature laughed. "Your threats do not scare me, elf lord. I am greater and stronger than you," the creature boasted as the orcs came into sight. With an evil smile, the creature backed away from the pair, moving toward the orcs. Before either elf realized his intent, a wall of flame ignited directly in front of Kelic to cover the creature's escape, causing Kelic to jump back and raise his hand to protect his face.

Jarmc released his arrow toward the running creature, as did another elf who had taken up a position nearby. Both arrows went flying past their intended target, hitting a pair of charging orcs instead as the creature disappeared behind his wall of flames.

Kelic was stunned by the creature's use of magic but had no time to dwell on the matter, as the orcs were upon them. Giving the order to retreat, Kelic and the other elves turned and ran as fast as they could toward their forest. All around them, orcish arrows and spears landed, including one arrow that hit Jarmc in the arm, making him cry out. Luckily, Jarmc was an experienced sentry, so Kelic did not have worry about Jarmc stopping to deal with his injury. Both knew that an arrow wound in the arm was nothing compared to the damage that orcs would inflict on them if captured.

A scream off to the left made Kelic pause as he saw another elf fall forward with a blackened arrow firmly embedded in his back. The creature might have won for the time being, but Kelic swore to the gods that he would make him pay.

As the last of the elves reached the forest line, arrows began raining from the trees, instantly dropping the entire front line of orcs chasing their brethren, causing them to fall to the ground screaming in pain. Knowing themselves now to be outnumbered, the orcs gave up the fight and disappeared back toward their camp, but not before retrieving the body of the one elf they had managed to kill. Their losses had been far more extensive; of the forty orcs in their party, only fifteen made it back to camp, but with a highly valuable prize in their hands: the body of a dead elf.

Inside the forest, Jarmc leaned against a tree, sipping water from his flask as Wa'tik bandaged his arm. He thought he heard Wa'tik saying something about how he was lucky. Jarmc felt anything but lucky as he thought of his day, a feat made harder as he slowly drifted in and out of consciousness. The arrow must have had been laced with some type of orc poison. As Jarmc lost consciousness, his last thought was his fervent hope that Wa'tik had the antidote on hand, as he had clerical powers to aid him.

Sometime later, Jarmc reawakened, relieved to be alive, and clearheaded. He wanted answers and knew he would not be able to rest until he started asking questions. Turning his head, he saw Kelic resting against a nearby tree, watching him silently.

"What do you think that thing wanted with Caed?" Jarmc asked.

Not wanting to discuss the matter of "that thing" in front of others, Kelic got up slowly and walked over to the tree where Jarmc rested, motioning to Wa'tik to give him privacy as he sat down next to Jarmc.

"I do not know, my brother. However, in my experience, hatred and theft are the most common reasons one attacks another in such a ..." Kelic paused as he sought the right word, "... personal way. Do you remember your brother ever talking about any enemies he might have made? Was anything missing off of his person? Anything at all?"

"I did not think to search his body before sending him back, but as for the other, Caed has not left our forest in at least three cycles. Frankly, I do not think he has had a chance to find anything special or meet anyone not of our people. What are you thinking. my lord?"

Kelic was thinking of the rumors he had heard about Caed, in particular, the ones about his dealings with magical items, but he decided that it might be best to keep silent about his thoughts for now.

In fact, looking around at the elves who were gathered around them, Kelic decided that he might need more privacy than could be had in the middle of a forest to say anything. He also needed to speak to their king before divulging more to Jarmc. Hopefully, the young elf would understand.

"We will speak of this matter more when we get home, my brother. There is much to discuss, and I know that you are concerned about Caed." Kelic smiled to Jarmc as he stood and started gathering his belongings.

That much was true, Kelic thought. Having an encampment of orcs practically at their forest gates was certainly a new development, as was their boldness in entering elven territory to attack his people. Something else was going on. Kelic wondered how much the strange events had to do with the creature they'd encountered. He suspected that the two were connected.

Seeing that Jarmc had followed his lead and gathered his bag, Kelic stopped to speak to Wa'tik, who was staying behind to keep watch along with a contingent of other archers before starting the six-hour trek on foot back to the village.

Chapter Nine

The sun was at the midmorning point by the time Kelic and Jarmc reached their home. The elves called their home a village, but in truth, it was closer to the size of a large city. Wooden buildings shaped like mountain caves dotted the trunks of the trees and branches of the forest that the elves had lived in for thousands of cycles. Kelic's own dwelling was a large cavern in the middle of the city, very close to the government caves and the royal caverns. Being the son of the first cousin to the king had never been a burden to Kelic. In fact, his position gave him more leeway to do what he loved: fight orcs and other darker creatures at their borders and beyond.

As he and Jarmc were waved into the gates of the village, the first thing Kelic noticed was that he didn't see anything different from normal. The village seemed to be operating as it usually did. Guards were at their posts; merchants were in the market. Outsiders like dwarves and men were milling about as well. There seemed to be no sign that the village had recently been visited by Lord Lugtrix. Kelic surmised that the winged stallion's magic must be even more formidable than he had thought if he could land in the midst of their village with Caed on his back without attracting any attention.

As the pair entered the third ring of the village the sound of singing could be heard coming from the temple, where the priests would be caring for Caed. Kelic could see the visible calm that came over Jarmc as they approached, even as his own senses were screaming at him to stay alert. Not only were soldiers posted before the doors (something he had never seen before) but the singing itself seemed wrong. The song coming out of the windows was one of warmth and not of healing.

Just before the pair reached the steps of the temple, a servant came rushing out of the doors to stand and bow before Kelic.

"Welcome back, Prince. I am glad to see that you are no worse for wear after your adventure, milord. Your immediate presence has been requested by our king. I was told to send you to his chambers at once. I will take care of Jarmc here."

Kelic gave the servant a long stare before finally nodding. "As our king wishes." Turning back to Jarmc, he squeezed his shoulder and nodded to silently reassure him of his support before heading off toward the king's chambers, still unable to shake the feeling that something was off.

He walked down the road that led to the king's chambers. Along each side, looking down, stood statues of warriors past that gave walkers the impression that they were being watched as they walked toward the leader of these elven peoples.

Kelic entered the royal chambers a while later as he learned the reason for the guards at the temple. The king was missing. From the looks of his now-blackened throne, there appeared to have been some type of a magical explosion.

Soldiers and advisors stood around talking franticly about the situation, even as Kelic was escorted by another servant into a private chamber off to the side, where his cousin Cufc, the heir apparent, sat in discussions with some of his own advisors. He recognized the mage Velus and the cleric Beca, but the rest were unknown to Kelic. "I heard that Caed's brother has been wounded as well. Is he expected to survive?"

Kelic blinked, unsure of who had asked the question. He was feeling quite drained at this point. He had been stuck for over an hour now in the small chamber but he knew by hearing and answering it would make things smoother for those asking questions, where he had been peppered with questions nonstop by the king's advisors, all while Cufc stood off to the side of the room, looking out a window. Kelic almost smiled at the kingly cliché, knowing that his cousin had heard every word thus far, until he remembered the news that had literally dazed him.

Lord Lugtrix had yet to appear in the village. Both he and Caed were now presumed missing. Kelic knew that it couldn't be a coincidence. However, right now, Cufc's advisors were more interested in learning more about the large orcish encampment at their forest borders than the whereabouts of Lord Lugtrix.

"My lord, are you sure that what you saw was hundreds of orcs?" one of the advisers asked.

"I saw hundreds of fires in their encampment. Far more than were required for the forty orcs who attacked us briefly. Whether they were all orcs or other beings such as the one we chased is unknown."

"Tell us more about the being that you chased. What did this creature look like," asked Velus, who was leaning against the wall beside Kelic. Kelic closed his eyes and forced himself to recall every detail he could of the horrid skull-faced being. When Kelic was finished, he opened his eyes as the mage showed a piece of parchment to Kelic, asking if the image looked like the creature he had described.

Astonishment came to Kelic's eyes. He couldn't believe that Velus was able to so accurately draw the image of the creature. "Yes, that's the creature I saw. Do you know this thing, Velus?"

Without answering, the mage turned and nodded to Beca, who rose from his seat and stepped to the side of the room with Velus, where they could converse privately. While they spoke in whispers, Kelic sat and listened to the others talk about what the village should do. Suggestions ranged from sending news to the human city to the west or mobilizing the army to maybe just hiding inside the forest and focusing on finding the whereabouts of the king.

As a warrior himself, Kelic understood the reasoning behind the last suggestion. Orcs were known to be strong fighters in open-field situations, but they wouldn't give the elves much of a fight within their forest realm. His thoughts were interrupted by the return of Velus and Beca to the table.

"Beca and I believe we know who or what this thing is. I dare not say his name here, but I know that we need to get our soldiers to the forest border and ready for anything. If our suspicions are correct, last night was just the first of more attacks to come." Velus's voice almost boomed inside the large room.

"Since when do orcs have the means to defeat us?" asked another of the advisors.

"It is not the orcs that you need worry about, but rather whom they serve. And," Velus paused, "we believe this creature took something from Caed that could be used to help in this attack."

Kelic frowned. "Are you saying that Caed had in his possession a piece of evil?"

Beca shook his head slowly. "Truthfully, my prince, neither of us knows what he had with him."

"Do you know if any of this business with Caed is connected to the king's disappearance?" Kelic asked.

Suddenly, the main door burst open and a soldier came running in, nearly out of breath from running.

Prince Cufc turned from the window. "What is the meaning of this unannounced intrusion, soldier? Guards!"

"Wait!" Kelic stood as two guards rushed through the doors to catch up to the warrior who had burst in. "I recognize this warrior." Indeed, the elf doubled over in exhaustion was one of the warriors he had left at the forest edge. The fact that he seemed to have run the entire distance meant that the news was indeed dire.

"Get this warrior some water," Kelic ordered the guards as he led the elf over to a bench and bade him to sit. .

"My prince … Your Highness," the elf said weakly, looking at Kelic and Cufc, "I am very sorry for disturbing you. But I have news from the border," the elf rasped.

Taking the goblet of water from the servant, Kelic knelt and thrust the goblet in the elf's hand as Cufc waved his guards off. As the elf drank deeply, Cufc placed a reassuring hand on his shoulder.

"Please continue."

The elf glanced at Kelic, who also nodded for him to continue. Taking one more deep breath, the elf explained, "My prince, the orcs we were watching were joined by yet another group of orcs. With their numbers rivaling that of a small army, they attacked our position along the forest border."

Both Prince Cufc and Kelic glanced over at Velus, who merely raised an eyebrow, as the warrior continued speaking.

"We fought them as best we could with the warriors we had. I was commanded to come and inform you and our king of the attacks. When I left, we were holding our own, but we were losing ground in certain areas." Only then did the warrior begin to notice the uneasiness of everyone in the chamber at his mention of the king.

All of the other chatter had melted away as the warrior spoke. Cufc knew that his quiet but furiously spoken words would be heard by all in the chamber as he stood up slowly.

"Ready the army. Orcs have never invaded our kingdom and will not be allowed to do so now. I don't care if we have to wipe them off the face of the planet. These evil things will perish before I let even one cross the first ring."

Kelic marveled at both the command in his cousin's voice and the speed with which his advisors jumped up to follow his order. Perhaps all of that staring out of windows wasn't such a bad tactic after all. On the other hand, he could not remember a time when his cousin was quite so angry.

Seeing Kelic's expression, Cufc smiled grimly at his cousin.

"I should have sent the army the moment I heard of the first attack. I wish I could go with you and fight alongside our warriors, but until my father is found, I must act in his stead," Cufc said, glancing over at the throne.

The large throne was the seat of royal power. For many, many generations, his family had only used the throne for peaceful objectives. Now Cufc needed to use it for a very different purpose.

Ignoring the blackened soot stains that marked his father's disappearance, Cufc sat on the throne, which instantly lit up the runes that were inscribed in their language along the sides and arm rests. The back rest shone brightly in a bluish glow. Cufc felt the power of the throne flowing through his limbs and into his mind. He closed his eyes so he could see the powerful images that were appearing in his mind more clearly. As he focused on the forest's edge, he saw the intense battle being waged between his soldiers and the orc army.

"By the gods," he whispered as he saw what looked like thousands of orcs attacking his warriors, who were fighting them off as well as they could.

Feeling useless, Kelic decided to give Cufc some solitude as he sought out his own chambers for a moment. As much as he wanted to return to the battlefield right away, he knew he would be of no use to his men if he didn't get some rest first. As he followed the advisors out of the chamber, however, its thick door slammed shut behind him, leaving Cufc alone and unguarded. As he turned to pull on the doors, a chilling scream reached their ears from inside the chamber.

For the next ten minutes, they worked to get the door open. Brute force proved to be a waste of time, as their swords and axes broke on contact with the enchanted door. Velus tried using his most powerful spells, but to no avail.

Soon the room went quiet. Those on the outside of the door watched in amazement as the bolts on the door suddenly fell apart, allowing the warriors to enter the chamber.

What they found sickened some of the guards to the point where they retched where they stood. Inside the chamber, they discovered all that was left of Cufc: a blackened husk of ash in the shape of Cufc sitting on the throne.

Chapter Ten

Despite his troubles, King Dia was almost sorry that the games were over. The competition this year had been the most profitable to date. He had also hosted the largest crowds ever. Dia wondered if he would be able to use the profits to finance updates on the city's defenses. Something told him that he would need a larger army and cavalry sooner rather than later.

In addition to Frei's report, there were new reports of orc movements on the northern borders, near the villages of Selkie and Mortlow. Even more worrisome were the rumors of a large gathering or army of orcs, goblins and other creatures sighted near his nephew's castle of Dagonor. The contingent was moving west toward the Forest of Levenori, where another group of orcs was said to be already encamped.

A cough behind him brought Dia back to the present. He turned around to see Frei and General Comitay waiting for him to discuss their next move. As he took his seat, Dia wasted no time asking the most pressing question of the moment.

"Do you believe that we can fight off three approaching armies of orcs?" he asked wearily.

General Comitay nodded toward Prince Frei, who gave his father an intense look as he answered.

"I do not believe that we can, Father. We had hoped that King Dago could handle the forces in the east while we tackled the group up north, but having heard no word from him ..." Frei paused.

"What if Dago fails?" asked Dia, looking at Comitay.

General Comitay raised an eyebrow as he looked between the two royals. "Then we will have a problem, Your Highness,"

Nodding, Dia stood and turned toward the window as he

considered their words. Frei and Comitay stayed seated, murmuring to each other as they patiently waited for Dia to give them their orders. A few minutes later, Dia turned back to the pair.

"We will have to trust that our eastern allies are managing the threats in their area. It could be that we have not heard from them because they are thusly engaged. Send our forces to the north. You must stop the orc army advance there. I fear it may be our only chance."

Prince Frei looked at his father and nodded. Dia knew at that moment that he might be sending his son to his death. He looked over to General Comitay. "How many men can we send north?"

General Comitay knew the answer but still checked his papers before answering. "We can send a thousand footmen with the prince as well as half of the cavalry."

"Half," Dia repeated as he mulled over the idea. It would not be enough. The orc forces were said to number in the thousands. There had to be something else he could do, some other forces he could call on. Frustrated, he pounded the surface of his desk, upsetting the neatly stacked parchments placed there earlier by Opto. One parchment in particular caught his eye: the list of winners. While Brigin'i City did not have the fighting strength to defend itself against three armies of orcs, thanks to the games, they currently had an abundance of mages on hand. Mages could use their expertise in magic to supplement his fighting forces.

King Dia turned around quickly and looked at his son.

"What is it, Father? Frei asked. "What are you thinking?"

"The contestants from the games ... there are mages among the winners." Frei looked at father and nodded.

"I have yet to send them on their final quest. What if I split the winning contestants into two groups? I could send half of the winners north with your forces, and the other half east toward Dagonor."

Frei walked over to his father and stared deep into his eyes. "Are you mad, Father? It is one thing to send the contestants north with my army. How could you think to send a bunch of ... contestants, alone into a nest of —"

"I have decided," Dia interrupted forcefully, silencing Frei's objections. Dia had not gotten his reputation for ruthlessness by being passive in the face of danger. He would risk every one of their lives to protect his son and city. Turning his intense gaze toward General Comitay, he folded his arms across his chest before addressing him. "Thoughts?"

Comitay shrugged. "You'll need the best of the group for the eastbound trip. With your permission, I'll assign some observers to determine the best arrangement." At Dia's nod, Comitay bowed deeply and left the chamber, leaving father and son together.

Frei wasted no time restating his case. "Father, I know you think this plan of yours is sound, but please consider the ramifications. You're talking about risking the lives of a bunch of competitors who are only seeking prizes. Have you thought of the future of the games if word gets out that winning might mean death instead of riches?"

As Frei continued talking, Dia sat silently, thinking about his son's words. In truth, he hadn't thought about the future of the games. It irked him to acknowledge that Frei had made a good point. The games would suffer if his final quests suddenly became deadly. He might even lose some hard-won alliances as a result. Still, he could think of no other options. His fighting forces were limited. There was no way to prevail against the massive orc contingent without magic.

"I respectfully ask to lead the group heading east," Frei said.

"What?" Dia replied. "No. I need you in the north."

"Then who will lead the group going east?" Frei persisted. "You must have someone in the group who knows your intentions." Then a face came to his mind, "How about Kalion? He has proven to be an exceptional ranger and leader."

"Enough," Dia responded. "I have heard your objections." Taking a deep breath, Dia tried for calm. "Listen, Son, I promise to consider your thoughts carefully. Right now —" A commotion at the door to the chamber interrupted the pair. "Sire!" Opto cried out as he ran into the chamber, visibly out of breath and sweating hard from his run.

"My king ... Shermee ..." Opto wheezed.

"What is it, man? What about Shermee? Spit it out!" Dia ordered.

"She's gone. Princess Shermee has disappeared," Opto wailed.

"What do you mean 'disappeared'?" King Dia asked loudly.

Taking a deep breath and swallowing hard, Opto nodded and continued on as best he could.

"The soldiers guarding her chambers have been found dead as well her ladies-in-waiting, my king. Please, come and see."

At that, Dia and Frei ran out of the chamber toward the northern tower, where Princess Shermee's rooms were located. Her private chambers, indeed all of the royal chambers, were guarded by some of his best soldiers. To his knowledge, there had never been a single incursion into the royal suites. Not even during times of war. As Dia and Frei approached the princess's chambers, Dia felt his initial worry turn into anger as he saw the bodies of the slain guards. However, what he found in his daughter's chamber turned his anger into a white-hot rage. The bodies of his daughter's ladies-in-waiting were burnt beyond recognition. Three young girls whom Dia knew and loved like his own daughters had been murdered most brutally. Frei bent down to investigate one of the bodies. As he touched the body, it instantly it fell apart, leaving nothing more than a pile of dust.

"What the ...?" Frei started.

The sound of metal banging against armor turned their attention back to the door of the chamber, where the city guard stood as Captain Marbod was fast approaching with a contingent of soldiers. Like the soldiers now lying dead, Marbod was a man whom both Dia and Frei trusted with their very lives. As he stepped over the threshold and saw the burnt bodies, Marbod stopped and sucked in his breath.

"By the gods!" he gasped, looking at King Dia.

"Report!" Dia ordered, having no time for routine niceties.

Marbod shook himself out of his shock. "I have given orders that no one is to enter or leave the city without being inspected by the watch. I've also doubled the guard in the royal chambers. So far, no one has reported any suspicious movements within the city at all. However ..." Marbod paused.

"What is it?" Dia asked impatiently. "Speak, man. This is no time to be coy."

Marbod stiffened but continued. "Well, sire, if I may say so, with the games going on, it makes it difficult to assess who may be a threat. The city is full of strangers, including many mages, sire, who are not known to be the most trustworthy of persons, with all of their strange powers. You do have to admit that this," Marbod pointed to the pile of ash that was once the body of a girl, "has the looks of magic."

Frei nodded. "I have to agree. I know my sister. There is no way someone could have come in and taken her by force without her yelling the castle down."

Dia nodded. He too knew Shermee. For all of her faults, she was no shrinking violet.

"My king," Marbod said, "I have heard rumors of movements of orcs. Might that have something to do with the disappearance of the princess?" Marbod could tell by the look on Dia's face that the rumors were true. Being captain of the city guards gave him access to a large network of informants. News like that couldn't be kept secret for long.

Dia looked at Marbod and told him everything he knew of the threat thus far. Marbod's eyes grew larger with each word until the king was finished.

"Three armies of orcs? By the gods!" Marbod whispered. Looking at his king, he continued. "I do not know how long you can contain the information about the orcs, sire, but no one will hear of them from anyone in my charge."

Dia nodded. "Thank you, my friend. Now, I must go tend to an even harder task." Indeed, Dia did not want to think of Shermeena's reaction to the news of their daughter. Then again, she probably knew already. As Marbod noted, it did not take long for rumors to spread around a castle of this size.

Leaving Marbod with the task of cleaning up the chamber, Dia made his way to his own chambers, where he knew Shermeena would be waiting. As he entered the room, he found her sitting on a divan surrounded by her ladies-in-waiting. Even from the door, Dia could tell that she had been crying. Dia stood patiently by the door as she dismissed her ladies. Once they were gone, Shermeena stood and began to walk toward him. Thinking that she was seeking his comfort, Dia held out his arms, only to be surprised by an unexpectedly strong slap to his face.

"How could you?" Shermeena snapped at her husband. "Who has our daughter? How could you let something like this happen?" she cried, even as she threw herself into Dia's arms.

Dia said nothing as his wife soaked his doublet with her tears. In truth, he had never before felt so helpless. More orcs than he ever knew existed were en route to his kingdom. Now his daughter had disappeared without a trace. Were the two events connected? He simply did not know.

He only knew that his kingdom was under attack from an evil that he could not understand.

Chapter Eleven

*T*he populace lined the main road leading to the arena, awaiting the winners' procession. Seeing their heroes walk past was one of the most popular features of the games, something the people truly enjoyed.

Captain Marbod crossed his fingers over his sword belt as he and his assistants stood above the crowds on a balcony, watching the parade. Ever since Shermee had disappeared, he had been placing guards undercover within the crowds to see what they could learn about the princess. Today, the bulk of his forces were posted at certain areas along the route to monitor and maintain control over the crowd, which numbered well over two hundred now.

With thirty winners to cheer for, the crowd was not only larger and more boisterous, but also far more raucous than in years past. And a little angrier too, Marbod thought. According to the betting shops in the city, this year's games had produced more upsets than ever.

Still, he anticipated that most of his problems would stem from those celebrating a bit too much. Brigin'i was a city of drinking and gambling during the games. No one loved such vices more than the exchequer. Marbod smiled to himself as he thought of the little man who had been beaming all week over the amount of coin this year's games had brought to city's coffers.

The crowd roared as the first of the winning contestants emerged from the arena, showing off their skills. Warriors waved and pounded weapons against shields; druids hit the ground with staffs or spears; mages shot bolts of everything from fireballs to lightning into the sky. Each action produced even louder cheers and roars.

Suddenly, Marbod caught sight of what appeared to be

a very drunk man running out into the parade to attack one of the contestants. Two guards had tried to grab him as he ran by, but he was able to slip through their hands. He ran straight for one of warriors, screaming as he took a swipe at the man, who was just able to jump back at the last moment and out of the way of the sword slash.

Marbod gritted his teeth in anger over the inability of his guards to stop a single drunkard. Turning to one of his assistants next to him, he growled, "Get down there and take care of the problem." The last thing he needed was a riot on his hands.

On the street, however, the "drunkard" was showing signs that he wasn't as drunk as Marbod had thought. Deprived of his initial target, the crazed man suddenly turned and attacked one of the dwarves who had come out of the procession to help the knight initially attacked. The dwarf took a full sword slash to the side of his head as the first knight jumped forward and with lightning speed pushed a small sword into the chest of the assassin.

Screams erupted from the crowd as the killer fell backwards to the ground. Blood pooled around the body as Marbod's guards worked to quiet the crowd and control the situation.

Thinking that the situation was rapidly spinning into chaos, Marbod yelled for all guards to prepare themselves as he ran down the steps and pushed his way through the crowds, only to notice belatedly that they were neither running nor screaming in terror. On the contrary, most watching seemed to be enjoying the spectacle. It occurred to Marbod that many in the crowd, most of whom had been drinking for quite a while, thought the attack to be part of the entertainment. Maybe the situation could be salvaged, Marbod hoped, as he broke out onto the parade route and walked over to look down at the now-dead body.

Seeing a guard nearby trying to hold back the crowds, Marbod realized that the first order of business was that of clearing the scene. Turning to another assistant, Marbod ordered, "You there. Get some soldiers and get those winners moving again. We need to get this crowd out of here." Turning to the crowd, Marbod pulled his sword from its scabbard and waited for the crowd to give him their attention. In as theatrical a manner as he could manage, he pointed his sword toward the direction of the castle and addressed the crowd.

"The quest has yet to start and already our mighty warriors are tested. What other trials await as our heroes seek the audience of the king? Move forth and discover more!"

As he had hoped, the promise of more action was all the motivation needed for the crowd to begin following the now-moving procession. Turning his attention back to the dead bodies still lying in the street, Marbod was interrupted by the soldier holding the knight who had killed the assassin.

"Sir, what do you want to do about this knight? He killed that man there."

Marbod had half a mind to let him go but knew he needed to find out what, if anything, the man knew about the assailant, something he couldn't do in the middle of the street. "Take him to the gaol. As a witness," Marbod stressed with a meaningful look at his soldier. "From what I saw, he was only trying to protect himself. And find the dead man's companions as well. I'll need to talk to them." Nodding, the soldier led the knight away as Marbod next sent a messenger to the castle to inform the king of what had occurred before having the bodies of the dead men moved to an herbalist shop. The king was not going like the fact that one of the contestants had been murdered before he was able to leave the city.

One of the guard messengers ran to him at that point and reported that the assassin was a drunk from a lower quarter of the city. He wouldn't be missed. Meanwhile, the dwarves who had come to the city with the now-dead dwarf had been located and escorted to the gaol to await his arrival. The messenger added that the dwarves were now demanding an audience with the king about the matter.

Marbod nodded and said nothing more as the messenger turned and ran back toward the tower, where the king was scheduled to address the contestants at the end of the parade route. Ordering his men to maintain order, Marbod headed for his meeting with the king.

The tower was the only part of the original keep that still stood today. Ten levels high, the tower contained over twenty rooms including the guards' room and audience chamber for the king.

As Marbod walked into the audience chamber he observed King Dia, Queen Shermeena and Prince Frei standing near the throne, which was elevated on a dais on the other side of the room, in deep conversation. Considering what had happened to Shermee, they seemed to be holding themselves up remarkably well. Another group of elven royals stood off to the side chatting among themselves. Marbod respectfully nodded to the group as he walked over to King Dia. After bowing deeply, Marbod quickly recounted the events in the street during the parade. Dia slammed his fist on the throne arm when Marbod finished. It was then that Marbod realized that Dia was closer to the end of his tether than he appeared.

"Marbod, you told me that you had everything under control, and now a dwarf from an allied kingdom is dead. Is there any reason why I shouldn't have you thrown in the tollbooth like your predecessor?"

"No, sire, there isn't. I lost control of the parade and will answer for that failure if that is your decision. However, I would rather discover the reason for the attack if you would allow me to continue. Meanwhile, order has been restored. The contestants are approaching this tower as we speak and are waiting for your audience."

Dia was angrier than Marbod had seen him in a long time, but he still managed to get regain his control with what looked like a physical effort.

"Damn you, Marbod. First my daughter's disappearance and now this. You had better bring me something useful, or I swear, I'll toss you in the tollbooth and not look back."

With that, Dia turned away from Marbod, dismissing him. Marbod needed no other cue to make his escape. As he left the chamber, his thoughts were of his family and what would happen to them if Dia sent him to the tollbooth. He would get the answers King Dia sought, all right, even if he had to make use of the tollbooth himself.

Meanwhile, Dia's thoughts were interrupted by the arrival of the contestants for the quest ceremony. Dia handed each winner a bag of coins as a reward for winning their respective events. With over thirty contestants, this was the largest group ever, but this also meant that he had more talent than ever at his disposal. If he could just send them on the quest, Dia was confident that he could find answers to some of the mysteries currently overwhelming him.

Dia stepped down from the dais after all the winners had been recognized. The laughter and talk among the contestants was joyful, and they all seemed to be having a good time, each hoping to win the as yet undefined quest. He could hear boasts from knights, warriors and even a mage about what they would do when they found the prize. King Dia had brought in a large amount of food and drink to celebrate.

As such, no one missed Dia when he left the room and headed up a small stairwell to another room, where the kingdom's state guardians and politicians had been waiting for him since his arrival. Dia despised the lot of them and knew that the feeling was mutual. Still, they had no choice but to deal with each other, and so Dia took a deep breath and entered the room, glaring at his enemies as everyone stood slowly and bowed to him.

"Your Highness, we have asked you to come and speak with us before you send out the contestants tomorrow," said Baron Parnland, who ruled a large amount of territory surrounding the city of Castoun, northwest of this city. A skinny man and one of the strongest and wealthiest men in the room, most people fell in line behind him when he had made up his mind on something. Even Dia liked him, despite his habit of interfering with the state's military business, which to Dia's mind, seemed to be happening more often than before.

Smiling at Baron Parnland, King Dia thought he understood their concerns. Money. It was always money. The barons, knights and guardians had for some time tried to overrule him on issues, but now it was personal.

As he motioned the gathering to take their seats, Dia decided to take the offensive. "Baron Parnland, may I ask what this meeting is about? As you know, things are moving fast, and I have many things to attend to."

"We are worried about the latest news of orc armies moving near our lands. Rumor is, they have been attacking and destroying towns in the north and east. Even the elves have been attacked east of here," said a knight seated at the table.

"Really? I have not heard of any attack from our friends in the forest. Where have you heard of this ... Sir Lual, is it?"

"Haven't you seen the smoke coming from their lands?" Parnland asked, returning Dia's look of innocence with one of skepticism. *That was what the smoke really was*, thought Dia.

Nodding at his name, Sir Lual answered, "Yes, my king. I have also been informed of other happenings within the mountains, such as cities being under siege by other dark creatures. As to my sources, well, it is pretty hard to ignore reports of these attacks now coming from travelers and survivors from those regions."

Damn, Dia thought as he saw his plans for maintaining secrecy unraveling. "Interesting ... please continue."

As expected, Baron Parnland brought up the topic of most concern to him. "On another matter, King Dia, we are all wondering why you have decided on choosing thirty winners this time. Our coffers cannot pay for that many if they all win. What do you plan to give them as a prize, if I may ask?"

Leaning forward so he could place his elbows on the large stone table, Dia looked around at each of the lords in front of him. He had to choose his answers carefully at this moment. Suddenly, an idea came to him.

"Lords and guardians of the state, I have decided to have thirty winners of the games not for the show of strength or for entertainment for our people but to help me find my daughter."

"Your daughter, the princess?" asked a young knight named Sturr. Although he had been knighted by King Dia only two months before, Dia suspected that his daughter had already had the occasion to enjoy his company based on his reaction.

"I have not put the word out, gentlemen, but yes, my daughter has been kidnapped."

Dia looked around the room to see the impact of his words and was frustrated to see genuine shock on the faces of the barons. He had expected someone to know of the kidnapping. Someone always knew something; each had his own spies who watched each other and the king as well. Still, he was warming up to his tale and pressed forward.

"I will have the winners of this year's games find my daughter. The thirty contestants will be broken up into groups and sent in different directions to not only find her wherever she may be but also kill whoever might be holding her or, if possible, bring them back here in irons."

Dia continued to look for signs of deceit but saw nothing but attentiveness on the faces of the barons. "As to how this will be paid, in addition to the normal winnings, I will be putting up my jewels and my personal treasures to make sure that things are taken care of."

"And will any of us or our people be ordered to accompany these people on this quest?" asked Baron Quin-toy, whom Dia had always thought of as a fat and lazy bastard.

"Of course not, Baron. None of you, your family or people in your employ will have to go, as I know all of you have more urgent business," Dia replied. *Like watching over your money and properties*, he thought, smiling slightly at the baron.

Hearing some murmurs of approval and seeing a few smiles and nods to each other around the table, King Dia knew that finances were the main reason he had been called here, as opposed to the orc problem that was arising on the borders. He could always count on politicians to think only of themselves and their own coffers.

For the next twenty minutes, Dia answered more of the barons' questions and concerns. After being asked the same question for the fourth time, King Dia slammed his fist on the table and got up.

"Gentlemen, I am sorry, but I cannot stay here any longer.

There is a celebration going on down below that I need to attend to. Soon I will need to inform the winners of Shermee's kidnapping. If you insist on arguing about this situation, then I suggest you leave and do it somewhere else. If not, you are all welcome to come downstairs and enjoy the celebration with me, the prince and our queen. Good day to you all."

At that, King Dia walked out of the room and headed downstairs. He was glad to see that the contestants were still having a good time for now. Dia knew that there would be little laughter after he announced the quest. Best to get the task over with, he thought.

"Again, I wish to thank the winners for entertaining the great people of Brigin'i at these games. I hope that all of you have had a good time here." Seeing the excited faces around him, King Dia continued speaking loudly for all to hear. "Because there are so many of you, you will be split into two groups. These groups will be assembled outside the city where they are to remain until the start of the quest at daybreak. I will post guards around each camp to ensure that the populace does not bother you too much ... well, no more than you want to be bothered." Smiling at the laughter and giggles, Dia signaled Prince Frei, who walked over to a large table that had been brought in earlier.

The Signing Table was part of an old tradition that his grandfather had started to be sure that each person sent on a royal mission was the same who claimed the prize upon returning. Dia had been a child at the time, but even he remembered the scandal that had occurred once when his grandfather had rewarded a knight with a large cache of coin and treasure, only to discover the body of the real knight a week later after it was returned by a farmer tending his fields.

While Dia waited for each of the contestants to sign the parchment, a messenger came up to him to remind him of the contingent of dwarves still waiting for an audience. Sighing, Dia left the contestants in Frei's hands as he stepped away to speak to the dwarves standing together in a small antechamber on the other side of the room.

King Dia regarded the group silently until he recognized the white-haired dwarf named Olan Orcslayer. Turning to him, Dia attempted to convey his sympathies over the loss of their comrade earlier in the day. Olan's accent was incredibly hard for Dia to understand, but he tried.

"The dwarf nam be Malor Spinebreaker m' lord a' he was one of me king's bestest warriors he was that. It was he me king gaveith the knowledge a' trust of this adventure too ya' know. He'th the wisest a' most knowledgeable of the world o'side."

Resting his hand on Olan's shoulder, Dia nodded.

"Kind dwarf, I am truly sorry for your loss. I saw your friend compete. He was a fine warrior. However, know that you will not be kept from this adventure due to the crimes of drunken fools. If there is one among you who feels that he can stand in for Malor, then I will agree to allow him to join the quest in his stead."

Olan thought about it and then looked up at Dia's eyes and nodded. "Yea, I do know a dwarf, m'lord. Me brotha', Holan. I'ma sure he be the best'est to follow in Malor's boots, as you say, yea?"

"Good, please go find your brother and give him the good news. Now, if you will please excuse me, I have many things to get ready," Dia smiled, glad to have the meeting over with.

Chapter Twelve

After leaving the dwarves, Dia ran into Opto and spent a while answering questions about maps, supplies and other things before returning to his throne. As he looked about the chamber, he noticed that some of the state guardians and lords had finally come down from the chamber above to attend the celebrations. He noticed that, interestingly, Parnland was not among them. Dia conceded that a few of them might have been genuinely concerned about Shermee but suspected that the bulk of them were just looking for something to criticize him about later, like not having enough food or entertainment, not to mention how much coin was being spent for this celebration.

Speaking loudly to get everyone's attention, Dia began. "Your quest …" Dia paused as the room fell silent. "Your quest will be to find my daughter."

Gasps and shrieks of shock erupted throughout the room. Dia had no time to answer their unasked questions now. "Each of you and any member who returns alive and with my daughter will be granted a piece of land with a suitable manor and staff to attend to your needs, along with a life pension."

Out of the corner of his eye, Dia saw some of the barons whispering to each other over his pronouncement, probably because they knew that he would take some of their lands to make up the new lands.

"What if the worst has happened, my lord, and she is dead?" one of the thieves piped up then.

Dia glared at the thief who had asked the question but understood what the man was really asking. If his daughter was dead, then why should they bother to return? He thought about it for a moment, then declared, "If the princess is found dead and you bring back sufficient proof, you will all still get the same."

Hearing many "ayes" and seeing smiles, he knew that had hit the right spot for them. Dia looked over to the lords who were now standing off to the right side, listening to his every word. Raising his eyebrows as if to dare them to contradict him, he continued. "So while I hope that you find enjoyment in this day's celebrations, please make sure that each of you is prepared and ready ... for ... tomorrow's ..." His voice trailed into a whisper.

Dia was suddenly struck with a sense of cold so intense that he felt as if he had stepped outside naked in the middle of a snowstorm. He looked over to his son Prince Frei and noticed that his son looked as if he were frozen in place. His eyes were staring at the king but not moving.

Dia rubbed his arms and blew into his hands to warm up. With the exception of a few contestants, almost everyone in the room seemed to be frozen in place. Dia walked over to Frei and touched his shoulder. Frei seemed to be caught in some type of trance that left him cold to the touch.

"My lord, what is going on?" asked one of the few contestants left unaffected. The others were looking around the chamber to see who or what might be doing this. A thief even pulled out his short sword and ran and hid behind a statue near the opposite wall.

"I do not know," Dia said quietly as he looked around the room. Suddenly, Dia heard what sounded like a howling wind, even though the air in the chamber was still. Out of the corner of his eye, he noticed two contestants pointing towards the dais. As he turned, he saw his throne glowing.

Dia quickly armed himself with a sword from one of his frozen soldiers, as did the rest of the contestants in the room who weren't already armed with blades. He motioned for them not to attack as he himself slowly walked up to throne. As he got closer, the light began to seem very ... beautiful to Dia. He wanted to back away but felt himself frozen in place like the others.

The sound of heavy breathing reached Dia's ears, followed by a loud voice that made Dia's heart almost jump out of his chest as it echoed everywhere.

"Hmm …" spoke the voice. "I can smell your fear... I can feel your fear," continued the voice, sounding as if it came out of the bright glow on his throne.

"Oooh, I do love it," the voice laughed echoing in the room, causing Dia to feel chills down his back when he heard a noise near his throne.

The glow of light on the throne slowly materialized into the shape of a man dressed in a black robe such as a mage or priest might wear, flames shot out from behind him causing Dia's throne to burn red then black in color. What sent a chill down his back was the silvery crown floating above the hood of the being now sitting on his throne. The glow from the crown blocked all but his mouth from view. At the moment, that mouth was smiling down at them.

Before he could even think of a word explosions of flames, clouds and sparks erupted as two other figures suddenly materialized from a bluish glow on each side of the throne. One wore a heavy, dark grey robe with a large hood that covered his head so nothing could be seen underneath it. Whoever — or whatever — it was held a staff that looked like a large snake of some kind. Dia felt his skin crawl when he tried to peer deeper into the hood and was instantly overwhelmed with a sense of darkness.

The other figure looked like a knight from times past. Taller than any knight Dia had seen, he wore ancient, battle-hardened armor that was rusted in places from the dents and scratches on his chest plate from battles it must have been in.

A death knight! Dia realized that he was looking at two creatures of legend, creatures that had been whispered about throughout the cycles but rarely seen, and seeing them now scared the hell out of him. Never in his life would he have ever imagined such creatures being within his lands, let alone his city. And while dealing with a death knight would be a difficult enough feat on its own, the presence of the other creature — an Illithid — was by far the worst thing ever for his kingdom. But now he knew. These were the things controlling and leading the orc armies along his borders. They just had to be.

An old soldier just off to his right grumbled and raised his huge axe before screaming a battle cry and charging up toward the throne. In his present state, Dia couldn't have stopped him even if he had wanted to. Just as the warrior reached the throne, the being sitting there simply raised a hand and instantly a flash of light exploded in front of the soldier. Screaming he flew backwards to land in front of Dia, leaving a trail of smoke from the explosion. The chest of the man was scorched with visible burn marks from whatever had hit him. He appeared to be dead, but Dia had no way to check him, as a bright flash of blue streaked across the room in the direction of a druid who had merely been whispering a prayer, causing the druid standing near the chamber wall to instantly change color, from flesh-color to grey, in front of Dia's eyes as he was turned to stone.

Dia couldn't believe it. Two men were dead within the space of a few seconds, and he could not do a thing to stop it. He screamed at the being sitting on his throne.

"Stop! Please stop what you are doing. Who are you?"

The laughter from the being on the throne made Dia clench his teeth in frustration. What he wouldn't give to be able to split this killer in two with his sword.

"Dia." The being stood up but didn't move away from the throne. "King Dia. High king of Brigin'i City. One of five kingdoms and states of the Northern Territories. I have been watching you for a long, long time... and I have come for my revenge upon you!"

"How is your daughter, King, hmm?" the being asked mockingly.

"My daughter ... who are you?" Dia asked quietly as his anger grew upon hearing word of his daughter but his voice sounded nervous to the creature standing at the throne.

"Who am I? Fool, I am the one who took your daughter. Oh,

she is a pretty thing, your daughter, so pretty. I think I might make her my personal slave. What say you to that?"

Dia watched helplessly as the being raised his hand and revealed a glowing sphere that floated toward Dia. As it got closer, Dia saw his daughter inside the globe. Whatever magic the being was using obviously allowed Shermee to see Dia as well, as she seemed to be screaming for her father.

Again, Dia struggled against the force holding him frozen as the being laughed and called the globe back to his hand his mind screamed from the terror of his daughter to what this monster had said about revenge.

"You see that I have your daughter, and I can kill her anytime I care to," the creature said sternly. "As well as your son." The creature laughed as a streak of blue light slowly inched toward where Frei stood frozen. Dia forced himself to quell his panic and think as the being threatened his son.

"Let my son go. Your argument is with me!" Dia yelled as the blue streak stopped its progress for the moment.

"You do not seem to understand, Dia. Your son is mine to play with now. I can do with him what I want. I have killed your contestants without such a thought. Why should I spare your precious prince?"

Anger battled with fear as Dia tried to keep the creature's attention on him. "If you harm my son, I will not do what you want." He quickly answered thinking if he negotiated it might stop the death in the room.

The creature laughed. "Ahhhh, Dia, you will do what I want whether your son lives or dies."

"What is it that you want?" Dia screamed as the being finally pulled the hood back. The crown above his head disappeared as if it hadn't even been there. Dia stared at the creature in shock. He knew that face, but from where, he could not recall.

"I... know... you," he whispered loudly.

The creature ignored Dia's words as he continued speaking,

quickly its voice changed as Dia could see its face shacking with anger as its eyes got tighter, mouth showing sharp and dirty teeth. "Remember, King, my companions here can kill you and destroy your city at will. If you want to save your city, you will do what I say, or within a fortnight, by all the gods, your city will be no longer... wiped from the lands forever."

Dia continued to focus on the creature's face. The face that appeared before Dia looked to be close to Dia's own age. Many blades had touched that face, but whoever this man was he had survived them all. Dia just wished he could remember how and from where he knew this man.

The blue light that had materialized before Frei disappeared as the creature turned to address the room. "Now, as for you winners of the games here in Brigin'i City, I order you to forget the task of finding King Dia's daughter. Those of you who do not heed my words will surely die. In fact, I expect you all to leave tomorrow and never return."

Of course, no one responded to the creature, but Dia instantly knew that death and dying overruled any prize money or titles that he could give them. He feared that he had just lost them in the quest to find his daughter.

The creature pulled out a huge piece of parchment paper from under his robes and threw it on the floor in front of Dia. "You will take all the coin that your exchequer has collected from these games and everything within your exchequer's cellar and bring it north to the castle of Lothaine. This will be your payment to me in exchange for a stay of execution. Else, my armies will destroy your beautiful city and the kingdom itself. Never let it be said that I cannot be merciful. If these conditions are met within a fortnight's time, I will release your daughter without you losing a thing, except your money," the creature laughed.

Why Castle Lothaine? Dia thought. There was nothing there except ruins and plague. Still, Dia had no time to think further on the matter. All he could focus on was ensuring that his city and people would not be destroyed now.

"What?" the creature sneered at Dia. "No argument from the great king?" The creature made a noise that sounded like an angry sigh. "Pity, I did so want to kill more of your subjects... and you!" Suddenly the creature laughed as if amused by a joke. "Of course, I jest. I need no reason to kill your people." The being laughed as he raised a hand again.

Thinking the creature meant to kill Frei, Dia could only scream "No!" as a flash of light shot from the being's hand. Instantly, the entire complement of state guardians and barons who were standing frozen in the corner exploded in red and orange flames, their screams echoing in Dia's ears leaving nothing but a black mark and dust on the floor where they had stood a moment ago.

Rubbing his hands together, the creature turned back to Dia. "Now you have nothing standing in the way of collecting the coin. Politicians are such problems, do you not agree, Dia?" the creature laughed.

An hour earlier, Dia would have been secretly pleased to hear of the loss of the guardians and barons who had plagued him for years, but now, all he could think of was getting this creature out of the room.

"Please, no more. I will do what you ask." His pride finally disappearing.

"Yes, Dia, you will. You understand now, do you not? I can and will destroy you, your family and everything you have ever known if you think to deceive me."

"I understand. But please, tell me who you are," Dia requested, hoping that his tone did not sound as pleading to their ears as it did to his.

With that, the being sat back down on the still-glowing throne as the Illithad standing to his left lifted the staff high into the air.

Suddenly, Dia's vision and mind were taken over with images of his city. Screams filled his ears as the vision revealed the populace of his kingdom running and falling over each other. Orcs, goblins and other creatures that Dia had never seen before ran through the streets, killing everyone they came across. The bodies of guards, soldiers and men-at-arms could be seen lying everywhere as blood pooled around them from the arrows, spears and swords sticking in them. More screams came to Dia's ears as babies were being eaten by what looked like trolls. The smell of blood came to his nostrils; heat seemed to be searing his skin.

Just as Dia was ready to beg for mercy, he heard "Methnorick is who I am" coming from the direction of his throne as the images suddenly stopped. Opening his eyes, Dia saw that this"Lord Methnorick" had disappeared. His throne was now clear but now burnt from flames. Also, he was now again capable of movement, as were the others in the room, many of whom now fell to their knees in anger and confusion as they took in the events of the past half hour.

Walking up to his throne, Dia was very, very angry. These creatures had come into his city and killed his subjects just to prove a point. Still …

"Who did it?" Dia demanded. "Which of you was able to rid the chamber of that creature and his henchmen?"

"It was a joint effort, Your Highness." Dia swiveled his head toward the voice and saw a small, grey-robed figure surrounded by two other figures similarly dressed. *Of course*, Dia thought, *mages*.

Right then and there, he swore to himself that if the city survived this attack, he would build a school for mages to rival anything that could be found in Blath 'Na City. However, what the mage said next nearly made Dia shame himself by weeping.

"I believe that we can find your daughter. This Methnorick should not be allowed to prevail. He must be stopped. I think we all agree to this."

Dia struggled to regain his composure. Thinking for a moment, he came up with his best idea yet in the hopes of getting their help.

"Are we safe, mage?" Dia asked. "Can I speak freely?"

The mage nodded. "My name is Harbin, sire. And, yes, we are safe enough for now."

Dia nodded as his pride came back with the anger within his body to. "Forget my earlier offer. This is now a life and death situation. Any of you who brings my daughter back will be brought into the kingdom as a duke or duchess and given anything you desire or need."

Seeing the contestants murmuring among themselves, Dia continued. "What say the rest of you? Will you join the mages in this quest?"

Dia waited patiently and prayed to the gods as the surviving contestants considered his words. One of the warriors, a former soldier Jebba, stepped forward. "Aye, I will go."

To Dia's amazement, Jebba's announcement seemed to inspire the others. Within moments, "ayes" filled the room as every one of the remaining contestants agreed to seek Shermee.

Dia was overwhelmed by such courage. "Thank you," he said quietly, holding back tears. Looking around the room, he motioned to Captain Marbod, who seemed still shaken himself. "Please go to the exchequer and bring back enough coin to double the prize money. You will ensure that all are equipped with everything they need. They must be ready to move within a day's time."

"Yes, my king." Marbod bowed before turning and literally running out of the tower to see to Dia's command. He hoped that the king knew what he was doing. Whoever this Lord Methnorick was, he was certainly powerful enough to kill anybody he chose. As a veteran of many battles, Marbod didn't scare easily. But he was scared now. Yes, he was certainly scared now.

Chapter Thirteen

*B*lath 'Na City was a booming civilization of culture, architecture and knowledge on the eastern coast. Three times the size of Brigin'i City, which lay many days west of Blath 'Na City, this city was one of the oldest settled cities in the northern territories.

The walls of the city had been expanded four times due to the city's growth. These walls were some of the largest and thickest walls in the territories as well. Made with the knowledge and oversight of the local dwarf smiths, each wall could withstand attacks from even the most powerful magic spells and heavy war machines. As an added defense, the base of each wall had been placed deep into the ground to prevent any attempts to tunnel in.

The port of the city was the largest of the territories, with the ability to house, supply and repair ships both large and small. The port area itself had its own governing body that oversaw the day-to-day activities. High cliffs on both the north and south sides of the harbor created a perfect cove for ships to enter and exit and provided high ground for establishing protection from pirates or worse.

An assortment of temples, churches and monasteries rose throughout the city. Each of the religious castes was afforded the ability to govern itself as long as its rules did not conflict with the laws of the city and did not oppress other citizens.

This diversity could also be seen in the city markets, some of the largest in the region, known for importing goods from all over the world. The universities, many of them more than a century old, boasted some of the top minds in not just religious studies but also science and magic. New students from all over flocked to the city each year.

It was no surprise, considering its size, population and strategic importance, that Blath 'Na City employed one of the largest bodies of footmen, men-at-arms and cavalry in the region. Over one thousand footmen and guards patrolled the city walls and areas around the city itself. Thanks to the massive amount of money that came in from the shipping interests, the city had no problem maintaining a standing body of men to not only guard the most important structures within the town but also be ready for any threat that might befall the city.

One of the buildings under constant guard was Blath 'Na Tower, the largest, oldest and most powerful building in all the territories, situated right in the middle of the city. Despite many years of weathered decay, the old tower still shined brightly during the day and glowed from firelight at night. Most surmised that magic was behind its appearance these days.

Blath 'Na Tower was run by a body of "advisors," who were well known to have a hand in everything that went on in the city. "Advisors," in fact, was a loose term since none of them had ever been voted into their positions. However, they had managed the city so well for so many years that the population simply conferred the title on them.

Within Blath 'Na Tower, advisor discussions were more like arguments about news of movements of darkness from the north and over the seas. For a few months now, since the middle of last winter's storms in fact, merchants and naval captains had been sending back reports of deadly clouds of mist and strange movements within the clouds of mist. That is, when they did not go missing themselves. Truthfully, there were even more whispers and talk of whole civilizations, human, elven, dwarf and others, just disappearing from where they had lived for years.

In fact, as the advisors reviewed the latest set of reports, a messenger entered with yet another report. One of the junior advisors stood to greet the messenger and take the report.

"Well, not only do we have these strange mists and missing

ships to deal with, but it seems that just north of our city, an army of evil beings has risen up from the ground to attack the villagers, destroying everything in sight."

One of the senior advisors piped up. "From the ground? Definitely magic. There is no way we can argue that now." Turning to the messenger, he asked, "Was anybody able to identify these creatures?"

The messenger looked at the advisor who had asked the question and shook his head. "No sir. Only one small child survived. She was found in a cellar, shaking and barely able to speak. This was the only information we were able to get out of her. I rode all night to bring you this information."

The same senior advisor spoke again. "You rode all night to tell us that some traumatized child told you about creatures coming from the ground? A tale that no one else can verify?"

The messenger reddened. "Aye, sir. The clerics there calmed her before talking to her. They insist that the information is accurate."

Seeing that the senior advisor was about to argue again, the junior advisor interrupted before he could reply. "I believe the best course of action at this time is to send a message to Whisleneck, the mage high tower, to see if they are aware of what is behind these attacks. Perhaps they can offer assistance."

The other advisors nodded in agreement. The young advisor turned back to the messenger. "Would you be willing to take this news to Whisleneck and return with their reply?" The messenger bowed. "Aye, sir. I will leave posthaste."

* * *

Then came the day when news came to the group of advisors that the Isle of Blakess, which lay a fortnight's sea travel to the northeast of the city, had been attacked, its towns and two castles overwhelmed and laid to waste. The isle's king had disappeared as well, and there was still no word back from the mages at Whisleneck. The advisors started to wonder if Whisleneck had fallen as well, but there had been no reports of any attacks to the west of the city.

No one had heard from the isle since word came of the attacks. Ships sent to the Isle of Blakess, both merchant and naval ships, had never come back.

The idea of such an overwhelming threat being so very close made one counselor state, "We need to close the port for the safety of the citizenry."

One counselor adamantly stated, "We must raise the levees and call on the army to protect our people."

Other counselors around the table started screaming out other ideas, like bringing the naval armada together to send to the isle to investigate.

Then there were those who wanted to keep things going as they were. The notion that the city could fall eluded most advisors, especially the older ones. They argued that the city had survived trade and openness and scaring its population now was the worst thing to do.

In the end, a compromise was reached in which they kept the port open but also ordered the levees to be raised and armed. The naval ships would be sent to check out the Isle of Blakess. In addition, the army would be also kept at the ready, using the public excuse that the time had come for more of the population to learn how to defend themselves as heavy snows hit the city hard from the western mountains.

* * *

In the middle of the night, word came by runners that Stych Castle, a large stone fortress and town situated south of Blath 'Na City, had been attacked and overwhelmed within a very short time period. According to observers watching from the hills when the attack occurred, every last man inside the town had been massacred and left for the vultures. Every house had been put to flames, and the castle itself was being pulled down brick by brick. It was a miracle that they had been able to escape without being discovered. They had been able to hear the screams of the dying for miles as they rode away to spread the news of the destruction.

As for who had launched the attack, the observers clearly reported a massive number of orcs being part of the attacking force, but also within their masses were giants — what kind, they could not say — and other types of beings they couldn't identify or describe.

Their reports were quickly followed by accounts from the port town of Laggtoun, situated north of Stych, as well as the town of Abynathor, just due west, of seeing flames. People from both towns were rapidly fleeing to Blath 'Na City in an attempt to escape whatever kind of force had the power to destroy an entire castle in an afternoon.

Blath 'Na City now found itself at end of its tether as all communication with other city-states and kingdoms had ceased, as did ships returning from the eastern seas, a fact impossible to hide from the many merchants who relied on their trade, not to mention the sailors' families.

Thus, it was through the news coming from their harbor that the population learned the truth. Now they understood why the levees had been raised and that the army wasn't just receiving training, but was preparing for battle.

While the games in Brigin'i City were coming to a close, many miles away, the city of Blath 'Na was in complete chaos. The advisors were operating in complete secrecy, refusing to divulge any news from the Tower about the situation. All that anyone would say was that the armada was still investigating the Isle of Blakess. Much of the populace was now deciding whether to leave for the mountains that lay west in the hope of escaping the coming threat or stay in the hope that the city's extensive military and massive walls could protect them from harm.

As town people from Laggtoun and Abynathor streamed into Blath 'Na City, the clerics in the city tried to calm those arriving in their temples as best they could. Truth was, they were quickly getting overwhelmed with frightened people and survivors. To make matters worse, many of these survivors were being pushed into army service, causing arguments to erupt as many resisted this. The continued silence from the Tower began to anger the people, who were starting to openly question the decisions of their leaders, especially when it came to the well-being of the people. Now not only had the two harbor towers been placed on alert, keeping further supplies from coming in, but the main gates had also been shut, keeping all further refugees from entering into the city.

At the same time that these things were happening, a dark, cloudy mist started moving in from the southern forests southwest of the city. Nothing seemed unusual about it until footmen out on patrol started choking and falling over screaming in pain. Mages from the towers within the city were called in and, within a few hours, had pushed the mist back. No one knew if this attack had been meant for the city, as it had been easily pushed back and away from the city proper. The toll, though, had been significant, with over thirty men lost to this mist.

As the sun disappeared over the western mountains, word came from a patrol that there was movement of creatures within the forests two miles north of the city's walls. The army and cavalry were quickly ordered into defensive lines outside the walls. Sergeants and officers could be heard yelling at their men to get into position. Bowmen inside the walls were placed along the ramparts and told to ready themselves. Trumpets were heard miles away as everyone was placed on alert. Citizens ran for their houses to find some type of cover.

As the men-at-arms and cavalry waited patiently, sounds of movement came. Then, slowly, signs could be seen as the creatures began to emerge from the forest and archers on the field, setting themselves up behind the army, constructed simple barricades and stopped and lit bonfires for their fire arrows.

Sintovmo Seabery, the marshal of Blath 'Na City, stood above the second line of soldiers and men-at-arms, watching the preparations and thinking of the impending battle. A veteran of many cycles of fighting orcs, giants and human kingdoms in the farthest reaches, Seabery had more experience and knowledge of warfare than any other man in this part of the world.

Though trained in conventional warfare, he had seen throughout the cycles how magic could change the course of a battle in the blink of an eye. Thus, he had ordered a few mages to cover the ground between them and the forest edge with flammable liquid that could be easily lit to combat those creatures who did not like fire.

The movements and shadows in the forests were soon accompanied by moans and howls, causing some of the younger men to visibly shake in fear. And worse, thought Seabery as the smell of urine hit him, he could tell fear was moving quickly through his lines.

"Damn civilians, always making a muck of things. Now their armor will rust," Seabery muttered to himself quietly, trying not to breathe in deeply.

Seabery's assistant, Usla, an older captain-of-arms who had been with him for a few cycles, smiled as he heard the marshal's complaint. He also hated dealing with civilians but understood why these young men were nervous. Truth was, he was a bit nervous himself, as no word had yet come confirming whether this was the army of orcs that had attacked Stych Castle in the south or something else.

Meanwhile, whatever was coming toward them now showed no sign of being deterred by the large army of over ten thousand men standing before Marshal Seabery. More worrisome, Seabery could see that these creatures were more intelligent than expected by not attacking right off. He decided it was time to take the battle to them.

Just as he raised his arm to signal the archers, screams, yells, roars and blasts from horns could be heard as the ground below him shook. As he held his hand high in the air, he watched creatures explode out from the forest in one great giant surge, running toward his army and city with all of the hellish gods following behind them.

"Gods help us," Seabery whispered quietly when he saw what was coming toward them.

"Fire! Fire! Damn you, men, fire your weapons!" he yelled as the screams around him grew in volume and intensity.

Chapter Fourteen

The campgrounds outside of the city's east gate were filled with contestants enjoying the free food, drinks and entertainment being provided by King Dia. Many were just glad to have lived through the games, not to mention their encounter with Methnorick earlier. Between the drinking and their raucous laughter, the activities at the campgrounds could be heard throughout the city.

In fact, it was the sound of the laughter that prompted King Dia to venture out to have a few drinks with those in the camps. He did not care if this Methnorick could see him or not. Brigin'i City had never been overwhelmed in its history, and Dia was sure that he could defend it again now.

News of orc attacks and movement blew into the camps that night, but to Dia's surprise, the news didn't seem to faze the contestants. Then again, having seen the destructive power of Methnorick, he was no longer fazed as he once was by the threat of orc attacks, either.

Jebba Plyhern sat next to the fire, trying to stay warm. He had always hated early morning watch. However, since he was the only one among them with a military background, he felt it his duty to watch over this admittedly skillful, yet mostly untested, group of champions. Shivering, he tossed another log onto the fire. Even with summer coming on, the dark early morning hours could be brutally cold. Furthermore, he had not gotten much sleep beforehand thanks to everyone in the campgrounds partying all night long, drinking and doing things that were, frankly, quite scandalous from what he could see and, most unfortunately, hear, so now he was both tired and grumpy.

Still, being on watch always gave him time to think. And right now, he was thinking about where they were traveling, the threat

Methnorick represented to King Dia, and most importantly, what he had volunteered for. Distracted as he threw another log toward the fire, Jebba overshot his mark, sending sparks into the air which landed on his companion's blanket. "Oops!" he exclaimed as he quickly ran over and stomped the blanket, hoping that he wouldn't wake Birkita.

Like Jebba, Birkita Kerwyn-el hadn't slept that well. Opening her eyes to the sight of Jebba stomping close to her, Birkita quickly jumped up.

"Sorry," Jebba whispered, "just a spark from the fire. Not to worry."

Smiling, Birkita returned to her pallet and fell right back to sleep. She felt fine with Jebba near her, and even though she didn't know much about him, she did feel secure enough to believe that he wouldn't kill her during the night.

Jebba felt the same way about Birkita, even though he knew nothing of her, either. Something about her just felt right to him, as if he could trust her with his life. He looked over at her sleeping form, marveling at how she had managed it, considering how few people he truly trusted nowadays. He had heard that she had fought some very hard battles against other rangers during the games, but it was the battle she had won after losing a hand during a sword fight that had added her name to the list of legends. The thought made him smile. She seemed to be fine now. The clerics in Brigin'i had been able to reattach her hand without her suffering a loss of feeling. All in all, she was a lovely looking elf.

The same couldn't be said for the creature stumbling into the camp at the moment. Jebba knew that the huge shadow coming out of the trees could only be the half-orc Bennak Mu'Hagan, one of the ugliest creatures Jebba had ever laid eyes on. Jebba really hoped that Bennak was as good as the stories told about him said he was. It was said that he had killed hundreds of orcs and goblins and even a few stone giants in his time and that fighting was in his blood.

Bennak knew that the humans thought he was older, but in truth, he was quite young. He had just passed his twentieth cycle when he left his people last summer. His large body bore the marks of a man who had fought hundreds of battles, and he made sure the humans knew it.

And in fact, Jebba was thinking of those marks. Scars literally covered Bennak from head to toe, yet he refused to wear a jerkin or anything on his upper torso that interfered with his movements. That was fine with Jebba. He didn't want this fighter having anything in his way when it was time to kill. With his long, flowing brown hair, piggish nose and dark black eyes, Bennak was larger in muscle and stature than the largest man in their contingent. Whatever quirks Bennak had, Jebba was glad he was fighting on their side.

Looking around the small camp, Jebba regarded the other companions in his group. His eyes fell upon the cleric Amlora Pizaeg. Probably a thief, knowing most clerics, Jebba sneered, then immediately cursed himself for his uncharitable thoughts. Not that Jebba didn't know firsthand of some clerics' penchant for greed, having been the victim of his own local cleric's thieving ways while grieving the death of his wife. But then again, that man was known to be so untrustworthy that most of the villagers had taken to hiding their valuables away whenever he came to minister to them. He had heard no such rumors about Amlora. She kept herself enclosed within a heavy cloak and didn't say that much unless asked.

A little ways over sat Meradoth Borynor, a man from some far away land he had never heard of or cared about, but who possessed skills the group needed. A mage in these times was a precious thing. This Lord Methnorick obviously had access to some powerful magic. The Illithiad with him proved that he had hold of a great power. Controlling a mind flayer wasn't easy, as they very defiant toward those they worked for.

Meradoth was a vociferous person too, always wanting to talk to people. Jebba had laughed when he had approached the shy Amlora and she just shrank away from his questions. Most of the others didn't seem to mind his questions, and Jebba had enjoyed watching people react to him.

Kikor Ru'nnn, an elf from the Hathorwic Forest just east of Brigin'i, was, according to Meradoth's quick observation, incredibly young for an elf and probably wasn't supposed to have left her forest. But, like he had told Meradoth, all beings had to try living sometime. Like him, Kikor was a warrior. It was her skill at swinging a blade that made her someone he wanted to get to know.

At least, that's what Jebba told himself. "As beautiful as deadly, according to those who saw her fight in the arena," Meradoth had whispered to him with a wink as Jebba stared slack-jawed at her flowing, silver-white hair, perfectly toned muscles and soft-looking skin when they first saw her from far away. Hathorwic elves were famous throughout the lands, having a reputation for being troublemakers, which was not always the best thing for their people.

Missing from the camp was Harbin Ituhwa, another mage, whom Jebba suspected would return with tales of having drinks with the king or someone else important. Harbin liked to boast that he could meet someone and get them to buy him a drink a moment later. Jebba had his doubts about the power of Harbin's appeal, but he did know that having a second mage could only increase their chances. And while Harbin was not quite as ... open as Meradoth (for which Jebba secretly thanked the gods), he seemed equally curious about people.

His last thought was interrupted by a sudden explosion from their fire pit. Being closest to the fire, both Jebba and Birkita were thrown backward by the force of the blast, which had been strong enough to not only produce enormous heat but also send fire logs flying outward. As the pair jumped to their feet, prepared for battle, a small giggle could be heard behind them. Turning toward the sound, they frowned at the sight of another companion in their group leaning by a nearby tree and laughing so hard that he had to hold onto it to keep from falling over.

"You should have seen the looks on your faces," Chansor Russfor squeaked, still overcome with laughter.

"Chansor, you nutter! You could have hurt one of us with ...

with whatever you just did," Jebba cried as he swiped at a piece of still-burning wood that had fallen on his shoulder. "Where in this world did you get the idea that something like this would be funny?"

Waving his hand as if he were still fighting off laughter, Chansor pushed himself away from the tree and ran toward Birkita and Jebba like a child, jumping around until he stopped in front of both of them with a big smile.

"Ah, well, I didn't really know what it was, but I knew it must have been something pretty interesting since a mage in the city kept it hidden in a small locked box. You should see your face, Jebba, he–he. Pretty flames it made, don't you think?"

Chansor looked over to where the fire was no longer in the pit but now a series of smaller fires all over the place. Seeing the burnt remains of bed rolls and their supplies made Chansor's smile disappear for a moment — but only for a moment.

"Only a thief would find something funny in someone's locked box," Birkita said under her breath as she walked back to her bed roll, or rather, what was left of it, and tried once again to get some sleep.

"She didn't like the joke, huh, Jebba?" Chansor whispered, leaning up to Jebba's face. Chansor was probably the smallest man that Jebba had met before, but from what he had heard about him during the games, being the smallest allowed Chansor to get through every trap that was laid out for his part of the games, getting through the course with such ease that it was like he was escaping from a piece of parchment paper.

"No, I do not believe she liked it," Jebba sighed. "You know Birkita." Jebba turned to look at Chansor and reconsidered. "Well, maybe you don't, but she seems to love her sleep, and you interrupted that."

Jebba looked up at the sky, knowing it would be light soon. "You should apologize to her." Seeing Chansor turn toward Birkita, Jebba quickly added, "Later. Just let her sleep for now."

Nodding to indicate that he understood, Chansor ran off

looking for another unsuspecting person to "play" with. Jebba watched him with a sense of bemusement. Maybe they would get lucky and Chansor would manage to steal something that could actually help his group in their adventure.

Jebba still had a hard time believing that Chansor Russfor was part of his group. Of all the thieves who had won in the games, he would end up with the one who acted more like a child or a fool than a thief. But then again, how does a normal thief act? Faced with this new riddle, Jebba returned his attention to the watch, and his thoughts.

* * *

Bright rays from the sun bathed the campgrounds as everyone woke up from the night's sleep. Soon, breakfast fires filled the campgrounds with the lovely smell of hearty food being prepared.

Groans could be heard from those whose heads really hurt, but most didn't complain. After all, it had been a good night to drink and think of good times ahead.

Bennak was one of those groaning the loudest. Imbibing over fifteen mugs of the local brew had not bothered him a bit. It was only after someone had passed him a pipe of what was supposedly the local weed that the effect of something had hit him. He had passed out soon afterwards, not even remembering his return to camp, but now woke to find himself surrounded by a few of Brigin'i's not-so-fortunate girls. Most likely the paid types, Bennak figured, judging from what they wore, or rather, didn't.

Cocking his head from left to right until he heard a satisfying pop and crack in his neck from the odd position he had slept in, Bennak rubbed his head as he stood up. "Ahhhh," he sighed, "it's going to be a good day." Looking around for some water to splash across his face, Bennak began his stretches, starting with his chest, even though it was still incredibly sore from a battle wound he had received during the games, before moving to his shoulders, all the while cracking joints and bones so loudly that he managed to wake a girl next to him.

Of course Bennak was well aware that he was far from handsome. He had heard the jokes about how his face was either cursed or the result of having been thrown off a cliff and hitting every sharp rock on the way down. But for some reason, when night fell, women flocked to him, though they mostly ran away the next morning — just like the ones next to him who were now waking up and scrambling to get away. Their screams and yells as they ran out of the camp didn't bother Bennak; he was used to it.

As the morning wore on, the last two members of the group, a man wearing a dark green flowing cape and Holan, a dwarf, finally arrived.

Holan, who had stumbled in, was of course as hung over from the drink as the others, Jebba realized. He grunted in welcome, not saying anything else as he walked over to the well nearest to their camp and threw the whole bucket of cold water on top of himself. His howls from the cold water could almost be heard across the city. Jebba shook his head, more grateful than ever that he did not care for drink himself.

Harbin, who had just recently returned himself, leaned over and asked Jebba if he knew the name of the now-screeching dwarf. "Holan, the dwarf who took the place of Malor after he was killed during the parade," Jebba replied hastily, as he was busy with the large amount of food in his mouth.

A cough drew everyone's attention to the other new man. Standing at the entrance of the campground as if it were an actual entrance stood the man with the cape. Jebba recognized the fine quality of his garment and wondered if they were in the presence of royalty. Across one shoulder was slung a leather bag that held a quiver full of arrows, a bow stave and other personal items. His chest was protected by a dull-looking piece of breast armor emblazoned with what appeared to be a dragon of some sort. Once everyone's attention was on him, the man raised a gloved hand and lowered his hood to reveal a smiling young face topped with long brown hair.

"Good morning to all. My name is Kalion Sa'un Ukka, but

you can call me Kalion. King Dia has ordered me to join your group and use my skills to help you along."

As Kalion lowered the bag from his shoulder, the source of his skills became apparent as everyone caught a glimpse of a long, sheathed sword and what appeared to be two smaller ones, which all knew to be powerful equipment from the crest that lay on their leather.

Kikor, who had been sitting across from Jebba, stood up, put her plate of food down and walked over to introduce herself, followed by most of the others. Of course Harbin knew of Kalion, explaining to Jebba that young Kalion was one of Dia's best trackers and rangers and having him was good for their group, even if he was from a powerful family and house.

"That would explain you having such a long name, friend — your family could pay for it," Bennak grumbled from across the camp as he approached the breakfast campfire.

Smiling, Kalion sat down next to Harbin, whereupon the two immediately started laughing and talking about some adventure they had once had involving some ladies in some far-off village a few years ago. Jebba listened intently as the tale unfolded and even smiled after a while; this Kalion seemed to be a good man, but Jebba was concerned about him taking over the group.

The pair was still laughing when the dwarf walked over from the well and grunted. "What's this, then?" he asked, gesturing toward Bennak. "We letting orcs and black elves in our group now?"

Jebba stood up and gave the dwarf a hard look. They had no time for petty prejudices. "Good dwarf," Jebba said coldly, pointing to Bennak, "this is Bennak, and he is one of us. Not some orc for you to kill."

Everyone seemed to hold their breath as the dwarf wrinkled his nose and stared back at Jebba.

"Fine!" the dwarf yelled loudly before throwing himself down in front of the fire where he started making himself some breakfast. The thought of some orcish man being near him still rankled him mightily, but he had a quest to complete, and the wisdom to know that he would need all the help he could get.

Kalion nodded at the clocked figure that stood off to the side near a tree arms crossed across is stomach, white long hair flowing off his head, Zahnz smiled and walked over and almost making the ranger bend over his heard the elf whisper a hello and quickly before he could say anything the dark elf returned to where he was moment before leaving the ranger and the dwarf both looking slightly in shock.

Everyone looked at each other with smiles on their faces. Even Bennak smiled a bit. Dwarves always could be counted on being grumpy, even at the best of times. Chansor was the first to walk over and sit down next to the dwarf, who was still grumbling under his breath about Bennak. Seeing the thief sit down, the dwarf grabbed for the small axe that he had placed next to him, but Chansor stopped him by raising his hand.

"I'm just here to ask your name, good dwarf, nothing else." The ever-smiling Chansor had always liked dwarves, thinking of them as good game for jokes and such.

"Hrrrr" the dwarf grunted as he moved his hand away from his axe. "Me name is Holan. Holan ORCSLAYER," he replied loudly, making sure that Bennak heard his surname.

Chansor smiled upon hearing the dwarf raise his voice. He would be good game for jokes. "Ahh, Orcslayer is it? Well, good, because we might need an orc slayer where we are going, I hear. If I see any, I will point them out to you."

Holan didn't have anything else to say to Chansor, turning his attention instead to stuffing his mouth with a mutton pie that he had bought at the market the night before. Seeing that Holan wasn't going to talk to him anymore, Chansor got up and walked over to where Birkita was gathering her things and placing them in her carry bag.

"I'm ... I'm sorry, Birkita, if I hurt you last night. I was, well, just trying to have some fun."

Birkita knew what he had done was for fun but also thought him deserving of a lesson, so she stopped what she was doing and looked directly into Chansor's eyes, giving him the hardest look she was capable of. "If you ever do that to me again, my little fellow, I'll make sure you are the first thing that Bennak over there eats for breakfast." At Chansor's gasp, she continued placing her things inside the bag, determined to hide her smile from Chansor.

Pulling his lips tight, Chansor risked a glance toward Bennak. Then he shook his head. Bennak didn't eat people ... or did he? He decided that it might be best not to take any chances as he walked over to where his things lay and also readied himself to leave.

Meanwhile, Harbin and Kalion had finished laughing about their earlier adventures and now continued their conversation in somewhat quieter tones as they talked a little longer about what was going on in the city and other places. Never one for much court chatter, Jebba joined Bennak and watched the others as they got themselves ready. "Bennak, it's going to be an interesting adventure, don't you think?" Bennak looked over at Jebba and grunted. While neither could have known it at that moment, this friendship would last a long time.

Chapter Fifteen

King Dia considered the news being brought by his heralds. More factions and contingents had left over the night, probably going home, he thought, having heard rumors about Methnorick. Still, a number had stayed around to enjoy the post-game festivities. Sitting in front of him was the list of winning contestants, most of whom were now both hung over and sore from a night of heavy drinking and womanizing. Dia would have preferred to have the teams leave as soon as they had agreed to volunteer so he could continue preparing the city for whatever might be coming from this Lord Methnorick, but he knew that any actions outside of the normal traditions would have instantly alerted the city to something being wrong.

He had, however, made arrangements for his son, Prince Frei, to go north with an advanced team of cavalry to try to stop any further orc movements. The horses and their riders made a quick exit in the hope of not being seen or heard by either spies or the populace.

Returning his attention to the list, he studied the team. Consisting of winners from each section of the games, the team was chosen based on the fact that many of the contestants in that team knew each other or had formed friendships during or before the games.

Meanwhile, the group heading east consisted of seven warriors, two mages, two druids, two clerics, one thief and one knight. Dia had heard from his heralds that the former soldier Jebba had established himself as a de facto leader. However, he felt that he needed a trusted ally to lead this group, for his daughter's life was at stake. His trusted captain of his special guard, Kalion, would serve this purpose. Besides, if rumors were to be believed, Kalion had feelings for his daughter.

However, there were a number of key warriors who showed Dia promise, and with what was ahead, Dia decided to have all the remaining contestants from the competition join his son in the north to assist in the protection of the city. Dia decided to place the elven warrior Osa Ardaka in command of the team that would join his son to the north. An unusual looking elf, he had captured Dia's attention at first sight, for unlike most elves, Osa was totally bald. This had the effect of making his pointed ears stand out more than usual, which in turn, made his other features seem even smaller by comparison. Dia had been impressed by Osa's performance in the second round of the warrior competition, where his skills with a bow were shown to be top notch. He hoped now that such skills would prove useful.

Another one who stuck out to Dia was Penelo, who had competed in the first round of knightly competitions and had shown considerable fighting skills with an axe and sword. However, Dia suspected that he might be a bit too overconfident about his fighting skills.

The most memorable of them all was the frost giant, Ame-tora. Representing one of the few giant clans that had come to attend the games, his cunning had thrilled the crowds as he outwitted all of the best warriors and traps in the warrior competition. However, something was nagging at the king, telling him to keep this one close by. He couldn't determine what it was, but he knew Ame-Tora should stay within the city.

Osa and Penelo would leave the next day behind his men-at-arms with those from the competition who had chosen to join the battle and meet up with Prince Frei north of the city, while the group heading east would travel in search of his daughter or track for answers to get them closer to finding his daughter.

∗ ∗ ∗

The trumpets sounded loudly enough for all in the city to hear. Each team set out from the southern gate with a fanfare from villagers out to wish them well on their quest, which the populace thought was just the common quest that Dia had cooked up for the team. Based on the details they had been briefed on, Kalion's group headed east once out the gate, while Osa led his group north to meet up with Prince Frei.

Both groups faced hard travel, but Kalion's group would have the opportunity to pass more villages, including larger towns with allied castles and a dwarf fortress with some of Holan's people who could help. More towns meant more opportunities for news and the ability to restock with ease.

The populace waved, cheered and blew horns from the streets and the city walls as the two teams left with huge carts following, each taking a main but ancient road, one west, one east. However, what none of the inhabitants of Brigin'i City realized was that there was another watching this fanfare and departure. One who did not cheer.

Chapter Sixteen

Clenching a gloved hand turned old and torn from age and travel and hard use into a fist, the spy watched and waited.

When he was done counting the number of members in each group and taking stock of their equipment, he got up and slowly began to make his way south, making sure to stay out of sight of any guards or footmen patrolling the roads nearest to the city until he came upon a hidden copse, where a large, black, leathery winged creature stood slowly munching on a wild animal it had caught earlier. The beak of the creature was as sharp as a sword and could kill a man in one strike. Seeing its master, the creature finished off its meal with a final big gulp and lifted its wings in preparation for flight.

Smiling, the spy grabbed the horn of the saddle and pulled himself up with a slight grunt. "South, my friend," rasped the spy. The winged creature cried a moment, then opened up its wings and lifted them high into the air. Following the western border of the Hathorwic Forest east of Brigin'i City allowed the spy to skirt all but the southern reaches of the forest, thus avoiding any attacks by elven archers or magic from within. Despite his power, he had been forced to learn that lesson the hard way when approaching the city days earlier. While the unexpected attacks had not slowed him down, they had caused his pet to suffer considerable pain when an elven arrow slammed into its right chest.

Two hours after leaving the outskirts of Brigin'i City and traveling around the elven forest kingdom, rider and creature saw the dust clouds of a large body marching north through a large, deep and long glen that separated the eastern parts of Brigin'i citydom from Castle Stych's northwestern borders.

A heavily guarded caravan rumbled along slowly through the heavy dust. Leading the contingent of orcs that stretched farther than the spy could see was a goblin holding a red banner with a crest of a blackened armored helm. At least a score of hill giants and heavily armed goblins marched within their ranks as well. Deciding that it looked like a prime opportunity to feed his pet, the rider ordered his pet to cry out a warning to those below.

"Orcs are always quick to kill," the rider whispered in his raspy voice to his pet. "They attack anything they believe will bring them either food or riches" he said as he drove his pet into the contingent, prompting the enraged orcs to attack, even as the captain of the guard ordered them to cease firing at him. None of the arrows hit him, as orcs were never that accurate at shooting, instead relying on massive amounts of arrows to kill their targets.

As the spy landed, he jumped off of his pet even before the creature had placed both claws firmly on the ground and ran over to the two orcs who had released arrows at him a moment earlier. As he approached the two orcs, the captain grunted to get his attention, running up behind him to explain that he had tried to stop them but they were just young and stupid. The spy turned around to face the captain, who instantly stopped when he remembered that he was dealing with a high-placed, dangerous person and instead raised both hands as if to say "sorry" before turning around and running off, leaving the young orcs to fend for themselves.

The two young orcs who had been stupid enough to release their arrows saw the reaction of their leader and tried to run off as well, but they were intersected by the rider's creature as the winged animal grabbed the closest orc and, in one motion, ripped into his chest with one of its claws while its beak stabbed into the helm of the orc's helmet, killing him instantly. The other orc screamed wildly as he turned toward the spy. Instantly, he fell to his knees and began begging for his life.

With a raspy voice that sent shivers up and down the spines of all watching the situation, the spy spoke. "Of course, orc," he said, just as his sword left its scabbard and severed the orc's head so quickly that those watching had only a moment to blink, sending it flying through the air, directly into the hands of an orc standing a few feet away. The orc screamed for a moment before dropping the head of his former companion and closing his own mouth in the hope that the man before him would not chop his head off as well.

Seeing that his pet was satisfied with its orc meal, the spy replaced the sword and turned around to find the caravan of the leader of this army. "Orcs," he spat out as he walked toward the caravan, which had stopped a few moments earlier, smiling as those creatures now hastened to get out his way. If nothing else, his pet surely had a way of making an entrance.

The huge brown leather and shield covered caravan was the mobile headquarters for the leader of this gigantic army. The general himself was a huge being who stood over everyone and everything except for the giants. He wore a leather helmet that was said to be made from the skins of men, elves and other creatures he had killed — a helmet with one eye hole, for it covered the head of a creature of myth to man: a cyclops standing over seven–and-a-half feet tall.

The sight of this "myth" leaning inside his caravan on piles of soft cushions atop a large bed covered with red silk failed to make the spy raise an eyebrow as he pushed his way past his personal guard and approached the general. For his part, Kaligor paid no attention to the spy's rude entrance into his caravan as he asked for a report.

"Do you believe the humans know of the master's plan yet?" Kaligor asked the spy as he gestured toward a small girl taken prisoner a few weeks earlier when her human clan was forced to join the army. Her chief had given her to him as a present in the hope that the general wouldn't kill her people. She gave him a piece of fruit which he took eagerly from her, laughing at her nervousness.

"No, my lord, I do not think they know a thing about Lord Methnorick's plan. Or this army," answered the spy, now leaning against the wall of the caravan to keep himself upright as the huge caravan bounced slightly with the movement. A gasp drew his attention back to the girl, who was now staring at him in horror as he spoke. Her sudden tears suggested that hearing his voice seemed more frightening to her than being in the presence of Kaligor, a thought that amused the spy.

The sound of a whip hitting flesh drew his attention back to the present. Grunting and curses could be heard outside as the hill giants pulling and pushing the caravan along the road were driven by their handlers.

"Dia Vaagini is no fool, though. Even if he knew of this army, he might not reveal his knowledge openly. He knows that spies are everywhere, and now that Lord Methnorick has visited him, he is sure to be sneaky about everything. Did you see any movement of men-at-arms or his prized cavalry?" the general asked as parts of the fruits spilled out of its mouth.

"Men-at-arms? Yes, I did see them, but not moving east towards this army, milord; they marched north," the spy rasped.

Hearing that, Kaligor stopped eating and leaned closer to the spy. "North, you say? How many?" The spy grabbed a chair just as the caravan took a major bounce, which was followed by grunts and yells from the giants outside.

Balancing himself in front of the general, the spy stated, "I would say at least a thousand men-at-arms, maybe five hundred cavalry as well." Watching the general's face, the rider continued. "Of course, a second and smaller group of contestants from the king's game went with them, but there are only about ten of them, including a frost giant, my general."

"Frost giant? Interesting that one of their kind would have been in Dia's games. He must have made an alliance with their king or something." At that thought, the cyclops stood up, knocking the girl next to him off the cushioned bed as he stretched his massive arms.

Her whimpers and cries made the spy smile a bit as he recalled his earlier thoughts. Maybe Kaligor would tire of her soon. She looked like she needed to be trained a bit more.

"I will have to have a talk with their king when we arrive

in their kingdom," Kaligor continued, interrupting the spy's thoughts again.

While the spy doubted that Kaligor would be allowed to talk to anyone, he said nothing as the cyclops walked over to a table with a large map on top of it marking Methnorick's progress. Armies had landed in the east near Stych Castle, and in the northern part of Brigin'i citydom, another army was marching toward its targets.

"North," the general repeated, looking at the map. "That would place this contingent of humans around here," he continued, pointing to a wooded area just north of the city. "If they march at a normal pace, they should get to their northern borders by the end of the week. I think our friends there should prepare a welcome for them, don't you?"

The spy smiled under his hood. Of course he would love to see the destruction of an army of humans. "My lord, I must report to our leader and inform him of everything I have told you. Is there anything you care to tell Lord Methnorick before I go, General?"

General Kaligor regarded the spy silently for a moment. "No, my friend, I have need of nothing. Please inform our grand and beloved leader that everything is going according to plan."

Turning back to the map, the general continued speaking out loud. "The Hathorwic elves east of Brigin'i City are under attack from my advanced guard as we speak. Blath 'Na City in the northeast is also under siege with the help of my cleric friends, and the far northern passes and fields are under constant surveillance. Everything is working as planned."

Kaligor stopped speaking out loud as he continued looking over the map. Speaking to himself now, he looked over the situation: *We have even managed to keep the dwarves below ground under intense pressure from our dark-skinned allies, which should be enough to prevent them from providing help to their aboveground allies.*

Rubbing his hands together, Kaligor smiled. Leaning back, he looked at the spy. "And of course, our trek northward has allowed us to gather many of the large man clans that lived west of Stych Castle, making our forces even larger with each passing day."

The spy almost smiled as he realized that the cyclops was actually fishing for compliments. "Yes, General, that is good news. Are we going to let the humans in this army live when we are done?"

Kaligor smiled at that but didn't answer. The spy took Kaligor's silence to mean an end to their conversation. He turned to take his leave again. "My master is calling for me, and I do not want to make him wait."

"Then be off ... although you should be warned that Blath 'Na City is not yet under our control, so the skies above will be watched there."

Bowing to the general, the spy walked outside to find the engineer of the caravan. Seeing him standing on a platform in front with two large Blingo'obins guarding him, the spy moved past the beings and jumped off the caravan before the giants could be ordered to stop.

He saw his pet flying in circles overhead and whistled. At the signal, his pet flew down quickly and landed in front of him with a loud screech. All of the orcs nearby scattered away, not wanting to anger either creature again as the spy again jumped on his pet's back and headed farther eastward to where the master waited eagerly for the news.

The crying sounds coming from the leathery winged creature as it flew away to the east echoed in the breeze as the orc army continued its slow march towards the largest-known occupied fortress between Blath 'Na and Brigin'i Cities: Bru Edin, known as the "Shield of the North" to the humans.

Bru Edin was one of the more newly built fortresses, having been built a mere one hundred cycles ago, and stood on top of an old volcano that had been dormant for thousands of cycles. Their fortress having been used as a base by elf and human warriors in the past, the inhabitants boasted now that Bru Edin could never be conquered. Kaligor was looking forward to making the people of the mountain fortress eat those words very soon.

However, it was the city just to the north of Bru Edin that Kaligor considered the real prize. Chai'sell, the city of honor and pride for the dwarf people, was over eight hundred cycles old. The city housed between five and nine thousand dwarf warriors, who provided more than enough protection for the three thousand workers and miners tasked with the common goal of finding metals both precious and hard. The dwarves of Chai'sell prided themselves on a reputation for producing the best armor and weapons in the northern reaches, a legacy that had spanned for more than six hundred cycles.

Kaligor knew that his goal of defeating both cities would not be easy. Combined, Bru Edin and Chai'sell had the ability, if needed, to call in over twenty thousand men-at-arm and warriors. Still, since leaving the middle kingdom of Sawla'mor and Stych Castle his army had been joined by smaller contingents of orcs and other creatures who now believed that this Methnorick was the new-found lord who could finally crush the human and elven dominance and solve problems throughout the world.

Chapter Seventeen

After a day of uneventful travel, the team led by Kalion came upon a small inn along the main road. Except for Kikor, most of the team, especially Meradoth, seemed surprised to discover the existence of such an establishment in the middle of the Hathorwic Forest. All, however, were secretly grateful for the opportunity to sleep under a roof that night, despite the quiet of the forest.

As far as Kalion was concerned, the forest was too quiet. Unbeknownst to the team, King Dia had warned him of reports of the eastern side of this giant forest being under heavy attack from a huge orcish army. While Kalion knew that elves had ways of avoiding humans when desired, given the nature of the threat, he had expected to see a steady stream of elves seeking refuge from the fighting, especially with his group containing of a fair number of elves. Yet so far, the western side of the forest seemed relatively normal but for the almost unnatural quietness, which seemed even more suspicious as he considered what looked like an empty inn.

Wanting to take no chances, Kalion decided to take a closer look.

"Meradoth, come with me. The rest of you wait here."

Everyone looked surprised to hear Meradoth's name called — none more than Meradoth himself, who quickly recovered from his shock and kicked his horse into action to catch up to the already departing Kalion. Once beside him, Kalion turned toward him and told him to ready a spell. "Just in case," murmured Kalion as they arrived at the inn and dismounted. Meradoth took both sets of reins, quickly tied them to the rail and took a deep breath as Kalion approached the entrance and stepped inside.

A moment later, Kalion returned to the door with a nod.

Meradoth released the breath he just realized he had been holding and turned around to signal to the rest of the group before joining Kalion. The inn had a simple but serviceable common room. There were at least ten long tables lined with benches and a large bar along one wall.

Despite the many candles burning in the inn, there were still a few dark corners; however, nothing seemed to be sitting in the shadows. Assured that there was no threat, Meradoth turned his attention back to Kalion and for the first time noticed the old man standing behind the bar. For the second time in the past five minutes, Meradoth felt himself overcome with shock.

"You're human. What are you doing in an elven forest?" Meradoth spurted out before he could stop himself, which earned him a frown from both Kalion and the innkeeper. Wearing what looked like an old surcoat of some kind, the old man had long gray hair and the look and frame of one who was once a strong fighting man. Meradoth wondered if the surcoat was a remembrance of past glory.

"You got a problem with humans?" the old man growled back. Sensing that he had insulted the old man, Meradoth glanced at Kalion, who merely crossed his arms and stared at Meradoth with an amused look, as if waiting for him to fix his flub.

"Of course not, good sir," Meradoth replied with an embarrassed smile. "I was just surprised to find a friendly face so far from the city."

The innkeeper stared at Meradoth for a moment before grunting out a curt, "Uh huh," leaving Meradoth with the feeling that the surly innkeeper would have happily spit on his toes after that grunt had they been standing outside.

Hearing the footsteps of the others, the innkeeper turned to back to Kalion. "Welcome to the Bloody Orc. What can I do for you and your ... friends?" he asked with a look of concern about the number of people entering the bar. Noticing the old man's increasing trepidation, Meradoth hurried to reassure the innkeeper of their intentions.

"Be calm, good sir. My companions and I are merely looking for some beds for the night. Food as well, if you are able."

"That depends. Have you coin for these beds and vittles?"

"But of course, my good man," Meradoth replied as he drew himself up, insulted by the notion that he was thought to be some kind of rogue. "We are on a king's mission. Not some lot of brigands." The old man glanced around the filling room, noting the quality of some of the garments before turning to stare at Meradoth again for what seemed like an eternity.

"Uh huh," was all he said to Meradoth before turning his attention back to Kalion, who couldn't quite hold back a smile as he nodded in agreement. Seeing Kalion's nod, the old man's face suddenly transformed as he pasted a smile onto his face and walked around the bar with open arms.

"Friends, be welcome. We have plenty of comfortable beds, good mead and my Domka makes the best pies in the entire forest. How long were you thinking of stay —?"

Kalion turned to see what made the innkeeper trail off. Just then Bennak and Zahnz walked in, dusting the dirt off their sleeves. Bennak was shirtless, as usual, and Zahnz's hood had fallen back, revealing the dark skin and long flowing white hair of his people. Seeing the pair, the old man dropped the cloth in his hands and ran towards the back of the large room.

"Dark elves! Orcs! Run for your lives!" screamed the innkeeper, in such a panic that he crashed into the door, instantly knocking himself out.

For a moment, everyone stared in shock at the unconscious innkeeper. Everyone, that is, except Bennak, who ignored the innkeeper and walked to the bar to pick up a piece of fruit. Turning back toward his still-stunned companions, he sat on one of the benches and bit into the fruit, completely unconcerned by the reaction of the others. Suddenly, Chansor giggled, followed by Meradoth, then Harbin, until the entire room erupted in laughter. Even Amlora smiled as she shook off her shock and hurried over to check on the fallen man. Meanwhile, the rest of the company began to help themselves to the fruit and mead that were resting on the bar.

"Bennak, did your stink scare the man, or did you scare him with your ugly face?" Chansor said, laughing. Bennak merely grunted at the insult that he had heard for nearly all of his life and continued enjoying his piece of fruit as Zahnz placed his hood back on and walked over to where Amlora worked on the innkeeper.

Like Amlora, Zahnz was a cleric. Such a profession was not normally associated with his people, but then, Zahnz was no normal dark elf. For one, he preferred life in the light on the surface. Most dark elves could not tolerate the light for longer than a few hours per day. Zahnz was one of the rare dark elves who had no sensitivity to light, thus allowing him to live among the other surface beings, as he had been doing for more than twenty cycles.

Zahnz had placed himself in the service of King Dia over fifteen cycles earlier and had helped negotiate the cease-fires of two small wars when his own city tried attacking Brigin'i. Being a natural politician or negotiator seemed normal for Zahnz, as was finding peace in being a cleric.

Amlora and Zahnz had finally roused the innkeeper and were helping him sit up when the door behind him opened abruptly, striking the man on the back of the head and knocking him out yet again. Amlora and Zahnz exchanged a look as Chansor howled in laughter, before returning their attention to the innkeeper.

A large, heavyset woman stood on the threshold, looking wildly around at the throng of beings filling the inn before finally spying her husband at her feet. The scream that erupted from her mouth as she fell to the floor, next to her husband, nearly knocked Amlora over as well. Even Holan, who was no stranger to noise, grumbled for someone to shut her up, as her crying and screaming bothered his ears.

"Dear woman, we did nothing to your man. He ... ah, just had an accident," Meradoth said calmly as he extended his hand to the woman and whispered a spell under his breath to quiet the crying wife.

Everyone watched in amazement as the woman looked at

Meradoth's outstretched hand as if it were a lifeline before placing her hand in his and slowly rising, now calmly looking at the diverse group of companions staring back at her in her establishment. She was an older woman, about fifty or so cycles old, with the look of one who worked very hard. Yet while Meradoth had quelled her panic, her eyes betrayed the fear she felt in their presence.

"We don't have much coin, but I have food, drink and some fresh horses. Please don't hurt us. It's only my husband and I and our young son." The scared voice of the woman could be heard by everyone now. Even Chansor had a look of concern as he ceased his laughter. Wanting to reassure the woman, Niallee gently placed her hand on the woman's shoulder.

"My lady, we mean you no harm. Nor your husband or boy. It is as my friend said. Your husband had an accident. He became ... distressed at the sight of some of my friends and ran into the door. We were merely trying to assist him when ..." Niallee hesitated. She was not sure how the woman would react to the news that she had knocked her own husband out. Nor did Niallee see any need to worry the poor woman further.

"Never mind that," Meradoth said softly. "We only want food and bed for the night," Meradoth explained, earning a smile from Niallee.

"You are not here to kill us?" the old woman asked quietly.

"Of course not. As I told your husband, we are on a quest for King Dia of Brigin'i and are just passing through the forest," Meradoth said with a soft smile.

Now that the woman seemed less frightened, Chansor returned to his old self as well, walking up to the woman with a big grin. "My lady, we plan to pay for everything here," he said, pointing over to Bennak, "even our dear and smelly friend over there."

Everyone in the room laughed as Bennak good-naturedly raised his flagon in salute, making the innkeeper's wife relax as she suddenly smiled at the prospect of telling her friends the unbelievable tale about the "polite" orc who visited her inn.

Mortlow

Kor Kor
Plains

Selkia

Du Idan
Selkie

Moors
of
Frost

Trois
Fields

River Brigin'i

Pilo Archs

Lake
Brigin'i

Levenori
Forest

Dagonor

Fle ors
Rocks

Brigini

Plains
of
Pawanee

Great South Road

Plains
of
Livi

She looked at her husband with a bemused smile as she heard him rouse himself yet refuse to open his eyes. "Dear husband," she murmured as she knelt down to stroke his brow before standing again to fix them all with a direct stare. "I will not have the lot of you thinking of my Aamonn as a coward. My husband has fought giants and lived to tell the tale," she added, looking at Bennak, who nodded back in acknowledgement as she walked behind the bar and grabbed a bucket of water that was used to clean dishes before returning to stand over her husband. "I'll not have you judging him based on a few ... problems."

With that, she gestured to Amlora and Zahnz to move away, before throwing the bucket of water onto her husband, giving Chansor yet another fit of the giggles as the innkeeper popped up shaking his head and spitting dishwater out of his mouth.

Opening his eyes, he glared at his wife. "By the gods, Domka, I swear you'll be the death of me!" The man shook his head again, trying to clear the fogginess that was in his vision until he spotted Meradoth.

"And why didn't you tell me that the orc and drow were with you? Can't you see that I am trying to run a business here?" Watching the innkeeper gripe at the friendly mage made everyone look at each other with smiles on their faces as Meradoth simply raised an eyebrow, shook his head and turned away.

Seeing that the innkeeper was about to follow Meradoth around in order to keep pestering him, Jebba decided to step in before his friend turned the annoying innkeeper into a frog.

"Kind sir, do you have the means to secure our mounts?" Jebba asked as the man looked away from Meradoth and began pouring yet another flagon of mead for Bennak.

Without looking up, Aamonn grunted and yelled, "Well, what are you waiting for? Get the boy, Domka!"

Jebba looked over to the innkeeper's wife and smiled as she frowned at her husband's back. Returning his smile, she turned to the room and said, "Please, make yourselves welcome. I will ready your rooms when I return." Pausing at the door, Domka turned around and said in a voice that dripped honey, "Oh, and husband, don't you dare let my forest pies burn while I am getting the boy," before slamming the door behind her, prompting Chansor to laugh at the look on Aamonn's face as he cursed under his breath and ran toward the direction of the kitchen.

The others were gathered around a large table drinking their mead and talking about the games when a boy of about fifteen summers walked in through the front door.

"You here for our horses, boy?" Harbin asked the wide-eyed lad. The boy nodded his head as he studied this strange group of the king's. Smiling, Kikor walked over to the boy and laid her hand on his shoulder.

"Then let's get to it. I'll tend my own horse then help with the others," she said with a smile that made the boy turn red as they walked out to tend to the horses.

Over the next few hours, everyone in the group drank and ate the pies that the innkeeper provided. The laughter and camaraderie continued as everyone at the table stared in amazement over the fact that Holan had eaten one less pie than Bennak, who was four times his size. While most of them had been more than sated after two pies, Bennak managed to eat five, all while insisting that the fifth was simply because he found Domka's pies the best he'd ever eaten.

Throughout the evening, Aamonn and Domka watched the group from afar, being quiet and serving them when needed. Birkita was the first to notice the strangeness of their silence and began to watch them closely, wary of a trap. After a while, however, it dawned on Birkita that they were nervous about something. Concerned, she rose from the table to join them at the bar.

"Is something wrong? You seem ... well, frightened again." Birkita motioned with a hand toward the others. "Have we done something to distress you again?"

Aamonn nodded and glanced at Domka, who dropped her gaze to the floor as she spoke. "It's just that we have heard rumors ...

whispers," she said, leaning closer to Birkita.

"Domka ... don't —"

"Silence!" Birkita shouted, quieting the room instantly without taking her gaze from the trembling woman. "What kind of rumors?" Birkita asked firmly, flashing the innkeeper a look that he had never before seen on a woman but knew better than to challenge.

Aamonn suddenly realized that this woman with the soft smile was dangerous. He glanced at the now-quiet group at the table with a new set of eyes and began to talk.

"The elves who live in the forest have been whispering about an evil force coming from the south and east for days. Then, yesterday, a runner came and told us that the evil was at their borders and that we should leave for the human city in the west. Now, today, you and your company come speaking of a king's mission. Yet you are not large enough to fight an army. And to go east otherwise is madness. Unless ..." he trailed off.

"Unless we are part of the evil force," Whelor piped up, having followed the innkeeper's train of thought.

"The thought had occurred to me," Aamonn admitted.

"And now?" Meradoth asked.

"Well, we ain't dead yet. Unless you were just waiting to fill your bellies before killing us," Aamonn spat out.

"Are you trying to make me kill you?" Meradoth asked through clenched teeth, rapidly tiring of this cantankerous old man who had had it in for him since he first stepped into the inn.

"No!" Domka screamed as she launched herself off the stool she sat on and stood in front of her husband.

Meanwhile, at the far end of the bench, Jebba and Harbin spoke quietly while everyone else focused on the growing argument between Aamonn and Meradoth. "You think we should have gone a different way, my friend?" Harbin asked quietly.

Jebba shook his head. "I do not. However, I do now wonder if we shouldn't have traveled as one large group. You saw what this Methnorick did in the king's tower. The innkeeper is right about our chances of success traveling east without more warriors. Do you not agree?"

Harbin looked more closely at Jebba's eyes and answered as firmly as possible. "You're looking at this the wrong way, my friend. Now I'm more confident than ever that the princess is this way. Why would you wish to compete against a frost giant for the prize?" Harbin laughed softly. Nodding toward the others, Harbin continued. "Look what we have here, Jebba. We have powerful magic, muscle, cunning and intelligence, something that the orcs do not have."

Jebba wanted to remind Harbin that the orcs might have Methnorick, but he had no time for further conversation as the group rose to go to bed, having reassured Domka that her husband was safe from harm by Meradoth.

Once the guests had retired to their beds, Domka left the common area to clean the kitchen area, closing the door behind her. Aamonn contented himself by counting up the coin he'd collected for the night. Tonight was a good night for his family, as he had decided to take his family west as soon as their guests departed.

He had moved on to cleaning the tables when Domka returned from the kitchen and trudged up the stairs to her own bed after kissing the head of their son, who had fallen asleep next to the fire. Aamonn hurried to join her when he heard what sounded like a horse at the front door.

"Not now. It's late, and I wo' not be helping whoever that is," he grumbled out loud as he walked to a window to see who or what it might be. Seeing nothing in the moonlight, he thought for a moment that his son hadn't finished securing all the horses as he heard the huff and chains of a horse again. Looking over at his son asleep by the fire, exhausted by the day, Aamonn dismissed the thought. What was he thinking? Moving to a different window, he pulled back a drape to look out onto the front porch. However, the torches that his son was supposed to have lit weren't burning.

"I'm going to have to hit that boy ... can'na do a simple job of lighting a simple torch, and now I'm going ta have ta do it." Grabbing a torch off the wall, Aamonn opened the front door, welcoming the rush of cold air as he stepped outside and away from the now-stuffy common room.

As he made his way to where the standing torches stood, he felt a chill go up his back and hurried to light the first of the torches in front of the inn.

The soft light cast a glow on the gathering area, revealing what he thought at first to be a wolf until he got closer and saw the armor and a hand. He dropped down and turned the body over to see who it was, gasping when he discovered the body of the elven runner who had come the day before.

"Oh gods, what happened to yea?" he whispered as he checked the dead elf for wounds. Not finding any, Aamonn saw the elf's messenger bag and opened it up. Searching through the bag, Aamonn found some elven food, a small knife and a rolled piece of parchment that looked like a message of some kind. Stuffing the items back into the bag, Aamonn lifted the body and walked back into the tavern.

Placing the body on the bar without making much sound so as to not wake his son, Aamonn checked the body more closely to see where the poor fellow had been wounded. Still not seeing anything made Aamonn wonder if magic had harmed this elf. "Hate magic," he whispered as he nibbled on some of the food.

"Hmm … elven food always has a special zest to it," he murmured out loud as he found the parchment and unrolled it. Seeing the elven writing, he cursed. "Of course. I should have known. What other kind of message would an elf have?" For a moment, Aamonn thought about waking up one of the elves staying upstairs, then decided against it. For all he knew, that woman Birkita might slit his throat if he tried to wake her. Still, this elf had died delivering this message. Someone needed to know, Aamonn thought, as he suddenly slumped down in the chair near him and fell into a drugged sleep.

Chapter Eighteen

The conquered castle sat on the top edge of a high mountain range looking over a jagged rock cliff. A formidable structure, each of its towers had high battlements that could stop any conventional attack. Its illuminated walkways clearly revealed signs of the huge army living and working within reach of the large keep that housed their lord inside.

Above, black storm clouds rained down heavily over the castle, accompanied by copious amounts of lightning, which seemed to strike the ground everywhere as Chenush approached.

From his vantage point atop his winged beast, he could see orcs marching around as goblins practiced with their bows and spears. Of course, these were no ordinary targets they were using. The goblins were firing on humans who had been lashed onto poles. Each time one was hit by either a spear or arrow, a high-pitched scream could be heard, even from where he flew, making Chenush grin underneath his hood.

"Probably the past owners of this castle," he mumbled. "Serves them right to be tortured." Chenush believed that weakness deserved to be punished, and this castle with all its battlements fell far too quickly. "Weak humans," Chenush mumbled.

Chenush jumped off of his pet's back the moment it landed and walked briskly to the stairs leading down into the tower, not bothering to look back at his pet as it cried out loudly before flying off in the direction of the mountains to rest until needed again. The walk toward Methnorick's chamber was quiet and uneventful. Chenush did not have to worry about passing any sentries as he made his way to Methnorick. The master would never have any orcs near him. Methnorick was the only being Chenush had ever come across who seemed to hate orcs even more than Chenush did, making Chenush wonder fleetingly as to why they served him in battle.

The thought was quickly forgotten, however, as he turned the corner and found himself standing before the doors of the main chamber. Like in the hallways, no one was posted here either. Methnorick had no need of guards, having other means of protection at his disposal.

Pushing the giant doors open, Chenush needed a moment to allow his eyes to adjust to the bright torch light coming from inside, which had been arranged to temporarily blind anyone coming through the main doors. Chenush smiled in approval as he heard the echo of his master's voice.

"Ahhhh, what news do you bring, my friend?"

Chenush felt his smile slide away. It rankled him when his master called him "friend." Chenush had seen Methnorick kill many of his so-called "friends" over the slightest infractions over the cycles.

As he stepped inside, Chenush looked toward the huge throne with elvish script chiseled all over it. Torches had been arranged to keep Methnorick hidden from view, regardless of how one entered the room. All he could see of his master even now were his legs as he sat upon the throne.

Sitting around Methnorick were five human women, including one who looked like the daughter of the former ruler of this castle. They each wore chains around their necks that were, in turn, attached to the bottom of the chair Methnorick sat in. Their clothes were sparse and tattered, and they appeared to be visibly shaking, either from the cold or from sheer fear. Chenush enjoyed the sight of them groveling by licking and kissing Methnorick's boots. However, he also knew that Methnorick did not like to wait for long. Falling down to one knee, Chenush answered his master's question.

"Master, King Dia has sent out forces to the north of Brigin'i City along with a smaller group of about fifteen marching east toward the elves, just as you said they would, in search of the princess. I also spoke to General Kaligor. He speaks of nothing but success, reporting that he has conquered all lands he has entered, killing nearly every man, elf and dwarf he has come across. Castle Stych has fallen, and he reported that all there are dead and the area is ready for your armies to land. Everything is as you planned it, my master."

"And what of Shermee?"

"She was still intact when I took my leave, master."

"And her current location?"

"On her way to Blath 'Na port to be transported here to you, my master. Safe and sound."

For a long while, Methnorick said nothing. In fact, the silence stretched so long that Chenush began to wonder if he had said something wrong. And then Methnorick spoke in a voice colder than any Chenush had heard before.

"See that she remains that way. Now rise."

Chenush stood, yet wisely kept his head down so as not to anger Methnorick further.

Methnorick waved his hand, and along the wall to his right, a large parchment map appeared. Chenush watched silently as Methnorick unrolled the map and held it by unknown magic as he checked out the areas that Chenush had just spoken about.

"Hmmm. ... What word of my army here in the north, my friend?" asked Methnorick as he pointed to the area north of Brigin'i.

Chenush lifted his head to look at the area Methnorick pointed out on the map. "Before observing King Dia's armies' movement, I made sure that they were moving to the position you ordered, my master. As of a week ago, they were waiting for his forces to approach theirs."

"Waiting! I did not order them to wait. Why are they waiting?" Methnorick turned around and walked straight up to Chenush. "Why are they waiting? I ordered them to attack at soon as they arrived," he screamed.

"I know not, Master, but General Orle'ak has his army well positioned in a large village overlooking an even larger valley and castle called Castoun. If Dia sends his army that way, they will have no chance, Master."

"Castoun, you say? Yes, I like that position for his army," Methnorick replied more calmly as he looked back at the map. Nodding to himself, he seemed to come to a decision.

"I need you to rejoin your army and prepare them for the final assault on these lands. However, before you go, I believe you have something for me," Methnorick said quietly. Chenush had almost forgotten about the objects that he carried within his side pouch. He reached in and pulled them out one at a time and placed each object on a nearby table. The first was a rectangular piece, the second a cube and the third a small pyramid with strange engravings. Chenush had picked them up as soon as he had arrived in this land, in the first small village he destroyed. All three objects had the same strange engravings.

Methnorick grunted and nodded. "Continue on with your mission, Chenush. I will see you when you return in front of the armies."

Chenush bowed his head and turned to leave, then stopped.

"Master, what are the objects for?"

Methnorick turned to Chenush with a strange look on his face. "I am not sure. I just know there are a total of seven to be found."

"But each object.. each has power that when put together within a larger device will bring total power for those that weld it.... but without these... there is nothing... nothing for me... nothing for the masters across the seas that will come if I fail!"

Chenush thought it strange that his master was not aware what the objects were to be used for. Perhaps he was not as vital to the mission as Chenush first thought. That would be something to consider later on.

"And what of the other contestants? Do you plan to do something with the second group as well, my master?"

Methnorick raised his eyebrows and smiled at this question. "They will be destroyed with Brigin'i. If they join the army and fight, they will be destroyed with the army. Either way, we need not worry about them."

Chenush smiled and again bowed and turned to walk out, stopping suddenly upon encountering two huge Blingo'obins. Hating how these beasts could sneak up behind him, he dismissed them from his thoughts as he quickly walked past them.

Blingo'obins were the largest of the goblin species. Each of these goblins stood over six feet in height, with such muscular bodies that looked almost human to some but for the greenish-grey color of their skin. Even their faces appeared more human than goblin. Legend said that magic had somehow merged humans with goblins in the past.

Methnorick cared nothing about their origins. He only knew that the Blingo'obins were twice as strong as other goblins and were also very intelligent for their species. Unlike orcs, Methnorick valued the presence of Blingo'obins in his guard.

* * *

Shermee awoke. Looking around she saw the rough wagon cover above her and felt the rocking motion as the wagon moved along the road. However, it felt much rougher than any road she had traveled on.

We must be moving through the forest, she thought as she looked around for an opening. The sides of the wagon had been tied down tightly so that nothing could be seen, giving her no clue as to where she was.

All of a sudden, the wagon stopped. Hearing voices in a strange language just outside, Shermee started to scream, only to realize that she was gagged.

The riders at the front of the wagon looked at each other when they heard movement in the back of the wagon.

The driver turned to his companion. "I think the princess is awake."

His companion grinned. "We are in the middle of nowhere, and no one will hear her screams. Maybe we can have some fun before we get her to Blath 'Na."

The driver shook his head. "No, you heard what we were told by Chenush, and he is one I don't care to cross. Plus, Blath 'Na is still several days north, and the boat is due to leave in two days."

His companion relented, having no desire to cross Chenush either. "Fine, then. But we should still check in on her. Suppose she has broken free?"

The next thing the princess saw was the wagon covering opening and two creatures who looked a lot like elves but with strange skin and huge smiles on their faces staring at her.

* * *

Chenush walked out of the huge tower and into the central courtyard of the castle and skirted by the orcs and other creatures who were there practicing and training. The rain that had been pouring down earlier had stopped, but mud now caked Chenush's boots as he walked along what was once a pathway. Prisoners were still being brought up from the dungeons deep below the castle. Their screams and cries of pain echoed throughout the courtyard.

He walked through the large portcullis in the front of the castle and saw the damage that Methnorick's forces had wrought during their attack as orcs and goblins worked on rebuilding the damaged portcullis.

Outside the large castle were heavily trodden fields where Chenush watched as large numbers of orcs and goblins continued training. Turning the corner, Chenush continued walking around the wall to the right of the castle's main gate where he came across a group of Blingo'obins as they were themselves leaving an area that held prisoners being tortured. The first creature looked down at Chenush and laughed.

"What have we here?" the goblin asked as he reached down and stopped Chenush by placing his huge hand on his shoulder. "You know you aren't supposed to be here without orders." Without saying a word, Chenush pulled out his blade from underneath his cloak and sliced into the hand that was holding him down, watching with satisfaction as blood spurt from the gaping wound.

The screams of pain from the goblin could be heard all the way to the courtyard. Chenush knew the creature could kill him but would not dare so long as he served Methnorick. He wanted them to know, however, that he was not afraid of them and would stand up to them if provoked. He looked at the remaining creatures from his half-hidden face, with his blade at the ready as the other Blingo'obins started to unsheathe their swords.

Still holding his arm, the Blingo'obin stopped his advancing companions with a quick shake of his head before turning back to Chenush. "You will pay for this, beast!"

Chenush smiled at that comment as he walked back to stand in front of the wounded goblin.

"Will I?" Hearing no answer beyond a growl of frustration from the wounded Blingo'obin, Chenush laughed derisively before leaving the wounded Blingo'obin and his companions to watch him walk past the prisoners held up by ropes on poles.

The wounded Blingo'obin watched as Chenush walked away and turned back to his companions, but not before whispering a now-sacred vow: "Someday you will not have Methnorick to protect you. Then we will finish this."

Chapter Nineteen

*D*omka woke up early that morning with an almost overwhelming sense of unease. Something was definitely wrong. Seeing nothing but empty space where her husband's form should have been made her even more nervous. Aamonn wasn't one to miss his sleep, especially with a group of travelers to tend to. Hastily donning her clothes, she tiptoed out into the hall and quietly opened the door to her son's room to see if he was there. Seeing his sleeping body calmed her somewhat as she closed the door and quickly but quietly made her way down the stairs to the common room.

Peering through the still darkened room, the sense of unease she had tried to tamp down flared back to life as she saw her husband's body lying on a table near the front door.

Taking a shaky breath to quell her panic, Domka rushed over to his still form, praying to the gods that he was all right until she was close enough to see his chest moving up and down. Shaking her head over her own silliness, she was about to turn around to start breakfast when she noticed a piece of parchment paper with funny-looking writing on it under her husband's arm.

Curious as to why her husband would be in possession of what looked to her like elvish writing, Domka eased the paper out from under his arm and walked over to the window to get a better view. Domka had lived in these forests and woods all her life and had learned to read and speak the local elvish tongue as a child. What she read made her start to shake yet again:

Lord and King Dia of Brigin'i, my dearest of friends, it is with a heavy heart that I send this to you. Our forest and kingdom are under attack from large numbers of orc and goblin forces. For four days now, they have attacked our borders and have so far not been able to get inside our forests, but our losses are rising rapidly.

I beg you to send help and soon. Your cousin King Dago has tried to help, but in doing so, his castle is now under siege, and I believe he will not survive long either.

To make our situation worse, both our king and high prince have disappeared. We have no word of what happened to them.

I do not believe that we will be able to hold our borders much longer, as we have been informed by spies that more enemy forces have been seen approaching our forest from the northeast.

I have ordered my people to gather at the southern reaches of our borders and make their way toward Pibor'ch Forest, where, hopefully, our cousins will be able to help. But it will take a ten-day march to get there, and we will certainly be under attack the entire way. Worst of all, I believe this army of evil will continue on toward your kingdom after it finishes with us.

Yours aye,
Prince, Lord Kelic

Dropping the parchment in horror, Domka ran back to her husband and began to shake him awake, screaming his name in his ears. "Aamonn, AAMONN! Husband, you must get up and make ready now!"

"Why 'ou so loud, woman? what's a ma'er 'it 'ou anyway?" He then saw that the parchment he had found last night was gone. "'ow ...'ou, woman, you 'ook that from me, yea?"

"Yes, I did," Domka replied tearfully. "Didn't you read it?"

Aamonn shook his head and frowned. "Of course not, woman. I ca'na read elfish, you know 'hat. Whats it say any'ay?" he said without much concern as he slowly sat up and yawned, holding his head with a hand.

"It says that the elves here are under attack and might not be able to keep the enemy back for long and that their king and prince are gone!" she said hurriedly. Aamonn stopped in mid-yawn as the events of the previous night flooded back into his sleep-fogged brain. Whipping around to face his wife, Domka was relieved to see that Aamonn was finally paying attention, even as he grabbed her arms somewhat painfully.

"What 'ou talking 'bout, woman? Under attack from whom?" Aamonn demanded, listening intently as she revealed the contents of the message.

"Gone? You think he meant murdered?" Aamonn asked quietly as he released his wife to retrieve the fallen parchment. He couldn't believe it. The elven king was gone, as was the king's son, two of the most-loved creatures of this forest. Who or what was attacking them now?

Hearing his wife gasp, Aamonn turned to see Domka holding a hand to her mouth as the other shakily pointed to the bar. "Now wha?"

Domka looked back to him slowly. "What is that on the bar, Husband?"

"Just the elven messenger who held that parchment you read," Aamonn replied as he ran toward the steps to rouse the king's contingent, leaving his wife to continue ranting about leaving a dead elf on their bar.

Hurrying to his son, Komenn's, room, Aamonn shook Komenn awake and ordered him to get their horses, along with those of their guests, ready for travel, as they would be leaving the inn as soon as possible.

Rubbing his eyes, Komenn sleepily asked, "But why, Papa? And where are we going?"

Aamonn looked over his shoulder as he hurried out of the room and replied, "West to Brigin'i. We will be safe there. Now go."

Aamonn then ran to wake the guests, although he began to feel that he need not have bothered with all the noise Domka was making downstairs. Sure enough, just as he raised his arm to knock on the first door, it suddenly opened, prompting Aamonn to jump back as Kalion filled the doorway before him with a fierce look in his eyes and a weapon in his hand.

Upon seeing the innkeeper, Kalion relaxed his stance and sheathed his sword. "What in the world is all the noise?"

Aamonn felt his cheeks redden over his reaction as he answered Kalion. "Sorry milord, my wife is in a bit of a panic." Handing the message to Kalion, Aamonn continued. "We received this late last night, after you had left for your rooms."

Kalion took the message and scanned it quickly, frowning as he read the contents. Apparently the orcish army was closer than Dia had thought. "Why wasn't this brought to me immediately?" Kalion asked, gazing at the innkeeper so intensely that Aamonn was tempted to turn tail and run right then and there.

Instead, Aamonn just looked down to the ground as he answered, "I am sorry, milord. I did not know the importance of the message until my wife read it this morning. The messenger died, you see, shortly after arriving."

Kalion regarded the keeper with a look of amazement, wondering how such a clearly idiotic man had managed to survive all these years in the forest. "Wake the others. Have them meet me in the common room immediately. And ready our horses."

Aamonn nodded, relieved to have finally done something right. "My boy is already in the stables getting them ready."

Kalion dismissed the innkeeper from his thoughts as he ran downstairs to question the innkeeper's wife about the messenger.

After reviewing the details of what had happened with Domka, Kalion headed over to the area where the team had assembled in the common room. Kalion had convinced Domka that food for everyone would be a good idea before they all headed out on the road, so Domka went back into the kitchen to make everyone something to eat. A few moments later, Domka served the guests while Kalion filled his companions in.

"We have to consider the fact that this could be the same force that this Methnorick is commanding," Hrliger said.

"If that is the case, is it wise for us to continue?" Jebba asked.

Niallee piped in, "Somehow we must warn Brigin'i of the danger as well."

"The innkeeper and his family will need to travel to Brigin'i. Why not have them take the message?" Chansor's voice sounded like a question to the rest.

"Yes, but it will take them a while to reach the city, for they will be traveling by cart with belongings," Kalion said.

"Why not send the boy on ahead?" Niallee asked. "That would do two things: get the message to Brigin'i and get the boy out of harm's way sooner. Once he is within the walls, he will be safe, and his parents will be shortly behind."

"Excellent idea, Niallee, but we don't know if the boy can ride," Hrliger said.

Jebba spoke again. "Are we even sure that we need to continue at this point?"

"Well, you are right. We don't know what is ahead of us, but we signed on to rescue the princess, and that is what we are going to do," Kalion stated. "We can't turn around at the first sign of trouble. Maybe, Jebba, if you are that concerned, you can take the message to Brigin'i?"

Jebba narrowed his eyes at Kalion. "No, I will stay with the group." He continued, mumbling under his breath, "Someone must be the voice of reason."

An hour later, every horse in the yard had been fed and saddled. The boy was frightened as he watched the group check their horses. He had only left the forest twice in his short life. He had never seen war and knew there was more to fear than his father was telling him. The whispers of such danger being the stuff of nightmares and legends made him shake with fear.

Zahnz was the first to notice the boy's unease. Not wanting to add to the boy's discomfort by approaching him directly, he signaled to Kalion, who to Zahnz's surprise, seemed to instantly understand the problem. He too had seen the boy staring at the team and recognized the look on his face from his own past.

Kalion approached the boy casually, smiling to keep the others from paying attention to their conversation. "I have seen that look. You want to go with us, don't you?"

Komenn lowered his head and merely nodded, ashamed to have been so easy to read.

Kalion placed his hand on Komenn's shoulder. "I'd be honored to have you on my team, but if you come with us, you will be missed. But I have a bigger job for you." Komenn's head shot up in surprise. He had feared that the ranger thought him a coward for wanting to accompany them. Kalion continued. "I need you to take a message to the king in Brigin'i. Tell him what has happened."

At this point, Domka gasped and put her hand to her mouth. "No, not my son."

Kalion looked at the woman. "There is nothing on the road between here and the city that will cause him harm, and this will get him within the city walls much faster." Kalion looked back to Komenn. "Can you ride? Are you up to this challenge?"

Komenn spoke with a shaky voice. "Yes, I can do this," he said as Domka lowered her head in defeat.

Komenn's family joined him as he started to ready his own horse for his journey and the group jumped up and settled on their mounts. The family watched them go down the road, riding east toward uncertain outcomes.

As the group disappeared in the shadows of the trees, Aamonn, Domka and Komenn ran back into the inn and gathered their final belongings. Within an hour, the inn was shut down and closed up tight. Komenn mounted his horse, said a hasty good-bye to his parents and raced down the road on his mission to deliver a message to the king. A few minutes later, two horses, a few cows, a mule and a wagon were seen traveling slowly toward Brigin'i City to the west. Domka cried a little and hoped that they could return soon. She loved their home and prayed that it would survive.

Chapter Twenty

Now that all in the group were aware of the danger that awaited them in the forest, Kalion decided that the safest way to proceed was with a warrior at the lead at all times. Thus, it was Winsto who first spied the group of orc and elf bodies lying on the side of the road two hours after leaving the inn.

Signaling the others behind him to wait, Winsto pulled his sword from its scabbard as he dismounted and cautiously walked over to the bodies, all the while keeping a watchful eye on the forest. Not seeing any visible signs of battle made Winsto even more careful in his approach, as he suspected that magic may have been involved. Checking the first body, Winsto could still feel heat coming from the elven body and knew that whatever had occurred here had happened recently.

Satisfied that the bodies themselves posed no additional threat, Winsto turned his attention back to the forest line as he signaled the others. Before moving forward, Kalion ordered Jebba, Bennak, Harbin, Holan, Kikor, Birkita and Whelor to fan out. Once they were in place, Amlora and Zahnz raced forward to check on the condition of the other bodies. They found that while the orcs had deep slashes in their bodies, the elves had almost no marks at all, except for strange holes in their heads.

Looking at Winsto, who was still scanning the forest, Amlora asked, "Do you think the elves were surprised by these orcs?"

Winsto shook his head. "No, I think the elves attacked these orcs but were, in turn, attacked by something else. Look at that one's face." Winsto pointed to one of the elves she had not checked. Amlora turned the elf over and saw that half of his face was gone. Only parts of his brain were still inside of the skull.

Gasping at the gruesome sight, Amlora whispered, "What could do something like this? Orcs don't possess this power." As Amlora continued checking the elf to see if she could find any other clue as to what had attacked him, there was a cry from Holan as he discovered the body of yet another dead elf a little farther down the road.

Unlike the other elven bodies, which were unmarked but for the unexplained holes in their heads, this one showed definite signs of battle. Jebba reached Holan first and was surprised to find the body of a small, young female elf, probably no older than Kikor. She may have been just as beautiful, but it was difficult to tell now that her body had been riddled with more than a dozen small arrows along her face and chest.

"Poison," Holan mumbled when he saw what the arrows had done to the elf's skin. Jebba nodded as he too saw how the elf's skin around each arrow had turned black. Just as he opened his mouth to comment further, Holan tapped his leg and pointed. Turning toward the outstretched finger, Jebba saw Bennak looking intently into the tree line as he raised his huge blade up into an attack position. Nodding to Holan that he understood, the pair began quietly making their way to where Bennak stood ready.

When they were about ten feet away, a small orc wielding a pole sword jumped out of the trees and rushed toward Bennak, screaming as it took a wild swing at Bennak, who easily maneuvered away from the clumsy attempt and countered with a swing so fierce that it removed the orc's head, sending it flying over Bennak's shoulder to land in front of Holan. A moment later, the orc's body fell to the ground as well, as a blackish stream of blood began to pool around the now-open neck.

Jebba was ready to enter the wood to see if there were any other orcs when Bennak stopped him with a hand on his shoulder.

"No, my friend, that was the last one. I smell no others."

Nodding, Jebba turned toward the others now running up as Bennak crouched down to search through the orc's belongings.

Meanwhile, Holan was already talking to Kalion, who had also seen Bennak raise his weapon and had been heading toward the trio when the orc attacked.

"What do you think? An advance party of sorts?" Jebba asked without turning after Holan told the group about the other dead elf they'd found. Despite his faith in Bennak's sense of smell, Jebba was still looking through the trees for another possible attack.

"They look more like a small foraging group," Kalion answered, speaking loudly enough for the rest of the group to hear. Gesturing toward the crude pole sword still held by the dead orc, he frowned. "None of them were even well-armed."

Jebba nodded. "I agree. An attack party would have had twenty or thirty orcs, and better weapons, too."

"You have an even bigger problem," Kikor chimed in, bringing everyone's attention to her. "None of them were archers."

Kalion nodded, having understood Kikor's words immediately. The rest of the group caught on a moment later, all except Chansor, who demanded to know why everyone else was nodding. Lowering her voice to a whisper, Birkita reminded Chansor about the dead elf Holan had found who had been killed with the arrow, prompting a loud "Ohhh!" from her small friend that made everyone smile despite the seriousness of the situation.

"Whatever these orcs were about, if they are this deep inside the forest, then the elves must be losing the battle. We should be extra careful from now on," Jebba said, still looking to the trees.

"Agreed," Kalion replied. "Castle Dagonor is about a day's hard ride from here. Perhaps they have more knowledge of the goings on in the area. We can strategize more after we get there and see what we're dealing with."

Jebba thought that was a poor move, thinking they should travel to the elven city deep within the forest. However, after a few moments of arguing he was finally overruled by the group, which decided to continue on the road toward the castle.

"Fine, if you all believe we should continue, then I say that from now on we move silently, armored up and ready for anything," Jebba said, trying to hide his fear of the thought of them riding headlong into a huge army of orcs.

No one spoke further as they mounted their horses and continued their journey. That is, all except Bennak, who chose to walk instead. He had never been fond of horses and preferred to be free to deal with any threats as quickly as possible. Besides, he was able to keep up with the others who were on horseback very easily.

The rest of the day was tense as the group focused on every sound in the forest, forcing their heightened senses to work overtime. Holan had the most difficulty, coming from a warrior background in which his role was that of attacker, not quiet reconnaissance.

The two druids, Niallee and Hrliger, rode quietly, talking to each other about the trees and animals. Every once in a while, they stopped to pick some berries or other foliage along the road in the hope that they would come across an animal that could provide information about what was going on in the forest.

Soon, Chansor decided to abandon his horse as well, complaining that it was giving him leg sores. Tossing the reins to Kikor, he jumped into the trees and began to run quietly beside the group.

"Where are you going, my little friend?" Birkita whispered quietly, just before he jumped over a log to disappear.

Chansor turned back to answer. "I'm going to hide in the forest. Who knows what I might find or see? Besides, I'm bored. A thief doesn't like sitting around, you know."

Birkita shook her head at him. "Bored? How can you be bored? You're in a forest that at this very moment is under attack somewhere, and you're bored?"

Chansor smiled widely at Birkita's frown, then turned around and jumped into the forest before she could say anything else. Birkita turned to Kikor, who merely shrugged her shoulders and lifted a delicate eyebrow before clicking her tongue and riding ahead with both horses. Chansor could take care of himself, she thought.

Everyone was relieved to have reached the halfway point of the forest without encountering any other attacks by the time they stopped to rest for the night. After staking out a position that would allow them to observe anything coming toward them, they broke up into small watches and lit a small fire for dinner.

There had been some concern about the wisdom of having a fire, but all admitted that a warm bowl of stew would be welcome. They had been riding hard all day at high alert, and having hot food would be good for their bodies.

As the rest of the evening passed by without incident, the team began to relax. All managed to catch a few hours of sleep as they took turns keeping watch. By the time Whelor and Holan took their turn, there were only a few hours left until dawn. The pair had been sitting quietly near the now-extinguished fire for only a few minutes when they became aware of a new sound in the forest and looked at each other.

"Did you hear that?" Whelor whispered to Holan.

"Aye, I do," Holan replied, quickly grabbing his axe.

Both men stood slowly, listening intently for the source of the sound as it moved closer. They relaxed somewhat when they recognized the sound of a horse galloping hard on the road. Holan couldn't make out where it was coming from but saw Whelor pointing down the road toward the east, signaling that the horse was coming from that direction.

"Why would someone be out on a horse at this time of the night?" Holan asked quietly. Whelor shook his head as the horse and the rider galloped past them at a hard and fast pace, waking up everyone in the camp as he passed.

"What was that?" Kalion demanded as he crashed through the forest to join Holan and Whelor on the main road.

"An elven rider, headed west!" Whelor replied.

"Another messenger perhaps?" Jebba asked as he stepped out of the wood behind Kalion.

"Could be," Kalion replied. "Unfortunately, we don't have

time to chase him down to ask. We need to move on, I think."

"This could mean that conflict we are riding into has gone horribly wrong," Jebba stated.

They were a decidedly quiet group as they broke camp after a quick breakfast and continued riding east.

As the sun broke over the horizon and the light poured through the trees, Bennak was the first to catch a whiff of a familiar, but dangerous, odor. Moments later, Kikor stopped and stood up in her saddle. Narrowing her eyes, she suddenly gasped and turned to the others.

"There's a large fire in the distance. Look," she said, pointing her arm in the direction of the blaze. Minutes later, the group watched in growing alarm as forest animals began running past them in an attempt to flee the fire.

Winged animals large and small filled the skies above as deer, hawks, squirrels and even a bear were seen running along the forest road edge. The smell soon became heavy as the smoke from the fire suddenly seemed to be everywhere.

"I have an idea, my friends," Harbin announced to the group. "I can jump ahead and observe what might be going on at the eastern edge, return and let our group know if we should continue on or travel another way."

"Are you mad, Harbin? You could appear right in the middle of an armed orc camp or something," Amlora said, sounding concerned.

"Worse, you could appear right in the middle of a battle or this fire itself," Kikor pitched in. "Or worst, since we don't know who is fighting whom, you could be mistaken for one or the other."

"All of what you say is true, but what would you suggest otherwise? Soon we may not be able to see anything at all. We have to know which way to go," Harbin replied, trying to sound confident in his idea. Truth be told, he wasn't feeling too sure about it himself, especially now that Amlora and Kikor had pointed out the potential dangers.

Niallee and Hrliger looked at each other. Seeing the fear on Harbin's face as well as the concern on her fellow druid's face, Niallee came to a decision.

"Wait," Niallee cried out, drawing everyone's attention to her. Nodding to Hrliger, she continued. "We can help guide your path so that you do not materialize in the middle of danger."

Harbin smiled at Niallee so widely that she blushed and looked away. Returning his gaze to the rest of the group, he gave them all a triumphant grin.

"There, it is settled. Let us begin." With that, Harbin withdrew a vial from a pouch that rested on his hip and, after inspecting it carefully, nodded to Niallee and Hrliger.

"See you soon, my friends," Harbin whispered. Closing his eyes, he began mumbling strange words that were unfamiliar to the group. Dropping a few drops from the vial he held onto the ground at his feet, Harbin suddenly disappeared with a popping noise. The others looked around, seeing that Niallee and Hrliger had their eyes closed and were mumbling strange words as well.

"I hope he will be fine," Amlora commented to no one in particular when Harbin vanished. "He is a funny but unusual man to have around." She thought at that moment about a joke he had told her the day before about giants and mice or something like that and how they both shared many of the same thoughts. This was the first time any of them had seen his skills as a mage since the games. Amlora worried about the consequences of using such a fearsome ability, despite the fact that Harbin had obviously proven his skills by winning his portion of the games. As Niallee and Hrliger continued to chant, however, her sense of uneasiness diminished.

"If there is one man in this group who can do what he claims, it is Harbin. Besides, I do not think he will just go to the east. Knowing him, he will probably go to Blath 'Na City or even travel back to Brigin'i City to eat some hot food or something," Jebba said as he dismounted to rest his horse. None of the others laughed at Jebba's joke but waited and watched the thickening smoke as the moments passed ever so slowly.

The sound of air rushing through a hole and another pop alerted the others to Harbin's return. Indeed, a second later, Harbin appeared in front of them, looking like he had been through a battle. Parts of his robes had been burnt in many places, his hair and face were nearly blackened with soot, and he appeared to be bleeding from a series of tiny cuts.

Amlora cried out and ran over to tend to her friend. As the group's cleric and healer, it was her job to make sure everyone remained in good health.

"Harbin, by the gods, what happened to you?" Winsto asked.

"I, ahh … I need a drink, if you please," Harbin mumbled as he walked over to a log that was near him. Amlora helped him sit down, then reached into her bags and removed some salves to apply to the burned areas on Harbin's face as the others gathered around him.

Amlora glared at Niallee and lashed out against the druid as she approached. "I thought you were supposed to keep him safe from danger."

Niallee raised her eyebrows and was about to respond when Harbin interrupted, placing a hand on Amlora's arm. "Niallee and Hrliger saved my life. I would not have found my way back without them," Harbin said softly, nodding at Niallee before returning his gaze to Amlora.

"Harbin, what do you have to report?" Kalion asked. Harbin drank deeply from the jug Amlora handed him before answering.

"You will not believe what I saw, my friends. … You just will not believe it," Harbin mumbled, looking at the ground.

"What did you see?" Kalion asked again, a little concerned that their decision to come this way might prove to be futile.

"Orcs everywhere … more than I could count. Elves too."

Everyone looked at each other. "You mean the elves are alive? And still fighting?" Kikor asked, leaning down to get closer.

"Most I saw were dead," Harbin answered softly.

Zahnz moved to sit down next to Harbin. "They cannot all be dead."

Harbin looked over to Zahnz and nodded to the dark elf. "Most I saw were." Harbin took another swallow from the jug. "Only a few were still alive and fighting the remaining orcs."

"What about the orcs?" Kalion asked

"Most of them were dead as well," Harbin answered.

"How did you get hurt?" Jebba asked.

"When I appeared, fields that I presumed would be lush and green were instead muddy and black from fire. Bodies and war machines were scattered everywhere. I just happened to be standing next to a war machine that exploded mere seconds after my arrival. The flames attacked my clothing, but I was able to get away before it totally engulfed me."

"War machines, you say? What types? How big? How many of these machines did you observe? You said that not all the elves were dead, did you see others?" The group began peppering Harbin with questions. Amlora pushed everyone back to give Harbin room to breathe.

"Harbin needs to rest, my friends ... please!" she spoke sternly to them.

"No, mistress, I need to tell them what I saw. We need to make a plan." Harbin continued describing the scene he had just left, answering all the questions put to him until Kalion clapped him on the shoulder and ordered him to rest.

Harbin was more than happy to comply with that order, falling fast asleep a few minutes later. Kalion motioned the others to the side so they could talk without bothering Harbin, who slept while Amlora tended the rest of his injuries.

"This is what I thought would happen if Harbin went there," Jebba said, leaning up against a tree.

Knowing that Jebba had not professed to think any such thing, Kalion ignored him as Winsto piped up.

"Orcs and goblins? Fighting together? I don't like the sound of that. I think we need to help the survivors, don't you agree, Kalion?" Winsto said as he looked over to the ranger.

"Think our numbers here can succeed against an army?" Kikor answered angrily. "You know that we cannot save them. So let us help who we can. The princess is counting on us. No one else can save her."

"I do not know about the rest of you, but sitting here talking surrounded by smoke, we might not be thinking as clearly as we should," Bennak added. "We need to figure a way around these flames, first and foremost."

Kalion raised a hand to quiet everyone. "Bennak is correct. We have a wall of fire ahead of us that we need to get around in order to reach Castle Dagonor. Since we cannot continue traveling east, we will go south for a while in order to skirt this fire." Kalion turned toward Amlora, who looked up and answered the question hovering on his tongue before he could ask.

"He'll be fine, Kalion. None of his injuries are serious. He is just exhausted from the travel spell. Give him a few moments to rest, then we can be on our way, but you should know that he will not be able to perform a spell of that magnitude for a few days."

Kalion nodded at her answer and returned to the others, ordering them to get ready to ride.

Chapter Twenty One

*I*t took more than a day to circle around the forest fire. In order to make up time, Kalion had made the decision to travel throughout the night. It had been a harrowing experience for them all, as the sounds of metal hitting metal, explosions and screams floated across the night sky. Not interfering in the various skirmishes they passed by was easier said than done, but they had moved steadily forward with the help of the mages and druids. Meradoth and Harbin channeled their skills to ensure that they didn't get too close to the fire line, while Hrliger and Niallee continued to use their uncanny connection with nature to keep the group safe from attacks.

As they slowly emerged from their hard trek through the forest to resume their travel on the main road, the signs of battle could be seen everywhere. Trees lay broken and burnt, many ripped out of the ground and ripped apart in places from explosions. The bodies of goblins and orcs embedded with elven arrows were some of the most gruesome sights. Only every once in a while did they come across the body of an elven warrior, which confused some in the group based on Harbin's earlier report until Kikor explained that elves never left a fallen brother in a battle if there was any way to retrieve him.

The group rode through the scene quietly, their senses reeling from the sights before them, until Bennak suddenly stopped and lifted his head, sniffing the air.

"Something lives."

Kalion turned to question him. "Orc, elf, what?"

"No, not orc or elf, nor animal ... something else," Bennak replied as the warriors within the group readied their weapons. Kalion gave the order to fan out.

Not being one to miss any opportunity to retrieve something

valuable, Chansor ran ahead to see what he could find. So Chansor was the first to break out of the forest edge. Chansor couldn't believe what he saw as his eyes scanned the landscape before him. Moments later, Whelor stepped up behind him, and he too stopped in complete shock.

"By the gods," Whelor whispered.

The destruction they had seen along the main road was nothing compared to the scene before them. It was just as Harbin had said. Hundreds, no, thousands of orc and goblin bodies literally covered the field. Some even seemed to have been ripped apart. Not far from where Whelor stood were the burnt remains of a huge war machine, surrounded by the burnt and dismembered corpses of giants.

Probably the machine's crew, Whelor thought as he continued scanning the field, counting four more war machines, all in the same condition.

Waving to the little thief now picking his way through the damage, Whelor signaled to Chansor that he was going back for the others. Chansor nodded back and motioned to Whelor that he was going out into the field to investigate further.

A few minutes later, a flash of movement off to his left caught Chansor's eye. Pulling out his short sword, he quickly but quietly made his way toward the source of the movement.

As he got closer, he heard what sounded like a creature in pain. Feeling a little less courageous now that he was almost upon the creature, Chansor hid for a moment beside the dead body of a hill giant. After all, it could be that the creature wasn't wounded at all. Maybe it was just trying to trick him. Still, Chansor knew he wouldn't be able to stay hidden long. The smell of the dead giant was already making his eyes water. He would have to move soon.

With that thought in mind, Chansor gathered his courage and leaned around the carcass of the smelly giant and saw something that made him shiver. A thin, armored creature was dragging himself along the ground not far away from where Chansor knelt.

"Looks like Bennak was right," Chansor whispered to himself

upon seeing the creature. Leaning back and looking up at the sky, he said, ."Not orc, nor animal."

Chansor peeked around the giant again and saw that the creature crawling had long white hair, just like Zahnz. One last peek allowed him to see the skin of the creature, confirming his suspicions that he was a dark elf.

So there are dark elves in the army, too. No wonder the forest and elves inside it took a beating, he thought, watching the creature slowly move toward something he couldn't see. Dark elves would have certainly been able to use magic against their elven cousins. Why dark and light elves hated each other, Chansor never knew, nor did he have time to think further about the matter, as the voice of the dark elf surprised Chansor.

"I can smell you, man creature. Come out and kill me, if you dare," the dark elf said weakly. Chansor had heard stories of the power that dark elves held in battle, so he didn't take the bait just then. Dark elves used trickery in battle, and this one might be tricking him into believing that he was wounded and hurt. On the other hand, the smell of the dead giant was quickly becoming unbearable.

Taking a deep breath, Chansor stood up and stepped away from his hiding place and immediately cursed himself for his cowardice. He could see that the dark elf was indeed hurt, judging by the spear stuck in his side.

The dark elf had stopped dragging himself along the ground and now lay on his back, resting on the body of an orc. Chansor squeezed the hilt of his short sword tightly and approached the fallen creature slowly. He could see where the dark elf's armor, clothes and face carried the signs of battle. Blood still trickled down his neck from a damaged eye socket. His armor looked like it had been hit many times by both arrows and other weapons. But the spear point looked the worst and must have been hurting the dark one a lot.

"Who are you? I didn't your know your people were here," the elf said weakly, staring at Chansor as he came to stand over him.

The elf laid his head back and looked into the sky, noticing for the first time the buzzards flying everywhere. He knew his lifeblood was leaving quickly and he didn't have long, and having this man standing over him just as he was dying didn't please him to say the least.

"Man, either kill me or leave me alone. I do not have long in this life and do not want you here," the dark elf demanded, his face wincing in pain.

Luckily, Chansor did not have to make that decision, as he turned at the sound of the group emerging out of the mist behind Whelor. Birkita immediately walked up to Chansor and placed her hand on his still-trembling shoulder.

"My friend, we are glad that you are well, but ...," she stared at the dark elf lying before her.

Birkita suddenly noticed the shallow breaths of the creature at their feet and pushed Chansor behind her, holding her sword at the ready. "Is that ...? By the gods, it's still alive, over here!" she screamed, making those who still stood nearby, staring at the carnage, race over to stand with wide eyes.

The rest of the team came running to where Birkita stood holding her sword against the throat of the dying dark elf. Kalion immediately moved to take her place, giving orders as he stared down at the elf. "Winsto, Zahnz and Meradoth, stay here. The rest of you go scout the field and see if you can find anything that might lead us to the princess. I have some questions for this elf."

As the others spread out in the field, Zahnz turned to Kalion and whispered, "I do not think this elf means to be truthful with you. I think you should let Meradoth cast a truth spell just to be sure."

Kalion looked at Meradoth, who merely shrugged and gave Kalion a half smile before acknowledging that it couldn't hurt. Kalion gave the mage the go ahead.

Meradoth started mumbling under his breath and waving his arms in the air. All of a sudden, he stopped. All looked down at the dark elf, and they saw a smile of contentment pass over his face.

Kalion asked, "What happened here?"

162

The dark elf started to speak and then stopped as blood started to seep from the corner of his mouth. Kalion looked to the mage and said, "Can you do anything? We need him alive a bit longer."

"You understand that I am not a cleric, right?" Meradoth answered. "I do not carry field medicines." Kalion narrowed his eyes and stared at Meradoth until the latter relented with a huge sigh. "Fine."

Reaching into his pouch, Meradoth retrieved a packet of herbs and a small vial. The others stood silently as he put a pinch of herbs into the vial, which he next filled with water from the jug at his side and capped before shaking it vigorously. Holding the mixture to the dark elf's lips, Meradoth tilted his head so the elf had no choice but to swallow. As he administered the elixir, Meradoth mumbled a few words. Almost instantly, the elf's breathing seemed to ease. Meradoth looked up to see three sets of raised eyebrows staring back at him. Shrugging, he gently placed the elf's head back on the ground before standing up and dusting off his robes.

Kalion had no time to wonder about what other secret talents Meradoth possessed, as he turned his attention to the elf. "Now, once again, what happened here?" Kalion asked.

The elf looked up and started to speak. "I was part of a transport headed east with the human princess taken from the city in the west."

Kalion looked to the others with surprise in his eyes. He wasn't the only one. The dark elf looked as surprised as Kalion at what had just come out of his mouth. Glaring at Meradoth for the spell that compelled him to speak, the elf continued with his tale.

"We were taking that damned girl to our Lord Methnorick on the Isle of Blakess. A boat was to meet us at the Blath 'Na port tomorrow evening, but as we came out of the forest, this battle was already underway. We saw many of our brothers battling by the side of the orcs and goblins, but it seemed the elves were winning." The dark elf heaved a breath, showing signs of pain as it shot through his body.

"We were trying to skirt around the battle when another

band of warriors moved up behind us out of the forest and attacked the wagon, killing one of my companions and leaving me for dead. By the time my other companion and I got to our feet, they were gone. Figuring that Methnorick would surely kill us once he heard of our failure, we decided to help our brothers on this field of battle. I guess that was a mistake as well." A smile appeared slightly, even as more blood leaked out of his mouth.

"Who or what took the princess from you?" Kalion asked.

The elf closed his eyes for a moment, then continued. "Men."

"Which way did they go?"

"East," the elf whispered, then coughed a few times before falling silent.

Zahnz crouched down beside the dead elf and began whispering softly for a few minutes, then drew his sword and plunged it into the dark elf. Winsto stared at Zahnz, his eyes full of questions as Zahnz continued whispering. When he was finished, he stood and turned to Winsto, ready for questions.

"I umm ... thought your kind did not really care if another falls in battle."

"My kind?" Zahnz looked down at the body of the dead elf. "Yes. I suppose that much is true. However, I have always believed my people are a lost people and need help. So I gave him a prayer in the hope that he finds that help wherever he goes now."

"But your people's gods and goddesses," Winsto pressed, ".are they not pure evil?"

Zahnz mouth cracked a small smile. "I see you have heard the bedtime stories. Yes, my friend, my people have their own gods. I cannot say their names openly, but that matters not since I did not pray to them. I prayed that this one find his god or goddess of light instead of one of the dark ones."

Winsto nodded. Personally, he didn't care about the dark elf beyond the information he had provided. Chansor had already stripped the body clean of anything valuable, as he had many others on the field to attend to.

Kalion, who was still mulling over the information provided by the dead elf, turned to Zahnz. "Zahnz, do you recognize anything about this, er, being?" Kalion asked as he too looked down at the body of the dead dark elf.

Zahnz didn't answer at first, but crouched back down to check the body.

"No, I do not know this elf. He does not carry any house or class badge, so I cannot tell you anything about his origins. However ..." Zahnz paused, peering at the body closely, his face showing signs of confusion. Something was off. "... there is a strange marking along the side of his face here," Zahnz continued, pointing to the area.

"Does this marking mean anything to you?" Winsto asked, looking back at the body of the elf just as Jebba moved up and joined the trio.

"Maybe. It reminds me of a house emblem that was once very powerful a long time ago. That is, until it fell during a small civil war," Zahnz said quietly, thinking of the past.

"When a house falls, another always takes its place. Depending on the house's new lord, they sometimes include a part of the old clan or house and make a new emblem to represent themselves. That, I believe, might explain this symbol, except ..."

"Except what?" Kalion pressed, crouching down beside Zahnz.

Zahnz looked into Kalion's eyes. "Except for the fact that the war I spoke of took place more than 1,800 cycles ago. At its height, it was almost as large as the Great Schism that nearly wiped my people out over 10,000 cycles before that. The civil war was large enough that my people lost close to 800,000 warriors."

"Eight hundred thousand," Kikor whispered, having stopped to listen to the story. "By the gods."

"Yes," Zahnz replied softly, closing his eyes as if to block the memory of such a massive loss of life.

"How many houses are there, Zahnz?" Kalion asked.

Zahnz smiled at Kalion, grateful for the change of subject.

"When I left, there were ten main houses and twenty smaller houses, with many more clans among them. Within my city, there were a number of smaller houses and one larger house that had the greatest position in the under-dark, as they were closest to the precious minerals in the lands."

Kalion nodded and was about to suggest that they had learned all they needed to know when a scream pierced the air. Immediately, all weapons were drawn as the team searched frantically for the source of the scream.

Chapter Twenty Two

*J*ust on the edge of the forest line, Birkita and Niallee were searching through the pockets of some of the few dead elves when they too heard the scream.

"What was that?" Niallee asked as she jumped to her feet and began scanning the battlefield frantically.

Birkita shook her head. "I don't know, but it didn't come from the battlefield. ... Look!" Birkita pointed to a spot in the sky.

Niallee gasped in shock as she followed the path of Birkita's outstretched arm and saw black shapes in the sky floating toward them. Her elven vision allowed her to see much farther than humans, and she could just make out figures riding on top of each creature.

"I make out three ... no, five creatures coming toward us," Niallee whispered. She looked over at Birkita, who was already turning toward the battlefield to warn the others. "How long before they get here?" Niallee asked as she ran to catch up with Birkita.

"I'd say we have about ten, maybe fifteen minutes, to get out of sight before those things reach this field. We need to move. Now!"

Nodding her head in agreement, Niallee chased after Birkita as they both ran back to where the others were gathered. Yelling so everyone could hear, Birkita told them of the impending danger. Everyone quickly grabbed what they could and ran toward their mounts.

Kalion looked around the area, trying to decide on the best means of escape, when he noticed what looked like the battlements of Dagonor on the eastern part of the battlefield. In fact, he realized to his dismay that this battlefield on which he stood was once the lush green western edge of Castle Dagonor. He had often hunted on these fields during his visits. Still, with those creatures approaching, Kalion did not have time to ponder the forces that could level an entire forest and make these fields turn red. They needed cover, and quickly. With neither time nor options left, Kalion pointed toward the castle.

"Head over there! Right now! If we don't get cover before those creatures reach this battlefield, the rest won't much matter. Let's ride!"

Kalion turned his horse and set off at a full gallop. The others followed suit and rode hard as a scream punctuated the sky. The sun lowered over the far west mountains behind them as the group crossed the charred bridge into the keep.

Castle Dagonor was not the largest nor the best positioned castle in the northern areas of the continent, but Castle Dagonor, named after King Dago's father cycles before, had been first built as a fortress to provide security for the lands that Brigin'i controlled in the east. This area had grown over the cycles as the city pushed its borders even farther east. A wooden fortress stood for many cycles until the ability to build stone walls made them grow higher and stronger, with four enormous towers providing sight and coverage.

Dagonor had a huge armory with cavalry stables, thick walls and a moat filled with very murky water, leaving no chance of any attack making it through. Kalion remembered someone once telling him the moat was filled with creatures as he had walked slowly across the ramp, seeing what he had thought were fins and tails of scary-looking creatures floating past.

No one had failed to notice the signs of battle as they approached the castle. The extent of the damage made the structure appear more like ruins than what Kalion had remembered as a thriving, functional castle.

Moving through the open gates, Kalion looked around the courtyard for a place to hide. To his relief, the stables still seemed to be intact. Dismounting, he urged his horse into a stall as the others arrived on his heels, now frantically searching for a place to hide as screams signaled the beasts' arrival over the battlefield.

"Hurry! Get those horses out of sight, now!" Kalion ordered.

Wrestling with horses that were now panicking with exhaustion and fear, the other riders worked frantically to calm and quiet them as the shadows flew over the battlefield. Meradoth lost his battle with his horse as it whinnied in panic and ran deeper into the courtyard of the castle. He started to chase the creature but was tackled by Winsto just as the first shadow passed over their position.

"Do not worry about your horse. Worry about yourself, my friend. The horse can take care of himself," Winsto said sternly to Meradoth, who nodded in understanding. Both looked into the sky as another shadow flew over them. They stayed absolutely still until the shadow left the area.

"What in all the hells are they?" Meradoth whispered to Winsto, who merely shook his head that he didn't know in response.

"Shhhh," Jebba whispered sternly as another shadow flew over them, screaming again. "Whatever they are, I don't want them to find us, so shut it!"

The group remained still after that until the skies finally cleared of the creatures a few minutes later. Not wishing to take any chances, they waited silently for another few minutes before deciding that it was safe to move around. After soothing their horses again, they assembled together in the courtyard to discuss their next move.

"I don't know about the rest of you, but I am quite tired of flying blind. We need to find some real answers as to what King Dia has gotten us into," Jebba announced with a pointed look at Kalion, who looked up to see everyone nodding in agreement with Jebba.

"I have to agree," Kikor added. "What is this place? How do you know it?"

Kalion looked away from his companions as he uttered a single word: "Dagonor."

Gasps and cries of shock erupted from the group as everyone began talking at once.

"Impossible!"

"What happened to the people? Where is the army that

protects it?"

"By the gods!"

"What are we supposed to do now?"

"Enough!" Kalion yelled, fixing the group with a look that reminded everyone that he was indeed a ranger. "We need to do what we came to do. We need to find the princess."

Kalion shared what he and the others who had questioned the dark elf had learned. "We know that she travels by wagon. We also know that the men who took her from the dark elves are traveling due east. We need only find the trail to track her. Since it is already nearly dark, we will stay here for the night. Come morning, we should be able to find her trail and track her from there. Agreed?"

Kalion was glad to see everyone nod. Well, almost everyone. Bennak looked around nervously. Kalion could see that the half-orc was not comfortable being in confined spaces but hoped that he would conclude that the castle would be safer than the forest with those creatures still out there. "Bennak?" Kalion asked quietly.

"Aye, Kalion, I agree. We wait 'ere."

"At least here we should be able to find some food," Holan said, winking at Bennak. "And maybe even some more answers."

"Fine. We'll take hour-long watches tonight. And Holan is right; we can always use more clues. We need to search the castle as well," Kalion said. "Birkita and Meradoth, you two check the right tower. Kikor, take Zahnz with you to check the left tower. Jebba and Holan, I need you two to take the first watch along the perimeter. Harbin, Winsto and I will check the main hall while Chansor and Niallee hunt down some food. Bennak and Hrliger, take care of the horses."

Amlora spoke up. "I think Harbin should rest and heal some more from his earlier ordeal. I will go with you."

Kalion looked from Harbin to Amlora. He saw that Harbin did still look a bit drained, then said, "All right, if you think he needs more rest."

At that, the group broke up. Chansor turned to walk away

when he suddenly stopped. Something was wrong. It took him another full minute of thinking and looking to notice that one of the group members was missing. He looked around some more just to make sure, but couldn't find Whelor anywhere.

"What's the matter with you?" Niallee asked as Chansor stood there just looking around as she walked past.

"Um, have you noticed that Whelor is not here?" Chansor asked.

Niallee looked around and suddenly gasped. "I haven't seen him, or his horse for that matter, since we left the battlefield," she said. In fact, she could not recall Whelor entering the castle grounds.

"Do we go look for him?" Chansor asked.

"No!" Niallee replied. "Kalion wouldn't want us to leave the castle right now. Those things could still be out there. We can't afford to lose anyone else right now. Let's just do as we were ordered and find food. We can tell the others about Whelor when we return."

Everyone went off on their ways. It took the combined efforts of Amlora, Winsto and Kalion to force the door open wide enough for Kalion to slip through the main doors of the central keep, where he immediately found why there were no sounds within.

Blocking the door were three footmen and a few sentries. Seeing them frozen where they stood quickly brought back memories of the attack back at Dia's castle. It was all Kalion could do to keep from screaming in rage as he moved the armor-clad, decaying bodies out of the way.

Horrified by the sight before her, Amlora covered her mouth with her hand as she and Winsto crossed the threshold. Most of the victims looked as if they had been in the midst of performing ordinary tasks prior to the attack. Now, everywhere they looked, there were frozen bodies of soldiers, footmen, merchants, peasants and even women and children, all showing signs of pain and horror. They had all witnessed Methnorick's attack on the barons, but none of them had thought him capable of using that awful power on such a massive scale.

Kalion whispered for everyone to break out and look around

for food and anything they could use on their trek. With out saying a word but nodding in agreement, they all separated and searched around in silence.

An hour later, majority of the group came together again in the courtyard of the castle, all shaking their heads to signal that they had found no survivors and relaying similar stories of finding frozen bodies. Then walking up Chansor broke the news about Whelor being missing, which caused even more anger and outbursts among the group.

"Where would the man go?" and "Was he discovered by those flying creatures?" were some of the quick questions asked as everyone tried to understand what was going on within this castle.

Winsto, in particular, had been inconsolable since entering the castle. No one could mistake the rage in his voice as it echoed throughout the castle. Seeing the others looking at him, wondering why he was so angry, he burst out screaming.

"This is murder! Whoever did this will pay for this atrocity! This I swear by my gods!" He raised his voice even louder with the last statement. If anything was out there, he wanted to be sure that it heard his pledge.

Chapter Twenty Three

Winsto was not alone in his anger. Everyone was affected by what they had just seen. "Kalion, you did say that there was a castle or something east of here, did you not?" Kikor asked gently, placing her hand on Kalion's shoulder and calming the situation down with her voice. She nodded at him as though she instinctively understood the torment roiling through him and the others.

While the others argued about what to do, Kalion sat down next to the tower on a small wall with his head in his hands to think. Unlike the other quest members, he had not been in the room when Methnorick had attacked the barons.

He couldn't believe that everyone within this castle was now dead. He had just been here about five months ago, and he clearly remembered speaking with King Dago about the upcoming games and the latest news of orcish movements. Seeing this castle and its occupants had driven him into a mild state of shock. Smiling gratefully at Kikor, Kalion looked up to see that almost everyone was waiting for his answer. Jebba, as usual, was acting disinterested, standing far away with his arms crossed and looking at the ground. Smiling slightly over how quickly he'd bonded with this bunch of undisciplined, aggravating, loyal misfits, he began to answer Kikor as best as he could as he fought his way out of his shock.

"There are two places that we could make for." For some reason he couldn't remember the names of them at that moment.

"There is a castle east of here as well as the dwarven city-kingdom just north of that castle." Holan smiled at the thought of visiting his brethren's underground kingdom. Kalion knew they were the closest, but what were their names?

"How far, Kalion?" Jebba asked, unable to restrain his curiosity.

173

"Both are a few leagues ... at least a few days' travel from here, maybe even a bit more. For cycles, King Dago has ..." Kalion swallowed, "... had problems with both the giants living in the mountains behind us here and the roving groups of orcs and goblins coming out of the hills, so it might be hard going without this castle's protection. We need to be extra careful with the horses and ourselves."

Kalion stood and walked over to stand in the middle of the group. Smiling as the names of those destinations finally popped back into his head, Kalion turned to share the information with the group, slapping his face in humor, which made a few smile.

"Bru Edin is the human castle that I was thinking of, and Chai'sell is your people's fortress built deep within the mountains, correct, Holan?" Kalion said, looking over to Holan, who nodded back with a large smile.

"Ah, yes. Chai'sell is well known among my clan as a place of wealth and strength." Holan kept the rest of his thoughts to himself — namely, that Chai'sell was also well known among his clan as a place of pride and greed. Still, he had every intention of taking the opportunity to visit, if possible. The things he would see, the stories he could tell afterward, would make him a legend in his clan.

Suddenly, Niallee came loudly bursting through the door, stopping for a moment to stare at the frozen people within before turning to the group, which was now silent and wondering at her urgency and waiting for her to speak.

"We've got problems ... and I mean bad problems."

"What is it, Niallee?" Kalion asked, all the humor suddenly stripped from his voice as he stared at Niallee with an intensity she had never seen before.

Flustered, she waved her hands around as she replied, "Part of that army we passed ... I think they are coming back this way!"

"How long? How many?" Bennak asked as he swung his mace up to on his shoulder.

Niallee bent down to place her hands on her knees. Amlora was the first to recognize Niallee's exhaustion and rushed over to her, catching her just before she fell.

"Foolish girl. How with the gods' help did you manage to cast another spell out there?" Amlora said quietly, mopping Niallee's brow. "What was it, a protection spell?"

Niallee nodded impatiently, weakly pushing Amlora's hand away to turn back to Bennak. "I would say within the hour, maybe less. I could not say for sure, but more than our number … a number of orcs and other creatures maybe coming to check on this place."

"An hour? What is a protection spell?" Holan asked, puzzled by her answer.

"I'm a druid, my friend. I protect the life in the forest, and it protects me in return," Niallee whispered before unconsciousness overtook her and she fell into Amlora's arms.

Holan grunted and turned away, not letting the others see his anger and confusion. He had never trusted druids that much. To him, talking to things that didn't speak was just … well, not right.

Kalion knelt down to where Amlora sat cradling Niallee. "Is she all right?"

Amlora smiled. "She will be. She has just fainted from the exhaustion of maintaining a spell for so long. I believe she cast a protection spell over this place, which required her to stay in constant mental contact with all of us as the beasts flew overhead earlier."

Amlora's softly spoken words made every warrior in the group look at the elf with a newfound sense of respect. Even Holan grunted and nodded, admitting to himself that maybe this druid wasn't really so bad on the whole.

"I am eternally grateful for her assistance, madam cleric. But my main concern is about the orcs approaching this castle now. If she does not awaken soon, she may have to be tied to her horse." Holan wrinkled his nose as he spoke.

"I want to go back inside and search the cellar and see what's there. Do you think there may be some food in the cellar?" Chansor piped up, earning a look of exasperation from the rest of the group that had him backing up toward the tower until a familiar face stepped out of the shadows, literally stopping everyone in their tracks.

"I would neither venture outside nor stay long within this place if I were you, friends," Whelor whispered from the shadows as he stepped out.

"By the gods," Birkita whispered as everyone else stared slack-jawed at their presumed-dead friend.

"Whelor!" Meradoth was the first to say his name. "Where have you been?"

His clothing, bent, dented and bloodied, looked as if he had just survived a battle.

"Yes, where have you been, Whelor?" Amlora asked, shocking everyone else into silence with the forcefulness of her voice. It was the first display of anger anyone had seen in the soft-spoken and serene cleric thus far. "You disappeared yesterday. We all thought you had been taken, or, or ..." Amlora dropped her head, unwilling to say more.

Whelor felt himself reddening as the faces of his group looked between him and Amlora. In that moment, he no longer cared to explain himself. Let them think what they want, Whelor thought as he knelt down, took Amlora's hand and smiled at her sweetly surprised expression.

"I am sorry, Amlora. I never meant to cause you undue distress. I saw a dark elf moving in the opposite direction just as I was entering the forest and feared that he would give away our positions if he wasn't stopped. I followed him into the mountains, where he finally turned against me. Luckily, I was able to kill the creature."

"Whelor ..."

"How did ...?"

"... kill one of the dark elves?"

"Good for you!"

Voices overlapped as several members of the group tried to talk at once. Kalion held up a hand for silence. "Did you happen to learn anything about what is happening here?"

"In fact, I was able to get some information from him. Do you really think we should talk about that right now, though? That army is getting closer to us as we speak," Whelor replied, reminding everyone of what Niallee had said a moment earlier as he stood up, looking over the rest of the companions

"Then may I make a suggestion?" Harbin asked as everyone turned to listen to what the mage had to say.

Harbin leaned on his staff as he continued talking. "We need to leave right now and keep moving toward the east before those beings get here. What do we all think of this?" Harbin knew the answer, but giving his companions the choice might lead them toward his thinking.

Everyone looked at each other, talking quickly, but no one noticed that Chansor wasn't with them anymore, as he had snuck past everyone and entered the tower while they all talked, wanting to find an adventure within it.

"Fight," came three voices, but most said "flee." Jebba wanted to stay, but he understood that whatever was coming toward them was more of a risk, for they didn't know who or what it was. It could have been the very thing that had killed everyone here.

"Whelor, do you believe the beings coming this way had anything to do with what happened here?" Jebba asked, thinking that might change everyone's answer.

Whelor walked over to where Jebba stood, shaking his head. "No."

Jebba nodded his head. "Ok, then, I say we gather up what supplies we can and head out." Jebba looked over to where Winsto stood, still angry at what had happened within the castle but now fuming at the thought of running.

Winsto was truly mad at the group's talk about leaving the castle when so many people had died here. This was not honorable, and being an honorable knight, this was almost unbearable for him, but he knew when he was outmatched.

While the knight thought to himself, a few members of the group started to walk toward the horses and gather themselves to ready and leave the ruined castle.

Dago Tower, named after King Dago himself, stood at over 800 feet in height. It was built on top of a large boulder that spurted out from the mountains behind the castle, giving it a higher stature than the rest of the castle around it. Standing on either side of the entrance were statues of the king and his wife, the queen, from cycles before, looking proudly down over their castle.

Leaving the main chamber, Chansor headed up a circular stairwell that went along the side of the wall, toward the king's private chambers. The stairs themselves were large enough for three knights abreast, but the king was also a cautious man, placing magical traps along it in case the castle were attacked, and Chansor could see a few as he walked up, noting that a few had been sprung recently.

None of these traps went off as Chansor moved up the stairs, not really caring about the tables, weapons or pictures lining the walls. He wanted to find jewels and other valuables in this place, maybe even a secret or two. Why not? The owners were dead now, so they won't care, he thought.

As he got to the third floor, he came around the corner to find three bodies that used to be some ladies-in-waiting for the duchess but now were just rotting heaps of dead flesh and bone. Almost tripping over the bodies, Chansor looked around to see where he was. He saw that it must have once been a floor where the king would meet visitors or others dignitaries, as there was nice furniture placed around the chamber, but absolutely nothing of interest to the thief was within this chamber, so turning around quickly, he continued up the stairs.

* * *

Below in the courtyard, Whelor and the others had started to gather up supplies as he explained what he had found out from the dark elf in the forest.

"Of course, he did not say much, but he did say that this

was only one army of many marching within the lands. He did not know who attacked this castle, as his people had found it like this the day before the battle with the Levenori Elves, which we saw the result of outside these walls." Whelor walked over to stand by one of the massive doors that led into the castle as he was explaining this.

"He wasn't that helpful really, saying that the army was at the elven door, probably meaning that the orcs and others were at their city deep within the forest or something. He also said many clans of orcs and goblins were gathered to attack the elven forest as well, with Brigin'i City next to be attacked after the leader of the orcs takes the elves down."

Jebba bent down and checked out the marks on the wall, not really hearing the comments from the large man.

"Interesting ..." Jebba stood back up and looked at Whelor. "You fought this dark elf. ... I'm impressed, my friend. They are not ones who die easily. You look fine and well for one having fought one of their kind."

Whelor had known that question would come sooner or later. "I was wounded, if you are wondering, but nothing too serious. I was just better and faster than he, mainly because he was wounded during the battle already, or so I believe." Then, to try to take the focus off him, he asked "Where is Chansor? I haven't seen him for a while now."

Just then, Chansor came around the corner with his arms full, jewels draping over his neck and arms. As the others looked at him with wide eyes, he stated, "What? ... They have no use for them anymore, and besides, we may need them for expenses."

The others just shook their heads. Kikor and Jebba tried not to laugh as they all turned toward the horses.

Chapter Twenty Four

Footmen walking the ramparts of the city's walls whispered uneasily about what was moving toward them. It was no longer a secret among their ranks that some kind of new orc army was marching toward Brigin'i City. Of the ten horse sentries sent out to investigate the dark clouds in the east, only three had returned, and they spoke of seeing the elven forest to their east burning, causing the morning sky to be clouded with the smoke of burning trees.

King Dia's advising council was still reluctant to acknowledge the threat outside of their walls, all believing that the massive walls would stop anything. They told themselves not to be bothered by such "rumors" and that they could tell the city's citizens and others to leave the castle and stay in the dwarf kingdom to the south until the rumors dissipated.

However, one within the group seemed to be apart from the others enthusiasm and pride of the city, Baron Parnland. a fat, overbearing man with large amount of lands to the north threatened by the orcs there, but he did not seem worried though he acted like he was. He knew what was ahead of them as he just sat quiet during the discussions around the table, smiling underneath his beard as he thought of his plans to come.

Outside the castle, orders had been sent out that all standing troops were to prepare for battle. Ramparts were readied and repaired where needed. Men-at-arms trained from dawn until dusk in open areas. Children watched and played along with each other as sword hit shield in practice. Extra men were sent to guard the small passes around their fortress within the forests and watch over the lakeside that lay just north of the city since cavalry and troops that had been sent north had not returned and the rumor had come that maybe orcs were trying to surround the city. The number of horse sentries outside the walls were doubled as well and were being sent in all directions to find information and to watch. The number of trained warriors grew thin.

Any generals or commanders with past experience battling orcs were tasked with supervising the building of catapults to add to the city's defenses in hopes of scattering their movements and forces if and when their armies reached the city. The forests northwest of the castle were cut down within three days, and the trees were brought into the city, where they could be made into weapons by the smiths and weapon makers. All of this activity was accompanied by a steady stream of people who decided not to wait and began making their ways out of Brigin'i City in hopes of finding a safe refuge among the dwarves who lived a fortnight away or in the far west, where a few deep canyons lay within the mountains beyond the sight of the city.

A few days later, as men continued to work hard, a lone horse rider was seen arriving in the late morning, riding so hard that dust rose behind him as he galloped through the gates after orders were given to open them up to let him through. Many footmen along the wall watched the rider jump off the sweating animal and, without stopping, run into the building that held the military command. As they wondered about the news that rider was bringing, many expressed their hopes that they were ready for whatever was coming.

Inside the command building, the generals listened to the messenger's report with a growing sense of trepidation as he relayed the fall of Castle Dagonor and that a massive army was approaching the city through the forest. If accurate, this information could change everything, a few mumbled while looking over the map before them all.

According to the messenger, besides the easy fall of Castle Dagonor, east of Brigin'i City marched what he described as the largest orc army he had ever seen. Elven forces were trying to stop it but were failing terribly, many having fallen or been scattered within their forests. Worse, it now appeared that orcs were being accompanied by at least twenty score goblins and many giants pushing heavy equipment, such as war machines.

He relayed that he and another scout had watched orc smiths rip down trees within the forest and were making more war machines. He believed he saw at least 20 being built before he was spotted and he and the other scout had to retreat quickly, the other man being caught and killed. The rider finished, looking at the ground.

What worried the generals even more, however, was the messenger's report about the strange pattern of darkening skies seen gathering over the forest and slowly moving west, covering the orcs below. What they had thought were storm clouds were in fact large, shadow-like creatures of unknown origin flying above this huge army together in a huge pack, making it look like dark clouds. The messenger had no idea what they were, nor had he wanted to risk capture trying to get a closer look.

After dismissing the messenger, who went off to find food and water, the generals quickly consulted with both the druids and mages who were in the room to see if either could shed any light on what these strange creatures might be, with no success. By night's end, the generals were forced to face the truth: Brigin'i City would not be able to defeat this threat on its own. With the situation now urgent, being told that orcs were moving south through the passes a league north, their quickest riders were sent to the dwarves and beyond in search of help and allies. Maybe the show of strength was what was needed now more than ever. If they could get to the city in time.

* * *

Bennak lay on top of a boulder that was part of the ruined castle's outer wall as the scene before him grew more alarming. The huge columns of orcs and goblins moving toward the elven forest were expanding as they marched by the castle. He had been watching them since the others had started to discuss options. He quickly began making note of their numbers and arms and wondering what was in the heavily guarded wagon train, which he watched with curiosity when he observed huge beastly creatures he had never before seen pulling and pushing this caravan wagon along the ground behind the army.

Of course, the one column turned into three, but numbers didn't matter to Bennak. All he knew that was this army seemed to stream out of nowhere and snaked along the ground like a beast stalking its prey.

He looked at the road to the left that headed out of the castle and continued east to Blath 'Na City. This was supposed to be their main destination before nightfall, a task that would now prove much more difficult with these creatures marching closely in the path. The orcs that Niallee had thought were coming toward this castle had stopped and were controlling the columns of their warriors like a constable would control a population.

Just as he finished watching, he turned to join the others when he saw Hrliger climbing up the wall of the ruins toward his position. When Bennak signalled him to be silent, Hrliger raised his eyebrows but nodded as he quietly peered over the ramparts to watch with surprise. He had only come to inform Bennak that the group was packed and ready to head out, but as he saw what was going on in the distance, the words on his tongue turned to dust, and he crawled closer to kneel next to the big half-orc.

"We still do not know what they are doing. And where did they come from?" Hrliger said quietly, trying to make out what the movement was in front of them. Being a gnome, his eyes were never the best above the ground, so he couldn't make out much, but even he could see the massive force before them.

Bennak didn't answer at first. He was still studying the movement of the army when he saw something moving within the orc and goblin ranks: humans ... coming up in the rear of the column.

"Damn," he whispered, "humans."

Hrliger grunted. "The sight of humans can only mean one of two things: either those are slaves from this castle or some settlements to the east, or somewhere there is a kingdom or city-state that has aligned itself with those nasty beasts."

Bennak looked back at the gnome, then back at the new sight, and thought about that for a moment. "No, there is another option. These could be the tribal men that live in the mountains to the south and east. In truth, they don't look organized enough to be warriors. One thing is for sure, we need a plan before leaving the safety of these ruins. I do not want to take on a whole army or have them give chase." He looked at Hrliger, smiling at his quiet joke.

Hrliger nodded in agreement. "Maybe together the other druids and I can do something to make sure they do not see us!"

Bennak answered with a grunt as he turned and slid down the wall. Hrliger ran to keep up with Bennak as they returned to the center of the ruined castle to find the rest of the group gathering up their equipment and feeding the horses. All but Meradoth, who still hadn't found his horse but insisted that he would take care of it and walked away without a word.

Seeing the big half-orc and gnome move into the clearing, the rest stopped what they were doing when Bennak called for everyone to hear what he had to say.

"An army of orcs, goblins and men, my friends, even larger than the group we saw dead on the battlefield yesterday, is marching itself west into the elven forest not far from us here, as if they knew for sure that there are no more elves to protect or stop it and that this castle is no longer a threat either," Bennak grumbled.

Bennak continued to describe what he had seen, saying, "The army seems to run as far as I can see. To make matters worse, they are currently close enough to the outside of these ruins that they could see us if we tried to leave."

This was answered by worried looks from most of the members of the group.

Bennak went on to say, "Not to worry. Hrliger here says that the druids should be able to cover us with a spell."

All looked to Hrliger, including the other druids and mages, with looks of surprise and wonder, making the gnome turn slightly red, even with his grayish skin .

Kalion looked at the druid. "You really think you can cover us all?"

With a shrug, Hrliger said, "Possibly, with some help." He looked to the other druids, who all seemed to be thinking of ideas.

Hrliger continued by explaining his idea and the exact spell he thought they could use to hide themselves from the orcs in order to pass by.

Now that she understood the gnome's idea, Niallee immediately agreed, saying, "Yes, I think we can do that."

Meradoth then said, "I believe Harbin and I can strengthen your spell with something I've been working on for a while."

Zahnz then spoke up, saying, "The question is which way do we go now? If the army is just outside the ruins we are in, we can't go back to the forest where they are heading."

"And what of those orcs that Niallee saw coming toward us earlier?" Chansor chipped in quickly.

"They seem to be controlling the columns like constables controlling crowds, so they are no longer coming at us but ..." Bennak answered.

Kalion cut in then. "Well from what we learned from that dead dark elf on the field, we need to head east toward Blath 'Na City. Hopefully we can find the princess there or find another clue as to where to go from there."

Bennak, meanwhile, had moved to the front gate to peer around and check on the status of the marching army and returned just in time to hear that they were still going to make their way east.

"It looks like the army outside the walls has left us a gap that runs around the edge of the ruins and will allow us to move southeast, but we still will be able to be seen. It will just mean that we will have to turn north once we get past the army. But it will be a trek, depending on how fast we can move," Bennak stated and then looked to Hrliger, who had gathered around with the other druids.

Hrliger looked around at all the others, then said, "Well it depends. I have never actually tried this spell for so many." Looking to Bennak, he asked, "How far do you think it is until we get past the army?"

"About a league," Bennak stated.

Hrliger's eyes grew big as he thought of the amount of travel they would have to do, so he looked to Meradoth, who had returned with his mount, only to hear what was going to happen. He also gasped about the length of time they would have to be under this spell, but everyone shrugged.

The mages and druids walked away from the group to devise a plan while the others moved the horses closer to the main entry of the castle ruins and waited for what seemed like days until the mages and druids were ready.

A few minutes later, the four returned, nodding their heads whispering that they think they have a plan.

Kalion looked from the horse to Meradoth with a questioned look causing Meradoth to smile and answer the look, "It seems he was inside the castle kitchen. Don't ask. I have no idea how he got there, but I saw him eating apples, so I grabbed him," Meradoth answered the questioning looks. As he showed them a bag of apples that he had grabbed when he found his mount, he said, "Will come in handy, don't you think?"

Handing the reins of their horses over to other members, they took up positions around the rest of the group as Meradoth turned to instruct the team.

"We are going to use a confusion spell to get past the orcs. You must remain inside the circle that we are creating around the group. None of us have ever had to maintain this spell for the time it will take to pass the army, so it is vital that you stay as quiet as possible to allow us to hold our focus, understood?" Meradoth finished with a pointed look at Holan, who merely grunted and nodded along with the rest of the team. "It will also be critical for the rest of the group to lead our horses so that we can concentrate on the spell."

Those who could all mounted their horses and readied themselves, each of those not involved in the spell taking the lead of a horse for one who couldn't ride at the moment.

Taking a deep breath, Hrliger started the movements and words of the spell as the others druids followed him and the mages' eyes closed in concentration. Everyone in the group was taken aback when leaves, dirt and even a few pieces of clothing began to circle their group like a tornado or storm, making it hard for them to see. As they completed the spell and fell silent, Hrliger nodded to the group, which moved slowly out of Castle Dago and onto the field.

The pace was agonizingly slow at first, which allowed the group to get a good long look at the enemy forces, who did see this unusual storm moving across the ground, but none of them stopped to investigate it, thinking it was just a field storm of some kind. It was as Bennak had described: orcs, goblins and men were everywhere along the battlefield, moving and marching slowly west. Every once in a while, some of the goblins and orcs marching along the main road would stop to look in their direction, but as the group made its way over the castle's old ramp and began to move east, none of the creatures had cried out, and no one wanted to test it by making any sudden movements for fear that their little storm might fall apart.

Moving slowly seemed to work well, a few mumbled, not wanting to break the spell or start a curse of bad luck, when suddenly, Winsto stopped, turned and, without saying a word, started to move toward the enemy, drawing his sword slowly out of its scabbard. "What you doing, Winsto? We cannot fight what is coming here!" Kalion whispered almost like a cry at the knight as the others quickly stopped to also watch the man leave.

Winsto stopped and turned in his saddle to answer the ranger quickly. "I am a knight of the Order of the Bleeding Shield, and I am not going to run away anymore, Kalion. I am tired of running and not fighting. These people did not do a thing against anyone, and look what happened here." Winsto nodded his helm back at the castle they had just left. "I will fight what is on this field … and die if I need to."

Bennak couldn't believe what he was hearing. "You do that and you will die. We know that from seeing the castle and the people we found there. You're just one knight,, Winsto, and alone, you can't do enough to damage or stop that army." Bennak pointed to the marching creatures not far from them.

Winsto smiled underneath his helm at Bennak. "I never took you, half–orc, as one to run away from a fight, either, but I must do this. Let me fight."

Bennak's anger started to rise at that comment. He only caught himself when he heard Jebba speaking just above a whisper to get a move on and leave the knight to fight his useless fight.

"I see there is no changing your mind." Winsto didn't respond as Jebba finished, "Well, I guess this is good-bye." The warrior then turned to follow the rest of the group.

Bennak, alone now, raised his hand at the knight's arrogance, wishing the luck of his gods, and turned his horse around to join the rest of the group.

"Do not do this, Winsto. Do not throw your life away on this," Kalion called over to the knight as the man kicked his horse slightly on the side and began to move away.

"Winsto is a knight. He knows what will happen to him, and besides, the duty of a knight of his order is to protect the defenseless," Jebba said sternly, riding up to the others. Jebba hated the idea of it as well, but what could he do?

"My friends, I must do this," Winsto said quietly back to the others as he lowered his visor, kicked his horse again and charged out of the storm cloud screaming something that the others couldn't hear, but that must have been a challenge of some sort, through the whirlwind of dust.

The black clouds that hovered above the marching army sent out a bloodcurdling scream that, even with the storm, made everyone cover their ears as five bursts of mist shot down to the ground near the entrance of Castle Dago, directly in front of Winsto. As the mist quickly cleared, armored creatures broke out, formed into a semicircle and charged toward Winsto.

Seeing Winsto raise his shield to cover his body, all knew that a battle was about to start.

Kalion couldn't believe they were going to let Winsto fight alone. He pulled at his reins and was about to ride forward to help the knight when Jebba reached over and grabbed the reins from Kalion. Looking at Jebba, Kalion saw him shaking his head at him.

"We cannot help him, my friend," Jebba said calmly. Kalion's anger started to get the better of him, but when he looked over to watch Winsto charge forward, his anger quickly turned to amazement.

"Winsto!" Niallee cried not far away, as did Birkita, who had been silent during the whole scene of moving into the castle, telling Kikor later that she had always hated going into the huge buildings. "The stone has always made me cold," she had stated.

They saw Winsto crash into three of the creatures hard, his sword rising up and down quickly. Steel on steel could be heard as the other creatures circled around to block everyone's view of the battle.

Horrible screams could be heard from the creatures and the beasts that they sat on, and Jebba was sure he saw flames coming out of the noses of the horses that carried the black-armored creatures. These screams sent chills down the backs of everyone in the group. They saw some of the beings break away and slowly trot straight at them, but they were transfixed by the sight of watching their friend dying.

Birkita could see blood from the swords whipping up and down around Winsto. Knowing it was Winsto's made Birkita sick, causing her to heave to the side. Turning, she rode down the trail, away from the scene.

The group knew that their escape wouldn't be hidden for long, but watching one of their own fight and die without any of the others lifting a hand to help made them all sick as they watched the armored mount that Winsto said he had brought up since he was born fall hard to the ground and Winsto's body fall as well, off to the side.

High-pitched screams of victory erupted from the black

warriors. The group watched these creatures move closer to each other and raise their swords high in the air as the screams made each member of the quest shake uncontrollably.

The rest of the beings turned and slowly rode toward the castle, leaving both Winsto and his war horse to lie dead on the ground in their wake. Winsto's sword lay a few feet away from his hand, with red blood pooling up, as well.

"Let's go, my man. Let's get the hells out of here, now!" Bennak cried to Kalion as he grabbed his reins. "The mages may not be able to hold this spell much longer." Turning his horse around, he rode away to follow the rest of the group.

"Ahh, Bennak's right. Lets leave now!" Jebba said as the creatures turned from the castle and began to move their way. "I think that they know we are here and saw what happened to Winsto."

Kalion was so angry that he almost didn't hear Jebba screaming in his ears.

"Kalion, get a move on, now. Those things are coming toward us."

"Kalion!"

"Kallllliiiioooonnnnn!"

The warrior wanted to fight the things so badly, but he knew he was overmatched. He had just seen a friend in full armor die within a few moments of fighting these creatures. Screaming at the things, Kalion turned and rode hard, following Jebba, Birkita and the rest down the path east, away from the castle and away from the body of their dear friend Winsto.

It took another four hours of silently dodging and hiding to make it to the outskirts of King Dago's land. By then, their tornado had taken on a life of its own and had gathered more debris as they walked. As they finally came to rest in a small grove, the sky opened up and more rain than they had ever thought possible began soaking them. Not saying a word, they dismounted. The rain was good because it covered the tears from Birkita and the others who couldn't hold their sorrows back. The four mages and druids were so exhausted, however, that they could barely dismount their horses. As the others assisted them, Kalion sat not far away, quietly leaning on his saddle and looking at the state of the land ahead of them.

So far, he saw nothing that posed any threat. The orcish and goblin army was far behind them now.

Chapter Twenty Five

Cold food, wet clothing, testy horses and damp fires plagued the group. Water was in everything now. Rain had been coming down hard now for two days, making the group, and their horses, miserable and cold. Bennak and Holan could be overheard complaining about how they must have made some god mad recently. "I wonder which one?" Holan commented a few times.

Finally, after hours of hearing the two complain, Zahnz couldn't take it anymore and yelled at them to be quiet. Not that it helped restore much peace, as the pair merely took to mumbling between themselves about how wet they were, when the group finally found some cover in a large cave opening.

No one much cared anyway at that point, as they quickly started up some small fires and rolled out their belongings to dry. Kalion quickly broke the team into groups, sending some to venture out to find food while others patrolled the area and guarded the cave. Kalion and Chansor were among those patrolling when they came across signs of a large army traveling westbound. Sliding over to where Kalion was hiding, Chansor opened his mouth to ask a question, only to be shocked by the warrior putting his hand across his mouth to quiet him.

Leaning over so his mouth was directly in Chansor's ear, Kalion whispered, "Shh ... There are dark elves out there. They will see our body heat if we move away from these bushes. Don't move a muscle."

Chansor watched with wide eyes as the army marched past with three or four dark elves placed within each section of the orcish troops. Kalion counted at least twenty of these dark elves as they marched by.

Where had they come from? He wished Zahnz were here. Once in a while he saw some of the dark elves move to the side of the road and speak among themselves before continuing on, but they were too far away for him to hear any details.

Kalion shook his head as the last of the group passed by. He couldn't believe that these creatures organized themselves so well without King Dia, the Levenori Elves or even Blath 'Na City's spies noticing it.

"What do you think?" Chansor quietly asked Kalion. At first Kalion didn't answer, so frustrated was he by the sight of the army.

"I think that we just saw the army that may destroy King Dia's kingdom forever ... and we cannot do a thing to warn the king," Kalion whispered furiously, not looking at Chansor.

"What about one of the mages?" the thief asked. "I'm sure that Harbin can get there and warn the king."

Kalion shook his head at Chansor's comment. "We need Harbin at this moment. Let us go warn the others." Kalion slid back as Chansor looked on for a moment longer, then moved to catch up to the ranger, who quietly moved between the trees.

The campsite was still nearly empty when they returned. Only Jebba, Meradoth and Holan were there, sitting around a small fire that the dwarf had been able to get going just a few moments earlier. Kalion and Chansor walked over and sat down next to the others and warmed their hands as Kalion reported what he had seen.

"You believe this army is on the kill, yea?" Holan grumbled to Kalion.

"Kill? Yes, my good dwarf. I believe we only observed a small part of of what could be the end of what we saw before near Castle Dagonor."

"Well lucky for us that they did na see us, and we got past it to continue on, yea?" Holan grumbled again.

As Kalion finished, the bushes nearby rustled, making the group grab their weapons, but when the bush opened, they all relaxed at seeing the big half-orc walk out.

Kalion was the first to find his voice. "Bennak! What happened to you?"

Plopping down on a log, Bennak drew in a breath and answered, "I was out patrolling the area when I saw an army of orcs go past. I followed them for a while until I was seen by a patrol walking the hills above my position."

"And then what?" Jebba pressed.

"I killed them all," Bennak said, shrugging, "then returned here to tell yea."

"Without bothering to wash their smell off? How was that even possible with all of this rain? Did ye just hide under trees the whole way back to keep the blood on yea as a prize?" Holan grumbled as he shook his head at the orc. "Now the whole of their army can just sniff yea out," he continued grumbling as Bennak frowned back at him before standing up, grabbing the rest of the rabbit on the spit and making his way toward the creek, grumbling to himself. He had tried to keep the blood on his body as proof of his kill. Leave it to Holan to make him see the foolishness of his pride.

* * *

Penelo and Osa walked south as fast as they could. Every once in a while they hid in the bushes and the tall weeds when they saw or heard orcs and goblin patrols running about.

After the battle in the north, the three remaining companions from the company that Dia had sent to join with the army finally came after two days of travel to stand on a large knoll looking down on Castle Bahn, the large tower fortress that kept the peace in this area. The sight they saw was not the one they had hoped for. The tower was smoking heavily from fire within it, and all around the tower's base danced orcs and goblins dragging many prisoners and throwing them into the fires alive and screaming, the sounds of which echoed throughout the area.

A woman, they could see, was being tortured while another not far away was being carved up. They had hoped to find a place of refuge and safety here after what they had experienced to get this far. Before they were seen, they turned and took their time to get around the tower's perimeter and the orc patrols they saw moving about.

Without horses, it took them several days of hiding and evading the creatures to get even close to the Brigin'i border. When they were finally spotted by one of Dia's horse patrols, faster than they could think, they were brought into Dia's kingdom and finally into Brigin'i City, where the clerics could take care of them.

The king, along with his generals and his sheriff, was interested in knowing what had happened, so the three were summoned before the king after being given a few patches to cover their injuries. The picture they painted of the battle, or rather, massacre, quickly showed the king and his advisors how the orc attack had surprised the army camp during the night, demolishing the entire army within hours. The sheriff said that a few other stragglers had been found as well, out in the countryside. Some had died from their injuries or the weather.

It would seem that not enough sentries or pickets had been placed around the camp, King Dia thought. The king had sent this army out a week before with his son in command to diminish the threat before it reached the city walls. He now wondered about his son and his safety.

The news about the fall of his northern borders made Dia both furious and sad. The whole area was now open to these orcs and whatever allies they might have coming from the east. He had lost over a thousand skilled warriors and cavalry, along with their equipment and horses, and maybe his son. Not only had Castle Bahn fallen, but now signs of orcs had been seen near the villages of Selkia and Mortlow, situated between Bahn and Brigin'i.

There certainly had been no shortage of bad news over the past two days, Dia thought, frowning. First, word had come that the Levenori Elves had all been destroyed and killed. The smoke from what had once been their forest kingdom had been drifting into the city for days now, causing many of the city's residents to flee toward the safety of the western mountains and the south.

King Dia had few choices left as he went over his options with the generals. He could only list three. One: to stay and fortify the city and castle, cutting down as many trees in the area for defense and to take away weapons from the enemy. Two: to fortify the castle and have the city's population leave for the west but leave a small number of defenders to give the rest a chance to get away. Or three: to have everyone leave for the west and destroy the city to leave nothing for the orcs to use in the future. The last option was the one that bothered Dia the most, but it was one that had to be placed on the table now.

The real last option of course was to pay the ransom and hope to the gods that Methnorick would keep his word to the king.

Based on the available intelligence, there were now two armies coming toward the city. It was estimated that the orcs who had destroyed the elves in the east would take at least another week to get to the outskirts of the city itself, maybe even longer if there were any elves left to provide some counterattacks. The estimates on the army traveling from the northern border were far sketchier. No one knew much except that they had been told by Osa, Penelo and the few stragglers who had made it to the city from that now-lost army that they were close.

"I believe we should stay and fight. Orcs have never prevailed against a castle like ours," one of the generals said making the rest nod in agreement.

"Yes, I agree," Dia answered back, grateful that someone still thought Brigin'i worth fighting for. "Orcs are good in open areas and in large groups, but they don't have the ability to besiege a castle like ours," Dia insisted as the generals argued back and forth.

Suddenly, an unexpected voice interrupted the proceedings, surprising everyone who turned to see the queen standing at the door,

"I too believe that we should stay and fight. Brigin'i is the heart of this region. Without it, where will the populace turn, and who will protect them? They have taken my daughter and, now, maybe my son. We must protect our home and our people." Many nodded their heads in agreement as Dia walked over to stand beside his queen.

"Then it is final. We shall stand and fight. He wanted a ransom believing my family... your families... our warriors and men across this city would retreat and run.. they can go the gods with my answer on this!

"Send the word out to the populace that a battle for the city is coming. Those who can may leave now, or they may stay and fight for their people and their kingdom," Dia said with confidence.

The generals saw that the meeting was over and got up as one and left the council chambers, leaving the king and queen alone.

Dia walked over to the large window that looked out over the castle and city beyond. How he loved this city and everything it stood for in this land. Now his family was paying the price for his arrogance, and he wouldn't stand for that either. Turning around, Dia smiled at his wife. She was everything to him. He didn't want her to die by the blade of some orc.

"My dear, I want you to go to the western mountains," he said quietly as he bent down so that he was eye to eye with her. "Our sons there could protect you, as their fortresses are enclosed within the mountains and are hard to attack. And you can lead those who choose to leave."

She smiled at her husband's concern for her well-being. She knew that he loved her with everything in his heart, but she was also afraid of what was out there, what was coming toward them. She had never been farther west than their family estates that lay a league away in a beautiful glen with a small lake next to it, but now she felt as though her world was closing in.

"No, my husband, my king, I will stay and fight and help where I can. This is my home, and I will fight for it." Still smiling, she leaned over and kissed her husband gently on his forehead and got up and left the room.

Dia was both happy and sad at her comments. "I love you too, my queen," he whispered to her as she walked out the chamber door.

Chapter Twenty Six

It took Brigin'i City only three hours to evacuate the population that wanted to leave, joining those who had already left days before. Supply trains of wagons and carts left the city in droves, most with civilians carrying older weapons. Many of the fleeing civilians were just using farming equipment as protection since warriors were needed in the city itself.

As day dawned, the city was so silent that it gave Dia shivers as he looked down from the castle. No sounds of children playing in the streets, no yelling from merchants, no sounds of music bouncing off the walls. But for a smattering of the city's leaders and a few country lords who had come in from the south, only the castle's footmen and men-at-arms remained.

The smoke coming from the elven forest even made breathing difficult for some of the sentries stationed closest to the wood. Pickets sent east came back reporting that orcs could be seen just inside of the forest. The orcs were watching them in return, even trying to taunt them into a fight, but, surprisingly, not attacking.

The forests north and west of the city had been torn down at a remarkable rate in preparation for the approaching armies. Workers labored to both strengthen the curtain walls from inside the city and soften the stone wall in response to news of heavy war machines being dragged through the forest. Other reinforcements included the placement of heavy amounts of dirt from ditches being dug for archers and spearmen, many being built with wooden spears in front of the ditches surrounding the city walls in the hope that they would stop, or at least slow down, foes larger than an orc, such as the giants who were said to be among these armies.

Dia walked the walls and the streets, doing his part to bolster the spirits of those who had stayed behind to help out. Having thought most of the children long evacuated, he was surprised to come across a young boy trying to warm himself by the fire of a torch light hanging from a post.

"Hello, young man, what is your name?" Dia asked as he came up behind the boy.

If the boy was surprised to see his king standing in front of him, he certainly hid it well as he jumped to attention with a smile. "Me name is Trvium, my king, of the house Clor-ium."

Dia nodded at the boy as he walked over to warm his hands by the flames as well. "Trvium, hmm ... isn't your father Travium?"

Trvium's smile grew even larger at the mention of his father's name. "Yes, me king, Travium is my father. Do you know of him?"

"Not too well, my boy, but your family's house is a fine one. Where is your father?" Dia asked as he looked around. "Why isn't he on duty with you?"

"Oh, my father went with the army to the north ... with the prince, my king. He is an excellent horseman."

Dia smiled at Trvium, despite his mind filling with horror over what had most likely happened to Travium ... and Dia's son if the reports were correct. "Well I am sure your father is doing well. My son is a good judge of character when it comes to horsemen."

"Perhaps one day I will be able to ride with the prince —" Trvium stopped in mid-sentence as he stared out at the eastern forest. Alarmed, Dia turned to look at what the boy was seeing.

Hundreds of torches could be seen coming out of the darkness of the forest. Dia felt a chill run down his back the orcs approached his city. Hearing the yells of others who also saw the sight, Dia quickly ran to the large bell that was used to raise alarms. Grabbing the hammer, he struck it hard, again and again, until the sound of corresponding bells echoed across the city.

Turning back to the young Trvium, Dia bade the boy to hide himself as he ran down the stairs to join his men in battle at the walls.

Yelling could be heard everywhere as soldiers, footmen and

archers prepared for the coming assault. War machines stationed every hundred yards behind the walls were made ready.

Torches and fires were extinguished along the wall to keep the orcs, who had terrible night vision, from seeing the soldiers lying in wait along the walls. Mages stood prepared with their spells and potions.

Instead of hiding as Dia had ordered, young Trvium stood with three other footmen as they looked over the wall toward the army, arranging themselves for the assault. One of the solders grumbled that the mages should be attacking them now to disrupt their preparations. The other solider responded that the mages were waiting until the attack began in order to repel as many as possible. Trvium listened to the two argue, wishing that he had gone with his mother. He had only wanted to protect the only home he had ever known, but now he was scared. He had never seen an orc. All he knew of them was that they were merciless killers who wanted to kill him and his people.

He looked below him and saw archers preparing themselves within some of the temporary ramparts that had been built for them as those sentries who were able to get away from the forest edge ran and jumped into these ditches. He was glad not to be down there with them as he wondered how afraid they must be, despite having volunteered to go outside the main curtain wall. Of course, the king's promise of extra pay had been the driving force for most of those now facing the first wave of orcs. Above and behind him, he saw more archers preparing themselves as well. A few mages had set up a trap in the middle of the field that made the passing orcs' footprints glow a soft blue that could only be seen from the city walls. King Dia was walking back and forth giving orders and encouragement to his men.

Trvium watched with horror as what looked like hundreds of footprints approached the castle, nearly wetting himself when the orcs suddenly started to taunt them with their screams. Behind him, calls for readiness from the sergeants and captains sounded over the noise.

"When they begin taunting, that means they intend to attack soon," a soldier standing next to Trvium grumbled quietly. "When they stop, be prepared, for that's when they strike," the man continued, smiling grimly at Trvium. Trvium regarded the soldier, who looked even older than his father, and nodded, hoping the man knew of what he spoke.

"Stop scaring the boy, Ulan," another old soldier said as he approached the pair, "he's here to show that his family has something to fight for." The second old man looked Trvium up and down and sniffed dismissively. "He'll probably run away the minute the orcs get here." Trvium was suddenly really scared now. Would he run or fight?

"Shut it, Cufic. You don't know this boy at all," Ulan snapped back. "At least he is here. Where's your —?"

Trvium had been looking at Ulan and therefore did not see what made his eyes widen as the old man grabbed him and pushed him to the ground. Lifting his head, he turned around to see what had alarmed Ulan.

On the ground a few feet away lay Cufic with an ugly looking arrow sticking out from his chest. The expression on Cufic's face was one of surprise and pain. Ulan himself dropped to the ground as three more arrows flew overhead. One hit Ulan in the right arm, making him groan from the pain before nodding to Trvium that he was fine and telling him to hide.

"Night arrows!" the old man screamed as loud as he could.

It was too late. All along the walls, black arrows flew into the city. Bodies were dropping from the ramparts, screaming as they fell to their deaths both inside and outside the walls and landing behind the archers below. The battle had begun. As he crawled behind a wall to hide, Trvium wondered if he would survive.

* * *

"What are you talking about, Chansor?" Amlora called over to the thief who for the past few minutes or so had kept chattering about some cave he had found, as the rain continued to fall. For two days now, they had hidden in the forest, trailing the orc army while avoiding their patrols. So far they hadn't been discovered, but now, some like Chansor were starting to get restless.

Kalion had reconsidered the idea of using a mage to warn the city. Harbin had tried twice to go and warn King Dia, but something had blocked him from doing it. That worried the group more than the presence of an army, especially when Niallee and Meradoth attempted the same spell with similar results. No one knew for sure what was blocking the mage's powers, but all suspected that the dark elves seen in the group might have something to do with the matter.

Food was also becoming a problem. It was difficult to hunt amongst an entire army searching the same woods. And now Chansor was annoying the increasingly frustrated group with talk about some hidden cave.

"Did you go into the cave, thief?" Jebba asked from his seat next to the small fire they had lit earlier.

Chansor shook his head, making Jebba snort at Chansor over his obvious cowardice. Still, Chansor wouldn't be swayed. "I am serious, Jebba; I think it would be a good place."

Bored with sitting still, Bennak jumped up and turned to Chansor, stretching as he spoke. "Then, my friend, why don't you and I go and check this place out since the others do not want to."

Chansor smiled. "Well, at least if there is anything in there that wants to eat me, Bennak will have first dibs on it!" Happy to have one as strong as Bennak for company, Chansor quickly grabbed his small sword out of his saddle bag along with a storm lantern stolen from the inn they had stayed in the first night.

The two walked for what seemed like a few miles. Just as Bennak was about to ask Chansor if he really knew where this cave was, the thief suddenly turned around and stopped. "We're here."

Bennak nodded quietly as he heard something scratching just inside the dark hole that Chansor pointed at. Raising a finger to his mouth to signal Chansor to be quiet, he pulled his large sword from his back and crept up to the entrance of the small cave.

The first thing Bennak noticed was that the cave was too

small to house more than five or six of their group. Nor was there room for the horses. Someone had used the cave once, however, as Bennak spotted burnt wood and ashes from an old fire and a pile of bones.

As Bennak emerged from the cave, Chansor jumped off a boulder and ran over to the half-orc. "So?"

"Well, for one, it is not big enough for the entire group. Still, I found nothing in there that could harm us."

"Oh," Chansor replied, somewhat dejectedly, "I really thought it would be a great place to hide for a while ... if they wanted to. At least it's dry."

Bennak shook his head as he smiled at the small thief. "Chansor, for one, you cannot get a horse past this entrance," he said as he pointed to the cave mouth. Next, whatever or whoever made that pile of bones made it somewhat recently as the bones showed signs of new wear and tear."

"How recently?" Chansor asked, curious now.

"I know not, but ..." Bennak raised his hand to silence Chansor as the thief's mouth opened to ask another question, "... it matters not since it is time to go back and find food."

"Sounds great to me, Bennak." Chansor laughed as he ran back down the trail with Bennak walking quickly behind him. They had barely stepped into the clearing before Chansor started regaling the others about their adventure at the cave. How the thief could find a cave so interesting was beyond the half-orc, but even he found himself smiling at Chansor's enthusiasm.

"Chansor says that you found bones inside the cave," Harbin remarked quietly as he walked over to Bennak.

"Aye," Bennak replied, keeping to himself for now the fact that the bones were not those of a creature at all, but those of a man. Perhaps he would mention it to Kalion later. Suddenly, his thoughts were interrupted as a branch not far from them snapped, causing the two to suddenly stop in their tracks as the bushes exploded and a deer shot out and ran in between Kalion and Chansor.

Kalion looked over at Bennak, smiling. "The race is on, my friend!"

Chapter Twenty Seven

For what seemed like hours, the enemy rained arrows into the city of Brigin'i. Soldiers, footmen, men-at-arms and civilians alike died under the shower of deadly bolts from above until they could finally hide in the buildings. Of the two hundred who started on the walls, no more than forty made it to hide from the deadly attack.

As dawn approached, another attack came, as huge boulders came flying in, slamming hard against the outside wall. Inside the city, Dia's generals were scrambling to counteract this unfamiliar enemy strategy. Never had anyone seen an army of orcs use war machines. Before today, their enemies had always only used brute strength, which was why the generals had felt safe placing archers on the walls in defensible areas, but now those same archers were dying as boulders fell upon them from above and behind, killing many as they were crushed.

Now as they had fallen back, the enemy began "The Haunt," a type of singing they did to both scare their enemies and also gather strength and courage among themselves. King Dia looked out from the castle walls over the city of Brigin'i, observing the damage that the enemy army had been causing for the past day with its continuing barrage of stones and arrows. Everywhere he could see, bodies killed by arrows or rocks lay along the streets and along the outer wall. They were being dragged away by footmen and civilians tasked with helping where they could as they dodged arrows still being shot into the city. Disease was the last thing this place needed, and the rising number of dead made the city susceptible to an outbreak. Now as he heard the enemy chanting, he wondered if they would even have to worry about disease. Up until now, the enemy onslaught involved those war machines just inside the forest edge, making it hard to stop them, but with the chanting, he knew that the direct assault was close at hand.

How much more can my beautiful city take? Dia wondered as he saw buildings everywhere cracking, many smashed and blown apart by the huge stones flying in, as the city's own war machines were doing their best in keeping up their own assault on the enemy.

Dia's two remaining generals (many of the others having been wounded or killed) had gathered high above the thick walls of Brigin'i to discuss the defense plans. However, as Dia stood there feeling hopeless, he realized the attack had up until this point been to reduce his fighting force. Messengers ran everywhere returning word and getting out word on where defenses needed to be thickened as archers were resupplied with arrows and weapons below were sharpened within metal smith buildings that were scattered throughout the city.

As one, the city worked hard to get itself ready, but it didn't matter, as the arial attack was taking a toll on the city. A report stated that over 800 civilians, warriors and footmen had been killed or wounded since the beginning of the attack, and many civilians who had stayed behind to protect their homes were missing, probably having been buried underneath the rubble of smashed buildings. This, added to the amount of damage being done to the tower war machines and other equipment defending Brigin'i City, indicated the city might break under the pressure.

At the high part of day two, the arrows finally stopped, giving everyone a brief reprieve and a chance to move about. Mages inside rested as best as they could, lying down next to archers who were resting their arms. Since the first assault began, they had all been doing their best to both defend the castle and attack anything they could see. The mages used bluish bolts of light and red lines of fire to ignite the forest in an attempt to push more of the enemy army out into the open, closer to the city, making them easier to attack.

King Dia moved down the main road that extended from the castle to the eastern part of the city. Moving quickly with his personal guards tagging behind, he saw a mage resting on the ground. The mage looked up as his king and the guards walked by, all nodding to him as they did. Dia, thinking suddenly of an idea, walked over and knelt down to ask the man to go on a mission for him.

"My friend, I need you to try to get to Blath 'Na City. Explain that things have taken a turn for the worse here, and find out where our reinforcements are," Dia whispered into the ear of the mage.

"My king, it might take some time to get there," the mage said as he struggled to stand. "I will need to pull together ingredients, and the spell will take time to prepare." As he looked at the King's face, he realized the importance of this mission. The young mage agreed and turned to walk back to his private chamber to begin working on the spell that would transport him to the port city far to the east. Dia watched the man for a moment, wishing him luck, and he himself decided right then and there that he would be at the forefront of the defense of his great city.

"Bachelor-at-arms!" he screamed, his voice echoing everywhere. Many who heard it knew instantly what was going to happen. Their king's voice told them all he was going to join the fight as they saw their leader move toward the main curtain wall.

As he walked up the stairs and joined the men along the battlements, King Dia looked out into the forest and said quiet prayers that some help would come soon. Over the past two days, the enemy had made significant progress in assaulting his beautiful city. One attack he estimated must have cost the enemy dearly, for even though Brigin'i had lost so many, the enemy dead outside his wall stacked up as well. They had attacked both the southern and northern walls at the same time, forcing Dia to divide his defenses between the walls. This made Dia think that the enemy attacking him at that moment had some assistance. It was too well planned for these orcish creatures, Dia thought.

Now Dia saw the tactics they were using taking form as the whole enemy army stood before him. He could hear the jeers and yells coming toward the city as the enemy — dark elves, giants and some indefinable creatures — taunted those looking out from the city battlements.

The enemy army used both catapults and a large group of mountain giants to hit one gate tower, demolishing it in three strikes. One rock hit the tower so hard that the walls began to crumble instantly.

On the third night, the night arrows continued, but with a focus on this heavily damaged tower. Within moments, the wooden gate was in flames, and as the defenders within the city could see, the flames moved quickly. Screams could be heard from the inside of the tower as the defenders tried to get out while others tried to throw water on it.

King Dia felt the hairs on his neck go up as he watched the tower burning, knowing that many of his warriors were dying within it. He looked down to think, knowing that his city was dying quickly and he needed a miracle to happen to save it.

Then, suddenly, the ground shook. Dia lifted his head as he watched watch the tower finally collapse. He ran over to get as close as he could before his guards stopped him. He stood helpless as he watched the defenders of the city being killed one by one. Dia shook his head, knowing that if the enemy did this to each of the main towers, the wall wouldn't hold up for long.

Dia felt a hand from one of the guards on his shoulder. As he looked up at the warrior and then toward where he was pointing, Dia saw that the orcs were attacking the north and south walls at the same time again. With the barrage of attacks from the wooden edge to decrease his numbers and now the attack on the city in two areas, the same two areas they had attacked the previous night, the enemy was working his city's defenses hard.

Everywhere, screams from defenders echoed in Dia's ears as he yelled for his archers to make ready. Warriors within the city were running to clear up the rubble from the fallen tower as many were passing pieces of it to get them to their machines that could throw them back at the charging enemy army. Everyone did what they could to clear the area and help those who needed it when, suddenly, all stopped working as a new sound interrupted their work.

Horns screamed out from the forests. Dia turned quickly to see the forests explode as enemy upon enemy charged out of the forests toward the city, screaming as they did with their banners and flags held high above their ranks.

"Make yourselves ready!" Dia screamed as loudly as he could as he rushed from his defenders toward the walls.

As he looked across the field, he saw that the orcs and dark elves were using mountain giants as shields. When they got closer, he could see that orcs and dark elves weren't just using the bodies as shields, but each giant was holding up a piece of large wooden shield, which seemed to be stopping his archers' arrows.

As his war machines began their counterattack by throwing out rocks, he saw only a few of the stones hit a giant, causing its shield to explode into pieces and killing the giant holding it as other rocks slammed onto the ground and rolled over many orcs and goblins trying to attack. There were many of these giants and many other creatures running behind them in large groups, as his war machines didn't slow the charge down. As he watched these huge beasts move closer and the enemy behind them try to cover their advance, Dia finally realized what they were doing now.

"By the gods ..." Dia mumbled, looking to the south and then east before turning back and screaming out new orders to his warriors around him. Running down the stairs, he screamed that a second wave was coming to the eastern wall as well. Servants, men-at-arms and warriors ran everywhere as the word spread quickly about the second wave now coming at the eastern wall. Dia starting screaming orders to his archers to use fire arrows. As the archers readied the fire arrows, others did their best to throw everything they had onto the field, including using the war machines that worked quickly to throw stone after stone against the giants.

As the king ran down the stairs onto the road below, he grabbed a warrior and ordered him to run to the castle and make sure the protection for the queen was set. Turning, he ordered his warriors to get the reserves that waited a few streets within the city to make themselves ready for any breach.

Grabbing the general who was in charge of the wall defenses, he quickly told him what he saw, but as he was talking to the general, the sky above quickly darkened. Everyone looked up as the sky filled with arrows. Dia looked at his general, cursing himself again for not thinking of a better way to defend his beloved city.

The general was also barking out orders as Dia turned and said, "Do your best, General!" The general nodded once as he watched the king run to the wall to see how the situation was progressing.

Dia ran up to the battlement. Grabbing the stone to steady himself, he watched as the giants approached the walls as the arrows from the orcish archers were giving cover to the larger creatures, killing many of his warriors along the wall who were defending it. A few of the giants, he noticed, were even carrying what could only be tree trunks, which took him aback for a moment.

Inside the city, the screams from men-at-arms could be heard as they ran up the stairs, only to be hit by falling arrows slamming hard into them, knocking them back and killing many instantly.

Captain Marbod and General Comitay were at the part of the city wall that looked directly down onto that section of the eastern wall. They stood in silence, watching the darkness coming alive before them. Looking at each other, they couldn't believe that the enemy was able to mount this type of attack. It was here that Dia found them as he was trying to get a better view of the fields below.

"Can you see the numbers of the enemy?" he asked, running up to them.

"Yes, my king. We ordered as many men as we could toward this area of the wall," General Comitay answered.

"And as many as we can afford, my king, and we have moved every machine to the south and eastern areas of the city, which seems to be where the most are approaching. Our archers are having a hard time diminishing their ranks, but we are making progress, my king," Captain Marbod added.

"The enemy is using giants as shields, and the giants have

trees as shields as well. We need to use fire arrows," the king said. He turned to one of the messengers in the room. "See to it that all archers are aware that they are to use fire arrows only!""

"Those stupid creatures might be able to get within the walls," he quietly said to the others as he leaned closer to the edge and watched his men-at-arms pouring out more arrows and throwing stones at the giants advancing toward the wall. "But we will fight on every corner and street to get them out."

Slowly, his machines were beginning to have an effect as giant after giant fell from the heavy stones and the large number of fire arrows hit them hard now as the distance closed, making the impacts harder. Dia even smiled when he saw a large boulder from one of his machines fly into what he thought might have been a hill giant and cut right through its body, taking the creature's head right off and killing a group of the enemy that was running just behind it.

Screams of warning were heard coming from the fallen tower as orcs and goblin warriors were trying to break through the quickly made defenses, but from where the king stood, it appeared his own warriors were doing well in holding them back.

Directly in front of them, Dia saw the massive form of Amatora whipping his huge axe left and right, chopping heads cleanly off, leaving many to fly into the air. Everywhere he attacked, the orcs gave way and retreated, letting Dia's own men take care of the others in the siege.

These counterattacks from Brigin'i were having a noticeable effect, as Dia and his warriors could even hear the screams from enemy sergeants and captains calling out for a retreat, and slowly, the giants walked backward, trying to protect themselves and the enemy around them. As they moved back toward the forests holding their shields up, many still fell from boulders slamming into them.

Looking at the battlements, the king could see that both walls of the city were damaged heavily and corpses, both human and orc, were lying everywhere, but luckily, most of the corpses were from the enemy. Green blood and red were mixing heavily as the enemy retreated, taking almost an hour to finally get all the enemy out of the gate tower's rubble, or what was left of it.

He was sure that he wouldn't be able get his warriors to fix the tower in time for the next attack, as he saw that the enemy would use that open hole in the wall to push any attack when it came. He sent word that all men-at-arms, footmen and anyone who could hold a weapon were to stand ready at that section of the city and be ready for the final assault by the enemy. Quickly, warriors who were being held in reserves deep within the city moved themselves to position just behind the rubble and readied themselves.

Dia watched his warriors move around and get into place as he looked out to the forest, making out heavy amounts of movement, as the enemy began preparing to attack again. Giants still holding the huge wooden shields stood in front of the enemy as they moved out of the tree line, and he could see other large-looking creatures moving the war machines to new positions to make a final attack. He could see that many were concentrating their placement near the fallen tower.

Looking over the walls that for cycles had protected his beautiful city and everything within it, he quickly remembered his thoughts from a few cycles ago when he had the idea of pushing the elven forests back more, but that was in the time of peace. Now Brigin'i was a total war zone with hundreds of his people dead or dying.

At least some had escaped, Dia thought as he continued to look out over his city. He knew that the clerics were overloaded taking care of those hurt and injured and water and food were coming up short in many parts of city. Rioting had even started at the western gate, as people still believing that they could leave that way were stopped by the guards. Three of his generals were out of the battle now. Two had been killed when the tower had fallen. One general had been below giving orders to reinforce the tower as it crumbled on top of him, and the other was inside commanding the bowmen. The third was taken out by the night arrows during the initial attack.

Most of his war machines were still standing, which was something Dia was very proud of. His engineers had designed the city's war machines to be stronger than any castle wall. However, the machines were running out of stones to throw, even with the rubble from the destroyed tower and other buildings that had fallen. According to General Comitay, his only war leader left, the enemy was going to make a final push using the strength of the darkness to their advantage, and this time he believed they would finally breech the walls. There were just not enough men left to protect all the damaged sections, the general relayed.

Looking out toward the forest, Dia could see whole battalions of the enemy — deadly goblins, dark elves and giants — preparing themselves. As the sounds of armor and feet echoed across the field, his archers again started releasing fire arrows in an attempt to slow them down.

The only source of relief at the moment, if Dia could really call it a relief, was that the barrage coming from the enemy archers had stopped, as did the rocks coming from the enemy's own war machines. It did give his defenders time to ready weapons and defenses.

"My king, I believe you should leave the wall before you are seen by their archers!" a shaky voice piped into Dia's thoughts. He turned around and saw standing there his personal counselor Bogwa, who himself had been wounded by an arrow, his right arm slung up now across his chest.

He knew Bogwa was just being protective, but Dia needed to be here with his fellow people when the final attack began.

"My dear friend, I cannot stress to you how glad I am that you are here, but you know that I cannot leave." Dia earlier that hour had changed into a regular man-at-arms uniform, covering his royal robes with the heavy armor. Now nothing would give him away as the king except that he still wore the crown of his forefathers on his head.

"Hmm, besides, I want to finally get my hands dirty fighting these ugly things that have dared to attack my city." Bogwa smiled at his king's stubborn defiance at what was to come. "I will not cower as my city falls. I will be here beside my men." With people inside dying, riots at the western edge of the city, and Dia's children all gone now, this man Bogwa still followed him. Dia looked toward Bogwa and said, "But you can do one last thing for me: see to the queen's safety."

Bogwa agreed with a bow and thought of how he would really hate to meet this king in the heat of battle, especially with the anger he held inside now. He could see the king's hand turn red as he gripped the sword his great-grandfather had forged many cycles before.

Deep within the forest, the huge caravan being pulled and pushed by giant creatures finally stopped and was lowered down as goblin and orc warriors ran around to make sure things were cleared and set. Crying out in some language none understood, a goblin leader watched as the large drape that covered the entrance flew back and the enormous shadow of the being who was inside stepped out.

The goblin ran up and quickly knelt down and waited until he saw the feet of the creature he knew rode inside.

"My lord general, our attacks have done a massive amount of damage to the walls, their warriors and more, sir, and a tower has just fallen, which should give you, my lord, the ability to move in," the goblin nervously said, relaying his information.

Hearing nothing except heavy breathing, the goblin dared to look up but quickly looked back down when he saw that the face of his leader was looking down in return.

"What are you orders, my lord?" the goblin nervously asked.

Without giving an answer, the leader walked past where the goblin knelt and toward the forest edge, causing the ground to shake slightly. Quickly, the goblin jumped up and caught up to stand behind the general as he looked over the battlefield before him.

"Is everything prepared?" the voice said, making the goblin shake as he tried to answer. "Send word to the ones above. The signal will be sent soon for their final assault."

"Ye ye yes, my general." Quickly bowing then running off to send out the orders, the goblin relayed everything he could, and quickly.

Watching the stupid creature leave his presence, the beast turned around and stood next to a large fir tree, using it to lean on slightly as he looked left and right but then leveled his vision at the castle city beyond where his army stood.

"Dia, I see you there. But this night, I bring the hells to you!" The eye blinked and the shadow disappeared as the moon shined through, showing the smile and teeth that were inside the large cyclops who led the armies against Brigin'i.

As Dia stood speaking to his servant, another messenger ran up and quickly gave the king a rolled parchment and then ran off to continue with his errands.

As he ripped the string and waxed seal that held the parchment together, Dia glanced at Bogwa. Bogwa looked at the parchment and saw writing that could only be described as elven in nature.

"Only the elves would use this type of wax," Dia mumbled as he unrolled the parchment to read what was written inside. His smile told Bogwa that it was good news. Smiling and nodding slowly, Dia handed it over to Bogwa so he could it read it as he turned his head to the north and east of the city.

"By the gods, could this be true?" Bogwa moaned moments later as he read the words, then continued reading the message again and then a third time, for he couldn't believe its contents. "If the Levenori Elves are still alive and this is not a trick from the enemy ... how did this get into the city? I did not see a rider and was not informed that one made it in." He looked up at Dia and then followed the king's stare to the north.

"That, my friend, is from an elven captain, an elf that I have known all my life and one whom I can trust to know that this message is true. And if he wrote this, then the elves must have played out a strategy with the enemy to make them believe they had killed them all or had scattered them in their forest and were too weak to counter their assault on the forests." He looked back to Bogwa at the last word.

Bogwa's mouth had fallen open as he listened to his king, but then realizing his expression, he pulled his mouth closed before he answered, "I am with you and everyone here in hoping that the elves were not completely slaughtered, but do you believe they are coming from the north as he wrote there?"

Dia grabbed Bogwa's shoulder as he walked him away from all others on the wall. "Bogwa, not only do I believe that they live, but I believe you are correct in thinking that they recognized the enemy army was just too large for them to fend off and decided to go deeper into their forest and the mountains beyond. Where, I do not know of course, but I know the elf who wrote this message. His name is Kelic, and for some reason, I remember him telling me over some grog that when pressed many cycles ago, his people had built a place within the mountains to hide their people in a time such as this."

Bogwa squinted his eyes, concentrating as he listened to Dia, but he didn't say anything until Dia was done.

"Do you believe that elven warriors will be able to counter the enemy enough to save the city?" Bogwa asked, looking to the field.

"If the elves will be able to fully attack the enemies where they stand ... maybe."

"But, my king ... you believe it might give us the chance to counterattack ourselves?"

Dia nodded his head slowly. "Maybe ... just maybe." Dia looked down at the message still in Bogwa's hand, then to the field.

"What do you command of me then, my king?" Bogwa knew he was about to get orders.

Smiling because Bogwa was so smart, Dia turned his head, looking from the enemy to his city below him as he thought of what he needed his servant to do.

"Have General Comitay gather all able people of our city to the eastern wall, but with largest number at the southern gate. If the elves do attack, then we need to be prepared to counter by sending our warriors out into the field through the southern gate in the hope that we can squash the enemy between our two armies." Dia patted Bogwa's back hard and then turned to walk over as a sergeant came running up.

"Make sure any cavalry that are still intact are made ready as well!" Dia said as he looked at the sergeant and then toward the forests, where he thought he saw something standing and looking back at him.

"Then continue on and protect the queen."

Bogwa bowed to his king without saying a word and ran down the stairs, looking for General Comitay as he remembered he had last seen him getting the defenses ready along the wall. It took Bogwa longer than he had hoped to find the general, but he found him standing at the top of the rubble of the southern fallen tower, yelling at his men, directing men-at-arms one way and archers another.

When Comitary saw Bogwa, he knew something was happening. He jumped down, and within a few moments of talking to the king's counselor, Comitay ordered what men he could spare to get themselves ready and to move into position at the southern gate, directing the remainder to the eastern wall.

Comitay slapped Bogwa's back as he ran by, motioning him to follow him as he ran toward the barracks, which was one of the only buildings left standing in the area. Once inside, they found warriors, men-at-arms and civilians preparing themselves for battle. Weapons were being sharpened and bow staves strung and tested to make sure they were ready.

Armor was being checked to ensure their leather straps were tight and that the armor was built correctly. At the back of the large building, they could see horses being shoed as fast as they could be brought in. To the side, they could see many of the fletchers were making arrows. Many arrows were not getting into the enemy armor, so the blacksmiths and fletchers were working together to make stronger points. Even two mages had joined their powers to give the arrow points some extra strength. This created an eerie glow that caused the entire area to take on this strange and unusual blue color.

The sounds from metal being shaped were deafening to Bogwa, but he didn't care. The city was on the verge of falling to an enemy that historically knew no mercy. Everyone in the city would die if the enemy got inside.

As he watched all this, a long line of men, women and older

children who had stayed within the city were gathering weapons, armor and whatever they were told to grab and went where they were told to go.

Bogwa could see the uneasiness of the people, many showing signs of fear at the thought of Brigin'i falling at the hands of the orcish army outside, but Bogwa could also see that this fear began to disappear when they were given something to turn that fear into anger, and it gave the man hope that Brigin'i might survive this onslaught.

It was there that the two found Opto, King Dia's personal assistant, and Captain Marbod, the sheriff, discussing the safety of their king and what to do if and when the city fell.

"Many cycles ago, the city builders made an underground passageway only known to the king's family, the command staff and a few others. The only problem is that it was built to go to the south of the city, and from what the observers have seen from the towers, the enemy has gathered and camped around where the exit is," Captain Marbod said, turning his head to see General Comitay walking up.

Nodding to the general, Marbod kept talking. "So the question is, Opto, where will the king and queen go when the walls fall?"

Opto didn't know what to do now upon hearing that the enemy had camped around the exit of the tunnel. From what he had researched in the past, the engineers had placed the stone door in an area where an army couldn't camp. "Stupid orcs" was all he could say then. Everyone nodded at that comment, but then each wondered if the tunnel could be discovered, and, if so, could they get into the castle and attack from within.

"Have you spoken to any of the mages ... maybe they have a ..."

Opto coughed to interrupt Marbod. "I have already. They say they do not have the power to get King Dia or the Queen out at this point. It would take two or three of them together to achieve a cloaking or disappearance spell needed to get them past the ugly things, and they are just too tired to try it."

"Our king has told me that he will fight the enemy on, so I know not if he will leave the city," Bogwa piped in then.

Comitay leaned back at what he heard, moaning. He didn't like that answer either but understood that things would not be getting any better soon. The mages who were left were getting weaker and weaker. A few, he had heard, had died, and one or two had even disappeared.

Captain Marbod, though, hadn't been in the city or the kingdom that long. He was a traveler from the southern Empire of Pendore'em and Edlaii. He had left when his family died from a plague that struck the empire many cycles ago and had met Prince Frei at the border mountains that were north of the empire as the prince was on a scouting patrol. The prince, seeing that he was a strong and kind warrior, asked him to come to Brigin'i and live there, offering to make him a part of his family. Marbod never looked back and had never left. He now had many fond memories that all involved the royal family. The thought of losing the city wounded him deeply, but not as much as losing his new family. With the loss of the prince, the King and Queen were his only family left. They must figure a way to get the royal couple out of the city to safety, and quickly, he thought.

After a few moments of silence, they all agreed that the king's personal guard needed to be ready to do what was necessary to savee the royal couple in some way. Just then, a messenger ran in calling out that the enemy looked like they had moved to their final position and intended to finish what they had started as quickly as possible. The four finally came to an agreement and nodded to each other. As Opto went to persuade the king to leave the city, General Comitay would join the forces at the southern gate, Captain Marbod would go to the walls and take command, and Bogwa would go to the Queen and get her ready for a quick exit.

Chapter Twenty Eight

The sudden blaring of horns erupted. As the unknown music began to drift in through the windows and doors, every citizen of Brigin'i stopped to listen and look north to where the sound seemed to be emanating from. All of a sudden, more music then erupted from the south, but much fainter, as if an echo were occurring, and then even more music started coming from the lakeshore.

The walls were soon crowded with spectators as they listened to the horns' haunting music. Everyone looked about to see if anyone knew what the horns meant or who might be blowing them.

King Dia, standing along the battlements with his arms crossed, knew that the horns could only mean one thing: the Levenori Elves were coming. Dia smiled at the thought that, at this moment, the enemy below was wondering who might be coming, so he looked down and pointed toward them, as he could see them getting nervous.

"Look!" he yelled.

General Comitay came running up to his king. "You know who it is, my king?" Comitay asked as he looked down on the enemy below. He knew the elven horns, but these horns sounded a bit different.

Dia, still smiling, turned and nodded to his general. "As I should, General. It is the elves ... our friends. They are coming to get revenge on the enemy." He pointed again to the enemy below. "See, the enemy is confused."

General Comitay looked below and saw that King Dia was right. The enemy was turning and dropping their weapons everywhere, showing signs of mass confusion. King Dia and General Comitay could see the columns of troops falling apart and hear the screams for order from the enemy leaders, which were of no avail, as many enemy fighters broke ranks and tried to run away.

Quickly, the archers along the walls began releasing arrows, taking out orcs and others who were running close enough to the walls. In the southern area, the giants were also falling apart, but since there were fewer of them, it was easier for the enemy sergeants to get them back in order with their whips. The goblins were also getting scared, as many could be seen running into the forest. Dia watched one die, who, not watching which direction he turned in, was stepped on by a giant. Dia could hear his scream from where he was.

As the horns continued, screams from the enemy lines could be heard as arrows soon exploded from deep within the forest in the north to slam quickly into the enemy ranks. Then the same happened from the south.

"Comitay," Dia leaned over and said in his general's ear, "open the southern gate and release our warriors when it clears there. I want Brigin'i to take part in this." Dia leaned back, smiling.

Comitay nodded and watched for a moment as enemy upon enemy was hit by arrows coming from the forest as well as from the city walls. He could see a few of the giants gathering together, and he figured from their expressions and actions they were attempting to figure out what to do. Based on his perception and military mind, he felt they had three options: charge into the forest, charge the city walls or try to run away.

It was the second choice that the giants decided on. Within moments, ten giants turned and charged as one toward the fallen tower of the city, each roaring so loudly that Comitay thought he could feel it. Comitay screamed down to his sergeants below to get men-at-arms to the tower area. His warriors scrambled as each screamed to his own people to get men to the tower as Comitay ran down the stairs and toward that southern wall.

Comitay quickly thought of his king's orders for the southern gate to be opened, but now that the giants were charging that way, he quickly paused before he headed that way, grabbing a few groups

222

of men who were waiting for his orders. As the giants approached, arrows fell from the battlements, causing only minimal damage to the giants themselves, for they still had possession of those huge wooden shields. As the giants hit the rubble of the fallen tower, a mage who had been nearby positioned himself to stop the giants and released three bolts of bluish energy toward them. The lead giant took the full brunt of the energy, making his chest explode open and slamming him back into two giants behind him. All three fell back down the tower rubble, screaming with such a cry of pain and anguish that a few of the warriors on the wall shuddered at the power of that mage.

Not far behind, a group of orcs that had been turning to flee saw the giants charging forward. They believed the tides were turning and that this might their best chance of surviving. This group of orcs turned and charged toward the fallen tower behind the giants, screaming as loudly as they could.

The mage turned his arms to release a blast at another giant pushing past his fallen comrades, but before the mage could send another bolt, he stopped short as two arrows slammed into his chest. The mage fell as the giant surged forward. Those along the wall looked south as forms emerged out of the dark recesses of the forest, which they were eventually able to identify as humans. Many of these human warriors stopped, lifted up bows and released arrows at the city. This new enemy caused much confusion as they came running up behind the giants. Until this point, the humans had hidden themselves within the forest, waiting for the order to charge at the city, but when it looked like the elves might turn the battle from their assault and then the giants began charging, they took the chance to charge and fight themselves.

Charging up the rubble, these dark-clothed warriors soon slammed into those defending the city. The mage who had killed the giants moments before attempted one last spell as he lay dying, but as he moved his hands to complete the spell, one of the human warriors jumped over a large piece of the fallen tower and pushed his sword deep into the chest of the mage as he spit into the face of the dirty-looking man. Both soon exploded in a huge fireball as the spell's anger at not being released consumed them. Their screams echoed as giants and humans continued rushing by the burning bodies to crash toward the defenders, who themselves were rushing up from the inside to defend the city.

Chapter Twenty Nine

A large bird flew over the city of Brigin'i, looking down to observe the battle below. If the humans, elves, giants or orcs fighting below had been able to see what the bird could, they might have formed a different battle attack or defense. However, they couldn't see the battle from above like the bird.

The creature saw that, from the north, the Levenori Elves were launching a swift and heavy barrage of arrows into the ranks of the enemy, which had caused them to turn and charge toward the elves when they finally got themselves together. Enemy after enemy fell underneath the arrow attacks as they tried to counter the elves who were hitting them from their right flank.

Flying in a circle, it saw huge goblin-type creatures that had been hidden deep within the forest out of eyeshot of the humans within the city now pushing their way toward the elves, using huge shields to deflect the elven arrows. So far it was working, and the goblins were making ground behind these large creatures.

At the eastern edge of the city, the bird saw that things were not going well for the humans within the city either. The giants who had made the sudden attack on the fallen tower had led their allies to charge toward the city's walls, causing the city's defenses to be thinned out along the wall.

In the south, the enemy was making its way into the city proper, pushing the defenders back and leaving the bodies of those who had died moments earlier lying everywhere. Many could be heard crying for help or for family members. As orcs, goblins and men ran over them, many stopped to finish them off. The bird could see scores of black-clothed humans within the orcish ranks storming into the city, making it hard to distinguish here and there as smoke made the human warriors look the same from above in the night. These human warriors though were charging in hard and were making ground pushing the defenders back into the city.

Across the battlements, defenders released arrows at both the enemy on the forest edge and at the invaders who had made it into the city and were now moving behind them. Every once in a while, a catapult from either side would launch a rock into the other's lines, killing or wounding many. The attacking enemy had moved their catapults just close enough to launch rocks onto the walls, trying to kill as many archers as possible and break more of the wall. So far it looked like it was working, as the walls were crumbling whenever a rock hit an area, causing those on the wall above to scream as they fell to their deaths.

The bird was flying off to the northern part of the city as an explosion and fireball erupted and blew up into the sky, making it change its flight quickly. Its eyes scanned the scene below as one of the enemy rocks had just flown over the wall and landed near a small tower that was being used by the mages as a storage facility. When the rock landed, it hit the ground hard, then rolled to crash into the tower, causing it to explode and shatter. The explosion caused the buildings around it to explode as well, sending hundreds of smaller rocks into those defending the city, killing many.

The bird looked down and cried loudly as it watched the explosion erupt into the air. Turning, it flew once more around Brigin'i, seemingly compelled to take one more look. It watched the scene unfold as its eyes scanned the battle and the city from far above, as if someone else were also looking through its eyes.

Far away, Methnorick sat on his throne in the dark, watching the battle through his pet's eyes on his tapestry, laughing at the destruction his army was causing Brigin'i.

"I told you, Dia, I would win," he whispered to himself. "Fight me, and this is what happens!"

* * *

226

General Comitay was down at ground level when the explosion occurred, causing him to duck down as his ears started to ring badly from the explosion. He shook his head quickly as his ears slowly started to hear sounds of screaming from the people around him. He looked up and grabbed one man-at-arms next to him, ordering him to find out what had happened as he turned and stumbled toward the battle forming on the streets of the city now. He stumbled, still misty-headed from the explosion. Looking up, he knew heavy fighting was going on at the fallen tower, and he had to get to there quickly.

The sounds of metal against metal and screams grew louder as Comitay came staggering up the street and turned the corner to find total chaos. He pushed through a few civilians who were running away from the battle as he saw the giants who had survived the charge sweeping their huge weapons, ranging from wooden clubs to axes, back and forth, sending many warriors and civilians alike flying. Screams were everywhere as Comitay pushed his way past the retreating civilians, trying to get to someone in charge of the situation.

Finally he saw the person he was looking for: a large muscular captain, who was fighting three ugly human warriors at once. The captain's uniform was bloody and ripped from where it had been struck. Red blood from the humans he had killed mixed with the black blood of the goblins and orcs he had killed previously. As Comitay moved to get to the captain, a one-eyed human jumped in front of him screaming, making him raise his sword up quickly deflect a blow intended for his head. Comitay and this enemy turned in circles, trading strikes with their swords. Comitay observed that the human, ugly and worn from years of living in the wild, was covered in bear fur and leather from animals and was carrying a large shield covered in leather and dotted with the blood of his people.

"I kill yea tra'r yo'!" the human screamed out, leaving spit running down his chin. Comitay, a skilled fighter in his own right, found this human was skilled as well, as hit after hit from his blade was slowly causing his arms to tire.

The two danced for an extended period, trying to break

through each other's defenses, until finally the general saw an opening. Not far away, a giant was looking for victims. He slowly maneuvered the human backward towards where thea giant was swinging his club. Finally, as he lifted his sword, he saw that the giant had turned to look over toward him grinning, believing he had a new victim.

Now seeing the two humans, the giant pulled back his arm and swung with all his might, hoping to kill them both at once. As the giant's arm swung around, Comitay fell to the ground to avoid the deadly swing. This move surprised the human warrior. The giant's club connected with the enemy's head, slamming him into a wall before he even realized what had happened. As Comitay lifted his head, the sharp sound of the club flew over his head and he watched the human, who didn't have a chance, explode on impact with the building.

Comitay laughed for a moment, but his delight didn't last long as the giant slowly turned his head, and seeing that he had missed one of the men, he turned to swing his club again.

"Ohhhh, noooo!" Comitay rolled away as the club slammed into the ground, making it shake hard and giving Comitay the chance to jump up and run away. The giant gave chase but couldn't go far as a barrage of arrows slammed into him from archers who had placed themselves on the top of a building not far away in the hope of stopping the assaulting enemy. The giant screamed from the pain as he fell back, trying to cover his face.

While Comitay stumbled away, grabbing the captain and ordering him and his men to make a defense retreat, the ground shook slightly as two huge legs moved past the general. He looked up, thinking it was that giant, only to find that, though it was a giant creature, this one was fighting against the orcs.

He stood and watched as the creature swung a club around, smashing it into the giant Comitay had been fighting moments earlier, striking him hard in the head and causing him to fall over. The giant who had saved Comitay stretched out his hand, letting out a blue wave of something, which wrapped itself around another giant, causing him instantly to turn into a frozen statue.

"Ice Giant!" Comitay cried, remembering this creature as he turned and looked down at the wide-eyed human general.

"Get your people to safety, NOW!" he moaned. Comitay nodded his head in response.

This triumph didn't last long, as this scene was replayed over and over near the fallen tower for over an hour until, finally, the number of enemy giants and their human allies was too much for the warriors defending Brigin'i and they slowly fell back deeper into the city.

Barricades had been put up quickly and were reinforced with reserves, who were finding themselves now at the front line in the battle. Along the walls and battlements, warriors and archers were still throwing what they could down on the enemy but to little avail, as the enemy continued to push deeper into the city. Those still out on the field realized that the city wall had finally been broken open and did what they could to turn away from the elves.

With elven arrows raining down, those on the field hurried to the walls of the city, but now the elven warriors moved out into the open in the south to push their blades into the chests of those who fought back as orcs leaders decided to sacrifice those nearest to the elves in order to get who they could into the city.

* * *

King Dia reached the edge of the wall and stood observing the battle in front of him. His generals were nowhere to be seen, except that Opto, his servant, had informed him that he had observed General Comitay in the courtyard before the tower fighting a giant earlier. When Dia's eyes showed his concern, Opto explained that he had survived somehow and was heard to be fighting a retreat near Merchant's Close road.

Dia nodded to Opto as he turned and observed the first wave of elven warriors emerge from forest edges to engage in full battle with the enemy. He saw the enemy was being slaughtered as their armor and shields were sliced through by elven blades and as arrowheads fell onto them.

Turning quickly around, he saw the enemy begin to move through his city, pouring down the roads like water, but he was sure his people could hold them off with the elves moving up behind cutting off their reserves.

Another explosion on the northern edge of his city brought him running to look over the edge of the tower and see a cloud of smoke rise into the air. As Opto stood next to his king, he also watched the cloud rise up into the air, knowing exactly what it was.

"My king, I must get you to safety," Opto said loudly over the sounds of battle.

Dia turned around, his eyes showing his anger at being asked to hide. "No!" was all he screamed, and Opto stood back in slight shock, but nodded that he understood.

"My king, may I at least suggest that we move the queen to a safer place?" a sergeant suggested, trying to show that he was in control of himself. Dia moved over and stood directly in front of his sergeant. Having his king that close made him nervous. The warrior swallowed and waited to be yelled at.

Opto piped up then. "Sergeant Helack, my king."

This introduction did not soften Dia's rebuke. "Sergeant Helack, my wife ... your queen ... is in the safest part of this city, and she will not leave there until I order her to or the two of us have died defending it." Dia turned and walked over to the edge of the tower to continue watching his city burn around him. Tears soon appeared in his eyes as he knew that it wouldn't last long — his people, his city, everything he and his family had worked for was now burning.

He could see that the Methnorick's forces were too great for his defenders and even the elves, as many of their warriors were falling beneath the forms of the giants at the northern end of the field.

He turned and looked at Opto, who, like the sergeant, stood silently and waited for his king to come to the conclusion they had already come to, both secretly wanting to escape from the city.

Dia walked out to the edge of the wall. Leaning against the wall, he slammed his fist on the stone as he looked out onto the battlefield. His belief that his city and the elves together could win the day instantly disappeared when he looked east toward the forest and saw the rising number of enemy fighters still moving toward his city, pouring out of the forest like water.

Staring beyond the forest, Dia could see the large blackish clouds moving toward his city, making him suck in his lips. He wondered what could be within the clouds, but he could guess all was lost if they got to Brigin'i. He turned back to look at the men waiting on him, and slamming his fist hard on the stone, he said, "My friends, we are to leave this place now. Get word to my queen that we are to leave the city within the hour!" At that, Dia walked over to the stairwell just as another explosion erupted just below the battlement, making it shake violently.

They moved away from the battlements, making their way past fallen warriors killed by arrows, rubble from fallen buildings or the few enemy warriors who had made it inside.

"When we arrive at the castle, you men will go and protect whom you can." Dia yelled as a loud wind flew past, spreading fire from a nearby building to other buildings. "Move any civilian still in the city to the western gate. So far, from what I have seen and been told, the enemy has not attacked that gate nor gotten through the city that far yet, so we might have a chance to get our people out.".

The guards nodded and kept watch as, every once in a while, a boulder or large rock would fly overhead into the city, causing screams to echo everywhere. When a barrage of arrows slammed into two of the guards trying to help him into a doorway, Dia blacked out as another pushed him through the doorway

* * *

It took the group about an hour to make its way through the crowds and scramble to get to the west gate of the inner castle.

Dia's guard numbers dwindled with each passing moment as they encountered orcs and goblin bands. The guards dragged the king with them until he finally woke. Dia shook his head as he saw building after beautiful building now reduced to rubble, not believing how much his city had been ruined since the assault had begun.

The situation was getting direr by the moment, when he and the few who were with him finally reached the large road that led to the gates of the castle that lay near the northern end of the city. As soon as they had run through the gates, Dia gave the order for the gate to be lowered. Knowing they had to prepare themselves for what was coming behind them, he grabbed Opto's shoulder, and both, without a word, ran up the stairs alongside the courtyard to get into the castle proper. He stopped at the top and watched his men-at-arms and warriors run everywhere throughout the castle. He would miss this place, he thought as he and Opto ran into the castle.

Chapter Thirty

*P*enelo was pulling his bloody sword out of the squirming orc's body when he heard the horns behind him. Not really caring about what they meant, he kicked the body back and slashed another enemy who was trying to attack him from his right across the face. The blade caused the enemy to stumble to the side, saving him from another blow from Penelo's sword, but in doing so, he also exposed himself to an archer up above them. An arrow suddenly appeared in his chest, throwing him back into three other enemy fighters who were coming up from behind him, making them all fall to the ground.

Penelo turned to see who had released the arrow and returned the warrior's nod as he looked around, hearing the warriors around him saying that they needed to get away now. Penelo grabbed the handle of a knife sticking out of the body of a human lying near him, and pulling it out, he quickly turned his body around and threw the knife into the leg of a hill giant who was lumbering toward them, before running away with the rest of the humans defending the remnants of that area.

Turning a corner, he stopped for a moment to rest and look behind him to see what the giant was doing. Peeking around, he saw the giant still yelling as he pulled the knife out of his leg, searching for whoever might have thrown it. Penelo giggled to himself as he watched the giant struggle but stopped when he saw four orcs push past the creature. He looked to his left and saw a few of the city's warriors running down a large street to get away, so he followed that way.

Halfway down the road, a nearby explosion rocked the city, making the pavement crack here and there and causing a few of the buildings to collapse. Penelo grabbed a footman who had tripped and helped him to his feet, when he heard a familiar voice pop up behind him.

"Interesting place for us now, do you not think?"

He turned and saw, covered in dust and blood, the elf Osa Ardaka standing and smiling at him.

"Osa ... I thought you were fighting in the northern part of the city." Penelo said as he looked over Osa's shoulder to see a few straggling humans run past them.

"Well, I was ... until it fell earlier, so retreating with the survivors, I made it here. Interesting place, do you not think?" Osa smiled at his comment as he looked at the scene around the two warriors.

Penelo smiled back, but before he could answer, he ducked as an enemy arrow flew past him, so he grabbed the elf's shoulder, and they turned and continued down the street, away from the oncoming enemy horde.

"I heard that the Levenori Elves are making a heavy counterattack from the north and south," Penelo stated, taking a big swig of water as they rested inside a battered building.

"Hmmm, yes they did, but I do not know if they were able to gain any advantage in the attack." Osa leaned against the wall, looking out for orcs who might come down the street they were on.

"I also heard that King Dia had closed the western gates for some reason," Penelo said, wondering if the rumor was true that the king would do such a thing. Osa nodded to Penelo's question but didn't respond as he took a drink of water and wiped some away from his mouth.

"I heard he did as well. I know not why, but he did close them, even though those gates are the only chance for freedom for those in the city. I believe he did it in response to rumors I heard that some of the enemy fighters were seen in the western forests. I believe he will open them to let everyone out once he is sure the road is clear." Osa looked back to the street and quickly flattened himself, motioning to Penelo to do the same as a group of enemy fighters came walking by outside, grumbling loudly in their language. They listened to them for a few more moments, and then they heard screaming down the road that caused the group to run toward it.

"Have you heard anything of Ame-tora?" Penelo whispered as he looked over at the elf for an answer.

"I know that the giant is still alive. ... Well, at least he was when I saw him last as we left the city," Osa replied, grunting as he thought about the big frost giant.

Seeing that the road was now clear, he turned to look at the other warrior. "We need to move now, my friend," Osa whispered to Penelo, who moved to the other side of a huge hole that was in the outside wall.

"This city is huge, but sooner rather than later, everywhere will be under the enemy blade, do you not agree?" Penelo said, quietly leaning back again when he thought he saw another enemy coming their way.

"We should try for the western gate then," Osa whispered, checking his side bag and his weapons. He looked over to the ranger, who was nodding and checking his belongings as well.

"And if it is shut?" Penelo whispered back

"Then we go over the wall." Osa smiled from the corner of his mouth. "I do not want to be in this place if it falls."

"Agreed," Penelo said as they both nodded to each other.

They both leaned out from the rubble. Checking again and seeing no sign of any enemy, they moved out of the building and onto the street. Moving quickly but slowly when needed, they made their way to the western area of the city.

* * *

It took them over two hours to get to the gate, hiding and killing when needed. As they got closer, the sounds of screaming and yelling began to float toward them, and when they came around the final corner to the main road leading to the western gate, they both

235

stopped suddenly to observe the scene before them.

"By the gods ..." The words came out slowly from Penelo's mouth. The scene before them was like a riot. Hundreds of civilians were scrambling to get through the gate, which instead of being open, was all but closed. They observed only a small portal open in the huge gates.

People were climbing over each other to get through the gate. Warriors and gate guards were doing their best to keep everyone in order. Dead bodies littered the roads everywhere. From people who had been trampled to others who had been wounded fighting in the northern, southern and eastern sides of the city, many had just been left on their own as people abandoned them to get to the gate.

Those wounded who couldn't move lay on the sides of the road, some leaning on the buildings and doorways, and from what Osa and Penelo could see, there were too many to count, leaving the two with no hope. The city was truly falling.

Mumbling a quiet prayer, Osa leaned over a body to check on him. Penelo shook his head slowly as he watched a group of rich-looking civilians pushing their way through the crowd not far away, making him squint his eyes as anger rose within his chest.

When another explosion occurred deep within the city, screams could be heard as a sudden rush of people scrambled to get out. Osa and Penelo stood and watched the total chaos. They could see the second door being pushed back and forth as guards tried to push it open until it finally gave way, making loud cracks as the mighty wood broke apart and fell onto the ground outside.

The rush of people toward the gates that were now opened increased. The people screamed and yelled, pushing harder to get out as the fire and smoke increased from the explosion moments earlier.

"The king told us we would be safe in the city," a weak voice said. Penelo looked down and saw the wounded warrior he stood next to struggle to breathe. That man's comment made Penelo and Osa look at each other in agreement. Dia had lied to everyone.

When the screams calmed for a moment, Penelo grabbed

his friend and said in his ear that they needed to get out now. Osa nodded in agreement as someone pushed him to get past. He followed the ranger as they ran down the street, pushing their way past a few civilians, mostly older people attempting to get to the gate.

They ran down two streets heading away from the gate, running into another, smaller crowd trying to move past a group of footmen who were preparing some type of barrier as the word spread that orcs were in the city and not that far away. As they came to another intersection, Osa looked around to look for an opening in the crowds when he caught the sound of crying near him. Looking down to his left, he saw a warrior lying on the ground, crouched in a ball, crying. Penelo, running past, looked around as well upon seeing a quick escape route up a crumbled wall of an old clerics building. He turned to the elf to motion to him and saw Osa standing over the crying warrior.

"Come with us," Osa yelled down as he shook the shoulder of the warrior. As the warrior looked up, Osa saw he wasn't a warrior but, instead, was a young boy of probably 10 or 12 cycles.

Looking up, the boy saw the elf looking down at him, smiling. Wiping the tears away from his face, the boy got up slowly, and taking the elf's hand, he stood up.

"Hurry, my friend. Come with us," Osa said quickly, hearing Penelo calling over to him to move. The boy nodded and followed the elf and ranger up the crumbled wall and onto a roof and ran with them, stumbling here and there, but with Osa's help, the boy was able to keep up.

After making their way along the tops of buildings, they they stopped for a moment to rest and check out where they were as Osa asked the boy questions.

Taking a deep breath for a moment, Penelo looked around, checking where they were. "Boy, what is your name, hmmm?" Osa asked, trying not to sound mad as Penelo scanned the scene around them.

The boy looked at the ranger as he took a water pouch from

the elf. "My my my name is Trvium of the house of Clor-ium, sir." The boy took more water, then gave the water bag back to Osa.

"I am Osa, and this is Penelo. We are ..." Looking over to Penelo, who smiled for a moment, he continued, "We were fighting in the eastern part of the city when it fell apart."

Trvium's eyes widened upon hearing who his saviors were. "You ... you're part of the games, are you not?" Seeing Penelo nod his head, Trvium felt at ease and knew he was a bit safer now. Penelo then looked back over to Osa, who continued to look at the boy and asked, "Tell me young Trvium, why were you hiding on the ground?"

Trvium felt ashamed, so he looked down as he quietly spoke. "I was up on the wall, watching. My king was there just before the first attack, overseeing that part of the wall when it happened. I even spoke to him!" The boy's face lit up for a moment. "At first he ordered me to hide, but then he ordered me to take a wounded warrior to where clerics were set up nearby helping warriors, which I did, but when I returned, the section of the wall had just disappeared." Both warriors nodded, as they had seen many parts of the wall collapsing.

"Everyone there was dead, so I ran." Seeing Osa nod a little, Trvium understood as he continued. "I thought the king was dead."

Penelo stood up to look at the huge amounts of smoke coming from the explosions. Looking to the north through the smoke, he saw the castle up above now had smoke coming out from inside. Even a few of its outer towers had collapsed, probably from rocks thrown by the orcish war machines. Penelo shook his head, as he couldn't believe this city of all places in the lands had fallen so easily. When he had arrived here, this place looked like it could take on the whole world and even the gods themselves could not bring it down. Then he looked at the boy and Osa and shook his head, saying, "Come, we must get out of the city now."

Chapter Thirty One

$\mathcal{D}$ia ran into the large bedroom, hoping to find the queen there packing, but instead, he found nothing. Quickly turning, he ran down to Frei's bedroom, believing that maybe the queen in her sorrow might be there, but still, nothing.

As Opto ran to get the servants out of the castle, the king ran throughout the royal chambers, calling out her name until, finally, he found her outside on the battlements, looking down over the city.

"Shermeena .... gods, what are you doing out here?" he called out as he ran up behind her and looked out to see smoke, fire and destruction.

Turning, the queen cried out, wrapping her arms around her husband's shoulders as she cried about the city's falling. "Shermeena, my love, we need to leave this place now," Dia said quietly as he looked down at the burning city.

From where they stood, the king could now see that, indeed, the southern and eastern walls had fallen in many places and that enemy continued to pour in. He had thought that the elves' attack would slaughter the enemy and distract them from his walls. Instead the enemy did the one thing he did not think of: continue attacking the city's walls to get away from the elves.

"My love ... please, we need to leave now," he repeated as he lifted her soft face, seeing tears running down it.

Over her shoulder, he saw an image only the gods could make, as the blackish clouds moving toward the city sent down mist to the ground. His jaw dropped as figures emerged from this mist, each sitting on a horse as they stood at the edge of the forest.

"Husband ... my city ... my family ... all gone ..." she whimpered quietly as he looked back at her, nodding that he understood. Turning his queen around slowly, he led her back inside the small chamber, as he wanted to get down to the escape tunnel quickly.

"Come, my dear," he said, looking down at her as they walked through the chamber and out into the hall. Her quiet sobs echoed from the room into the hallway until suddenly she stopped, looking up and gasping, causing Dia to look at her confusedly until he heard a familiar voice.

"So ... this is where it ends!" The words caught both quickly. Dia could see the form before him move as he quickly pulled his queen behind him and drew his sword out from his hip to point it at the form moving out from the shadows to stand before them.

"Gods!" The whisper left his mouth as the form came into view with sword drawn, smiling from the corner of his mouth.

"Baron ... Parnland, what are you doing?" He was dumbfounded that one of his trusted councilors and landowners was threatening him at sword point.

"My king, or should I just say "Dia," this is the end of Brigin'i. I have made sure of it!"

Confused by the words, Dia, not lowering his sword in the slightest, looked directly into the almost-red eyes now looking back at him. "What have you done, Parnland?"

Smiling again, the baron slowly walked to the king's right to stand near a table that held up a bust of an ancient member of the king's family. Turning, he looked back at them, smiling.

"Dia, it was I who gave the enemy information about the weakness of the city's walls. It was I who gave them information about your armies' movements. And it was I who gave them information on where you would be at this very moment." At that, the baron lifted his sword again, this time closer than Dia had expected, as it got within a hand's length of his face when he lifted his own blade to counter Parnland's.

"I have closed the only way out of this city, leaving your people with no escape. They will join you both in the heavens all too soon." Dia blinked, unable to believe the betrayal.

"Now you will either follow me or die in your castle, along with the queen next to you. It matters not to me, but this ends now." Parnland gripped his sword tightly, knowing that, if nothing else, the king would fight for his queen when threatened, so Parnland had to be ready for anything.

The anger within Dia rose quickly, but then he felt the soft but tight hand of the queen next to him and knew that he couldn't take a chance with her life. When he spoke, he squinted his eyes, looking directly at the baron before him.

"From this moment on, Baron, I will hunt you down and make sure your life is put to an end." Parnland smiled and gave a quick whistle, letting the king know he was not alone.

Dia gasped as more figures walked out of the shadows. As they came into view, he saw that his worst nightmare had come true:. dark elves were inside his castle.

As four elves moved closer, all staring at him with their nasty-looking faces, Dia turned slightly and whispered to the queen, "My dear, when I give the word, I want you to run." She nodded as she prepared herself to make a run for it down the stairs that were not far away as Dia gripped his sword, getting ready.

"NOWWWWWW!" he screamed as he whipped his sword up and around, attacking the nearest elf, who blocked the king's blade with his own, then turned and struck back hard, knocking Dia off balance only slightly, but enough for the other elves to move in.

Moving back and forth, Dia was able to swipe his sword across the neck of one of the dark elves, making the elf fall back, gasping from the wound and using a hand to cover it as blood splashed on the stone floor below his feet. Dia turned to attack the three others as his sword was quickly knocked out of his hand, causing him to cry out from the shock surging down his arm.

The elves quickly moved in and began punching him hard in the face, causing him to fall down to his knees. They roped his hands tightly as his vision blurred for a moment. Then his sight came back as he looked up, seeing the traitor baron standing not far away.

The scene before him sent a massive shiver down his back as he saw what had happened. "Nooo!" was all he could scream as Parnland pushed the still form of his queen, Shermeena, the love of his life, to the floor, pulling his sword from her beautiful body. Dia watched her still and silent form fall to the ground.

As the elves finished with the bonds, they lifted the king up roughly, making him wince from the pain. As he looked at the queen's body lying on the floor, tears filled his eyes.

Parnland walked over and slapped him hard in the face. "I told you this would end!" he said as he grabbed Dia's bent arm and roughly pushed the king down the hallway. He looked back at the still form of his queen as they passed a group of his personal guards and servants lying dead on the floor, scattered as they had fought or had tried to get out of the castle. As the dark elves kept an eye out for any more guards, they moved quickly out of the castle with him.

* * *

Reaching the top of the wall, Penelo, Osa and the boy Trvium took one final look at the city of Brigin'i, then moved to climb over the battlements and scale their way down to land hard outside the western gate on the lush green grass.

The three of them quickly jumped up and ran as fast as they could across the open field until they found shelter in the woods that stood about a mile to the west of the city. There they fell to the ground and hid behind the trunks of some trees and watched as more and more smoke rose and took over the skyline around the city.

The ground, even from this distance, shook as more of the city exploded. Screams echoed everywhere as smoke and rocks continued to fly into the city. Osa was thinking that King Dia must have brought out the worst evil to have this done to his city, while Penelo looked over at The Great Northwest Road, which snaked just south of their hidding spot and was now crowded with the few remaining refugees scrambling to get as far west as possible.

"Look!" Osa whispered as he pointed toward the city. Squinting his eyes, Penelo couldn't see much, as the smoke from inside the city walls began to move across the field. The boy, lying next to them, lifted himself up as he also tried to look, but his eyes weren't as strong as the others', as the smoke and the hard run made them burn and water.

"Orcs ... fighting against warriors of the city at the western gate there. It looks like they are giving these refugees a chance to get away, but I can see that someone we know is standing above them all."

"Ame-tora?" Penelo asked. Seeing the elf nod, Penelo pulled out his sword and walked out of the forest's edge. Then he turned around to look at the others. "Then I think we should join them, do you not think?"

The shock at the thought of continuing the battle made the boy shake, but Osa nodded as he got up and pulled out his sword to make ready to join his comrades. When they noticed that the boy wasn't beside them, both looked down at him.

"Boy ... Trvium ... go join your people and protect them. If we cannot stop the enemy, they will all be killed," Osa said, using his sword to point to the refugees on the road.

Trvium got up slowly, looking from the two warriors before him to the refugees moving quickly into the forest.

"Are you sure?" he whispered as he stopped and looked back at the two warriors, making both Osa and Penelo smile and nod.

"Go ... and hurry, my friend" Penelo said as he turned to look at the last stand of the city, seeing that it might not be going the way of the defenders since the enemy had been able to encircle them.

Nodding, Trvium moved toward the refugees on the road that wound itself west. He stopped and turned back to the two and said, "I hope to see you two again soon, and thank you!" Seeing them nod back and wave him off, he turned and joined his people as Penelo and Osa picked up their feet and ran down the field. Soon Trvium couldn't see them anymore through the smoke.

* * *

Chansor lifted himself up on the horse he was using and silently walked it alongside the others as the memory of losing their friend crept into everyone's mind that morning. They all had just passed a statue of some ancient warrior king along the road. "Probably the old border of Brigini'i," Kalion piped in.

What made everyone quiet was that the king looked like Winsto in both face and armor, making even Birkita's eyes tear up as they all sat on their mounts observing it until, finally, Bennak kicked his horse, getting everyone to follow him as the sun rose slowly behind them.

* * *

Ame-tora whipped his axe around, chopping the heads off of three orcs who had moved within his arm's range. Turning around, he could see Brigin'i's warriors fighting more orcs. His eyes grew larger when he noticed new warriors he had hated since he was a young one. Seeing them, the giant grew angrier, lifting his right hand up as he spoke the one word that no creature could survive unless he was the one who had spoken it.

Instantly, the burst of sound and light erupted out of the giant's hand as water like streams of ice flew across the field to slam into two of the dark elves, causing both to die, encased in freezing ice that only left their surprised faces visible.

Seeing the giant fighting for those within the city made one goblin roar in anger, as he could see that this creature was turning the battle against them. Pulling his club out of a man he had just killed, the goblin, standing over eight feet in height, charged at the ice giant, who at that moment was stepping on a goblin who had moved too close. Upon hearing the scream from his right, Ame-tora turned just in time to block the club that was swinging toward his chest. The two fought each other, taking hard hits from one another when Ame-tora noticed familiar figures not far away running into the battle.

244

Osa charged into the fray and headed toward Ame-Tora, killing three orcs who didn't notice him as he ran past, whipping his sword quickly across their throats and chests. Penelo was not far behind, dispatching a few orcs and goblins as well.

Osa, charging up behind the goblin who had just swung hard at Ame-tora's thigh, jumped up onto the back of the creature and took his knife out before stabbing it hard into the neck of the goblin, causing him to scream out and drop his club. The ice giant paused for a moment to watch.

"Osa?" he gasped out of his dry throat. His surprise was again sparked when he turned to see the human warrior Penelo also join in, stabbing his own sword into the chest of the huge goblin. When the goblin fell to the ground dead, which caused those orcs and goblins nearby to turn and run away, the elf jumped off and moved over to look up at the ice giant, who was still surprised to see him and Penelo.

"How are you, my friend?" Osa asked, his smile making Ame-tora finally breathe in and laugh. The elf could see the battle had taken a toll on the ice giant and that he wouldn't be able to continue much longer. Looking around, though, Osa saw that the big creature had done a nice amount of damage to the enemy, with bodies littered everywhere.

"I think we should get ourselves away, do you not think?" Osa asked as Penelo joined them. "The city is dying, and even though we won this small battle, the city has fallen, and this field might soon be filled with more uglies than even we can handle. At least we have given those people fleeing a chance to get into the forest."

The elf pushed his sword into its scabbard as he heard movement through the smoke coming from the east. "We should leave this place ... and now!" When he could make out the smell that came with the sounds of movement, Osa said, "Our friends are returning, and I would think in more numbers."

Both Penelo and Osa moved through the bodies of the dead as the sounds of marching boots could be heard, but it took a moment for Ame-tora to get the picture that all was lost now.

As he dragged his axe across the ground, not caring if it dragged over a dead orc or human as he did, he thought to himself, *How could this city, once proud and strong, fall so easily!* His thoughts were interrupted when the calls from his friend brought him back to what was going on, telling him to move quickly.

Seeing that the giant hadn't joined them yet, Osa screamed, "MOVE!" for he could see through the smoke that the enemy was now gathering and beginning to make its way along the western edge of the city again. Finally, the giant pulled his axe up and over his shoulder to secure it on his back.

The three made their way to the forest edge southwest of the city, checking as they went to make sure they had left all of the enemy behind. All were tired, covered in blood of various colors from those they had killed and from their own wounds, as they moved into the forest, leaving the screams from the city and the smells of battle behind.

Ame-tora stopped and looked down at his friends. "Where do we go?"

Osa, kneeling on the ground, looked up. "I think we should go toward the empire in the south ... but it will be a long and hard travel for all of us."

"Harder for you!" Ame-tora said, smiling. "But I do not know if my kind will be welcomed there."

Penelo, blowing out some air, looked up at his friend. "If not, we will find another place, maybe within the mountains that border it!"

Standing up, the elf looked at his two friends, then back out of the forest to see the smoke from the city that had been so kind to them since they had walked in many weeks ago to join and fight in a game that would have made each rich beyond his dreams. Now as he looked back at the rising smoke, he pulled his pack tighter on his back and looked to the south and began walking. Soon his comrades turned and began to walk as well, beginning their long trip south.

* * *

Whelor, Birkita, Zahnz and Hrliger rode their horses at a slow trot as they came over the high rise of the hill and continued on, leaving behind the rest of the group that decided to stop and take in the scene before them.

Bennak smiled slightly but then started making his way down after a few moments, followed closely by Jebba, as the others were just glad to let him go so they could have peace from his gripes for a moment.

"You think we will make Blath 'Na?" Kikor asked as she leaned back on her saddle to stretch her back for a moment.

"Blath 'Na? I was hoping we could make it at least to the Bru Edin you spoke about." Chansor giggled and looked over at Niallee, Amlora and Harbin as he thought of the food and jewels that a human city always had.

Kalion sat quietly as he listened to the others talk for a while, seeing that the mountains to their left stood quiet like they had for hundreds of cycles before. Snow capped the tops, and he could just make out the massive funnel of smoke that always seemed to be rising from the volcano that lay in the middle of these mountains.

"I think I'll walk my wee horse for a while," Holan said as the others watched him slip from the saddle with difficulty. When he had adjusted himself, he grabbed its reins and quietly began walking on the road to follow the others.

"He hopes to get to the dwarven city and find it well and good, of course" Meradoth whispered to the others.

Kalion, still not speaking, looked to their right and saw flowing fields of green and lush forests, knowing that inside them could be anything: orcs, goblins, dark-skinned elves or even Methnorick himself.

"Let us leave and continue on. The longer we sit, the better chance she has to get away." With that, Kalion kicked the sides of his horse, causing it to jump slightly but walk down the hill. The rest

247

did the same as the sun rose over the trees in front of them, causing its bright warmth to cover them all as they made their way into an unknown future.